JUDGMENT AT SANTA MONICA

JUDGMENT AT SANTA MONICA

E.J. Copperman

**SEVERN
HOUSE**

First world edition published in Great Britain and the USA in 2021
by Severn House, an imprint of Canongate Books Ltd,
14 High Street, Edinburgh EH1 1TE.

Trade paperback edition first published in Great Britain and the USA in 2022
by Severn House, an imprint of Canongate Books Ltd.

severnhouse.com

British Library Cataloguing-in-Publication Data
A CIP catalogue record for this title is available from the British Library.

ISBN-13: 978-0-7278-9098-6 (cased)
ISBN-13: 978-1-78029-812-2 (trade paper)
ISBN-13: 978-1-4483-0550-6 (e-book)

All Severn House titles are printed on acid-free paper.

Typeset by Palimpsest Book Production Ltd.,
Falkirk, Stirlingshire, Scotland.
Printed and bound in Great Britain by
TJ Books, Padstow, Cornwall.

To Jessica, Josh and Eve
because there is no one else who compares.
And in the memory of Parnell Hall

PART ONE
'Friends'

ONE

'Is this the sock in question?'

I held up a long, ugly argyle knee sock and showed it to the witness, who was Elizabeth Corcoran, my second college roommate. I couldn't remember where I'd gotten the sock and was trying to remember the charges that had been brought against Liz, who was also the defendant.

'I can't be sure that's the *exact* sock, but it was one that certainly looked just like that.' Liz had always been good at assessing the situation, so she knew to answer the questions directly and not incriminate herself. In . . . something . . .

'And where did you find the sock that evening?' I asked, again unsure as to exactly where that question had come from.

Liz looked up at the judge, a stern-looking man I didn't recognize. 'Do I have to answer that?' she asked.

'You have to answer unless you feel the response will incriminate you, in which case you would invoke the Fifth Amendment to the Constitution,' he answered.

Liz nodded, not the least pleased with that idea. 'What was the question?' She was buying time as I was trying to figure out why she looked exactly the same as she did in college, which was fifteen years earlier.

The court reporter, a dowdy-looking woman in her fifties who bore a striking resemblance to my Aunt Helene, repeated, 'Where did you find the sock that evening?'

Liz swallowed hard and gave me a look that I couldn't read. Was it anger? Remorse? Pity? Then she took a deep breath and said, 'I found it tied on the doorknob of our dorm room, Sandy.'

They tell you as a lawyer never to ask a question that you don't know the answer to in advance. And I *did* know the answer to the question I was about to ask, but I couldn't for the life of me figure out why I would be stupid enough to ask it.

'And what significance did seeing that sock on the doorknob have for you?'

Liz's look said it all: *Really? You want to go there?* But I had asked the question and it was her obligation as a sworn witness to answer it.

'It meant you had a boy in our room, Sandy, and I shouldn't come in because you were probably in bed with him.'

Yup. That was what it meant, all right. Mike Denton. Wow. What a jerk. Hang on; what was this all about, again?

I looked up at the judge, who for some reason was now my mother. 'Is that true, Counselor?' she asked. Or demanded. It was hard to tell.

'Mom,' I said.

'You'll refer to me as Your Honor or Judge,' my mother insisted.

'Your Honor,' I corrected myself. 'This information is not material to this case.'

'Oh, I think it is, Ms Moss,' my mother said. 'And I think you know the consequences of this offense.'

My stomach was a knot. 'No,' I moaned.

'Yes. You are grounded for a month and your father will be speaking to you about the dangers of premarital intercourse. You're also held in contempt of court and sentenced to a year of community service followed by a public hanging.'

I opened my mouth to protest but no sound came out. It was like a dream where . . .

Hey, wait a minute . . .

I woke up sweating, but not sitting up straight in bed with my eyes wide like in the movies. The ceiling fan was on low so there was a gentle breeze, but my blanket, which I'd lugged all the way here from New Jersey less than a year ago, was made for winters in the Northeast, not late spring in Southern California.

Maybe that was why I had that bizarre vision in my sleep. It took me a full minute to remind myself that none of that had actually happened, that I'd clearly just been having a really odd nightmare, and that my mother was well aware that I was not as pure as the driven snow and hadn't been for some years now.

But Liz Corcoran was definitely going to get a testy message on Facebook.

Well, I wasn't going to fall back asleep, not after a corker like that one. So I stretched for a moment and then got out of bed and got dressed for running.

It should be noted that for the first thirty-plus years of my life in New Jersey I never went running. Not until I moved to Los Angeles, where everyone is so fit you figure they're hiding all the fat people in a community dungeon, did I take up the practice. I have a very low tolerance for dungeons.

And I sincerely hate running. Putting on sweats and sneakers is fine with me – that's my natural state of fashion – but then going outside and pushing myself back and forth on the streets, up and down hills and back again without ever reaching a desirable destination? That's a form of self-torture that I could easily have lived without. Not as long probably, but more enjoyably.

You might very well be wondering why I put myself through it, and if I had a defensible answer I would offer it to you. But the fact is I was running because I compared myself with other women in the area I lived, came up short in my own mind, and was taking steps to try to narrow the gap. And my thighs.

I didn't tiptoe through the living room even though Angie was sleeping in the other bedroom just off the main area. My best and longest-tenured friend, Angie had flown to LA just a few weeks after I'd moved in, the circumstances of which I've explained elsewhere. She'd shown up as 'protection' for me under extraordinary circumstances and then stayed because she decided she liked it here and besides, I couldn't be trusted with my own safety.

So I'd given up the one-bedroom apartment and moved to a two-bedroom three flights up in the same building. Angie had insisted on the smaller quarters and promised to pay her half of the rent (prorated to reflect the fact that I had the bigger bedroom) as soon as she found a job. She was negotiating with Dairy Queen, for whom she'd been working in New Jersey, and was told they might be able to find her a similar position in Santa Clarita or Redondo Beach. Angie had said that was great and then we quickly googled maps to try and figure out where those places might be. We still really didn't have the lay of the land in the City of Angels.

It had been months and Dairy Queen, which insisted it didn't want Angie to leave its employ, had not yet found a job for her other than distributing soft serve, which was about six levels below where she'd been. Angie was, let's say, exploring other options.

She almost never sleeps so trying to keep quiet as I passed was a pointless exercise as I prepared to exercise, which I was beginning to think was also pointless. Life is cyclical.

Sure enough she stuck her head out while I headed for the door. 'Running?' she asked.

'No. I'm going on a hot date at seven in the morning dressed like I'm training for the Olympics.'

'Pick up some light cream.'

I gave her my best withering look. 'Where in this outfit do you think I keep my wallet?' I asked.

'Who told you to buy sweats with no pockets?' Angie asked.

'They were all the rage.' They were discontinued and $12 on OldNavy.com.

'You got your phone so they can call me in case they need someone to come identify the body?' Angie's mind tends to go dark at odd times.

I nodded.

'Good. You can pay with that.' Angie went back into her room and closed the door.

I was out on the street and starting to raise my heart rate before I had digested that. I love Angie more than if she were my own sister (and my sister knows that) but I was chafing a little at the way she was counting on me for . . . everything. I don't begrudge her a thing and she was looking for a job so paying for stuff like cream wasn't at all a concern. It was the casual assumption that I would, without a please or thank you, that was gnawing at me this morning.

Or maybe it was the case I was going to court with in another four hours.

I ran up whatever street this was (who pays attention when you've got GPS on your phone?) considering how to convince a judge that my client, a forty-two-year-old mother of three, should not have been charged with prostitution because she had been 'flirting' online with a man who turned out to be a woman who turned out to be a vice cop looking for violators. Madelyn Forsythe was the most suburban woman in the world and honestly had no idea she was doing anything other than indulging what she considered to be a slightly naughty impulse.

The problem was that cops are cops and the charges were

pending about a month after Maddie had divorced her husband, who had been indulging *his* naughty impulses with a dental hygienist for eight months and oddly was not brought up on any charges whatsoever. If justice is truly blind, it's also fairly tone deaf.

I had agreed to represent Maddie because the firm I work for, Seaton, Taylor, Evans and Wentworth (formerly Seaton, Taylor, Evans and Bach, but that's another story) wanted me to. We're a family law specialty firm but, since I used to be an assistant county prosecutor in New Jersey, I tend to get the cases that have a Venn Diagram overlap with criminal matters. So I would go to court for Maddie over her charges, which were ridiculous. Prostitution involves the exchange of money as well as bodily fluids. Maddie had demanded neither.

But I knew, after some months, the judge who'd be hearing the case, and he was not likely to care about the particulars. A woman 'soliciting herself' online while her children slept in the next room? She'd be in jail and her kids would be calling the dental hygienist 'Mommy' before I could introduce the explanation. But just to be sure I had put the cop who arrested her on my witness list. Let her explain why she thought Maddie was a sex worker.

I was about half a mile from my apartment and playing Strauss's 'Tales From the Vienna Woods' in my earbuds as I ran. Since I was a little girl I have always tested myself against the music in my head. If I reach that tree before this chord change or that part of the pavement before the tempo picks up, I can consider myself a winner. And since I get to set the rules, I win almost all the time. It's like a constant race. I don't even notice myself doing it all the time.

No, I don't know why I do that. It wasn't making me run faster. People are weird and I am a person. But I do it all the time. If I can beat that car in the street to this tree, if I can get down the stairs before that lyric, if I can make it to that line in the pavement before the guy walking toward me . . . it all seems to matter somehow. It's one of the ways I motivate myself, I guess.

I made it past the one lone palm tree on the street before Strauss decided to start a new movement, but just barely. At only a half-mile I had pretty much exhausted myself, which was sad but better than the week before, which was sadder. There was a little *tiendita* on the corner where I could pick up the cream for Angie, so I took a break, checked my pulse (I had one) on my watch and walked inside.

The dairy case was in the back of the store. I walked through and nobody noticed the sweaty, poorly dressed woman because they had, you know, lives. I stopped at a cooler a few feet away and took out a bottle of water – just water, not flavored or jazzed up with nutrients – for myself. Then I found a small carton of half and half (Angie would have to cope; it was a tiendita) and took both to the counter.

Standing there was Angie.

'What are you doing here?' I asked her.

Angie's face was emitting beams that were equally concerned and elated. 'You'll never guess who called me. Is that half and half?'

'You came here to tell me about a phone call? You could text, you know. And yeah, it's half and half. If you can find light cream in a tiendita, be my guest.'

The guy behind the counter looked over at me. 'Far cooler,' he said, pointing.

Angie gave me a look. An Angie look. 'Far cooler,' she repeated.

So we walked over to the far cooler, stopping just long enough for me to replace the half and half I'd taken out less than a minute earlier. 'How did you know I'd be here?' I asked her.

'This is as far as you can run without collapsing,' she said. 'I used to be a personal trainer, remember?'

'You used to work at Planet Fitness. You wiped down the machines.' Sure enough there was a refrigerated rack three sections away from where I'd been where there were various varieties of milk and one of them was light cream. Angie reached over and took a container then handed it to me because I was the one with the money.

'You got me off track,' she said. 'Guess who called.'

'Who?'

'*Guess.*'

'I don't want to guess. Who?' There was a bead of sweat rolling straight down my spine and all I could think was that if

I stayed with Angie and carried the cream, I could walk home instead of running.

'Come *on.*' Angie loves games. I hate games. Except for trying to beat the music in my head to the next tree. That's a game, right?

'Beyoncé,' I tried.

Angie's eyes widened to the size of silver dollar pancakes. Or silver dollars. 'That would be so *amazing,*' she said.

'OK, who?'

She rolled her eyes; I was clearly not playing along in the way she'd rehearsed it in her head. 'Patrick McNabb.'

Oh no. Not again.

TWO

'Sergeant LeRoy, thank you for testifying today,' I began.

'I was required to appear,' Sergeant Antoinette LeRoy answered. This was not going to be a fun cross-examination and Madelyn Forsythe's freedom pretty much hinged on my getting it right.

When I was a prosecutor I had tried a few prostitution cases. Very few. Most of the time these things are negotiated with the public defender assigned to the case and they never see the inside of a courtroom. But in this instance Brian Longabaugh, the deputy DA assigned to the case, wasn't in a mood for barter, I guess, and I had not been willing to trade much because my client was so obviously innocent. The charges were, to be polite, absurd.

'Sergeant, when you were operating undercover as a man named Randy and you entered into an online conversation with the defendant, who thought she was talking to that man, did she ever demand payment for sexual acts?' I'd be damned if I was going to call them sexual 'favors'. A favor is when you take out somebody's garbage for them on Thursday morning because they have a sprained ankle. That was decidedly not what LeRoy and Maddie had been discussing.

'Demand?' Sergeant LeRoy repeated back to me.

'Yes. A charge of solicitation requires that the person in question demands payment for sexual services. Did Madelyn Forsythe ever say, in your online conversations, that she required payment for sexual acts?'

The deputy district attorney raised a hand instead of standing up. 'Objection.'

What was there to object to? I'd asked a question.

'Mr Longabaugh?' Judge Amos Coffey sounded as startled as I felt.

'The sergeant was operating undercover,' Longabaugh said. 'She could not ask whether Mrs Forsythe wanted money before the defendant broached the subject.' He looked at me. '*That* would have been entrapment.'

Longabaugh was new to me. I'd only tried one criminal case in Los Angeles before and the prosecutor in that one had been Bertram Cates, who would have disappeared if he turned in profile. Longabaugh, on the other hand, was one of the few people in Southern California not to work out obsessively, eat lots of kale and know his cholesterol numbers off the top of his head. He had a rather prominent midsection and had swung it around with some alacrity while getting LeRoy to recount the dogged pursuit of human traffickers, a category that did not even alleged-ly include Madelyn Forsythe. But she had said Maddie had solicited her (in the guise of 'Randy', the horny internet surfer) for sex.

Judge Coffey looked weary. 'Overruled, Mr Longabaugh.' The prosecutor, looking disappointed, lowered his hand, which he'd forgotten he'd raised.

'I was operating under cover,' LeRoy parroted back, perhaps thinking that was a defense of her handling of Maddie's case, which had been remarkably poor.

'Of course you were,' I admitted because it didn't seem important. 'Now, when you were involved in the sting operation online . . .'

'Objection to the term "sting operation" as prejudicial,' Longabaugh said. He again had not even risen from his chair, as the prominent midsection probably was putting a decent amount of stress on his knees.

'Sustained,' said Coffey, one of the many men in this case

who seemed to believe that it was OK for guys to scour around online for sex but not OK for women to do the same. 'Please refrain from the use of that term, Ms Moss.'

'Certainly, Your Honor.' Turning my attention back to LeRoy, I said, 'Sergeant, when you were online searching for people involved in prostitution, how did you identify yourself to those you met in the chat room "Lonesome Lovers"?'

LeRoy's eyes betrayed more anger at me than you might expect for such an innocuous question, but the jury probably couldn't see it from their detached vantage point.

Her voice, however, gave away nothing. 'As per my undercover assignment, I identified myself as Randy, a male in his forties.'

'And Ms Forsythe showed interest in Randy?' I asked.

Police officers have to testify in court pretty frequently, so LeRoy knew how to behave. Her answers would be short and to-the-point and her demeanor would be unflappable. You couldn't flap her with a six-foot spatula.

'Yes, she did.'

I gave a glance to the jury, who appeared to be taking their civic duty seriously, having been unable to duck out of this session. Sometimes they appear disgruntled, but this panel had been carefully selected and was excited by the idea of a crime involving (at least theoretical) sex. Two of the men on the jury kept looking over at Maddie and smiling. If I could prove she was not in fact a prostitute they were going to be severely disappointed. I had tried to block both of them unsuccessfully from the panel.

There was also a buzz of noise at the back of the courtroom, but I didn't turn back to see what was causing it. Maybe someone had fallen ill, in which case the judge would put us in recess, or maybe someone had spilled their coffee, in which case everybody would get out of the way and eventually some maintenance worker would be called to clean up what was left. Probably after we were finished with this trial.

'How did Ms Forsythe express that interest?' I asked LeRoy.

I had not broken the rule about asking a question to which you did not know the answer in advance because I had read the transcript of the online chat conversation that had taken place between Maddie and LeRoy. And LeRoy knew that.

'She said she was available every night of the week,' she responded. 'She said that she was hoping to find a man like Randy and that she could be very responsive if he were willing to meet her qualifications.'

One of the men on the jury licked his lips.

Coffey, surveying what had become a fairly noticeable disturbance in the back of the room, said to no one in general, 'What is going on back there?'

The bailiff, a very nice man named Matt, started up the aisle toward the disturbance, but my stomach sent up a little acid when I heard a voice calling from the back, 'So sorry, Judge. I promise we won't make another sound. Everyone sit down, please.'

That voice. The one with the British accent that had started out Cockney and ended in the upper classes. That easy jocularity, just-another-guy voice.

Patrick McNabb.

The crowd that had gathered around him – a small one, but it was a courtroom – had no doubt been clamoring for autographs. Patrick had been a big star on *Legality*, a TV drama that pretended to be about the law, and was now an even bigger star on *Torn*, about a private investigator with (get ready) multiple personality disorder. Which was about as plausible as Patrick showing up in the courtroom exactly when I was trying a case.

I'd come to Los Angeles about a year before, ready to put criminal law behind and deal with 'family law', which is mainly divorce cases and their aftermaths. I'd just been assisting on Patrick's divorce when it became a murder case (he was accused of killing his estranged wife with a bow and arrow) and the firm, with its curious sense of humor, had assigned me his defense.

Let's just say Patrick and I had become friends in the process, despite his constantly driving me nuts with his insistence on participating in his case given his vast experience of playing a lawyer on television. But I'd gotten him acquitted anyway.

In this courtroom all his fans sat down, some grudgingly, not having gotten the moment they'd sought out, and Patrick was visible, smiling with his charming ease and crinkling his eyes just to remind me that he could. He actually looked at me and waved. In a courtroom.

I turned back toward Coffey. 'May I have a five-minute recess,

Your Honor? I think I can make the commotion go away.' And I'll admit I made a point of staring at Patrick while I said those last two words.

Coffey made a little exasperated sigh. He probably had a tee time coming up and didn't want this hearing to go on much longer. 'Exactly five minutes, Ms Moss.' He actually used the gavel, interesting in that – aside from Patrick's posse – there were maybe eleven people in the courtroom to hear it.

I thanked him and walked to the back of the courtroom, even as I saw Longabaugh make a gesture of futility with his hands, wondering why he had to put up with such nonsense. I decided at that moment to beat him badly in this case and to kill Patrick McNabb as soon as Angie could figure out how to best dispose of the body.

'Sandy!' Patrick was in an ebullient mood, which was typical when his life wasn't in danger. Of course, I'd known him mostly when his life was in danger and he had *still* been ebullient most of the time, so go figure. 'How wonderful to see you again!'

I did not return his gleeful tone. 'Patrick,' I hissed, trying to keep my voice from rising in volume. 'What are you doing here? I'm working.'

'Yes, and you're doing a wonderful job of it.' Patrick, largely because I managed to keep him out of jail for the rest of his life but not only because of that, thinks I am a legal genius. It's one of the myriad areas in which he is wrong.

Maybe I'm being too hard on Patrick. He's really a very nice guy and a good actor and we'd gotten very close during his trial. We'd even kissed once just after the whole thing was over. And then Patrick had let me drive him home, thanked me, and not gotten in touch again until this very morning in this very courtroom. While standing next to a stunning blonde who was drawing as much attention as him, I thought, because she was wearing a shirt – if you could call it that – that left little to the imagination.

Maybe I'm *not* being too hard on Patrick.

'First of all, no I'm not doing a wonderful job. At the moment I'm losing a case that shouldn't even have made it to court. And you didn't answer the question. Why are you here, Patrick?'

'Because you are wonderful,' he answered. Seeing that hadn't made my face light up as he must have anticipated, he added, 'and my friend Cynthia here is in a dire position. We *need* you, Sandy.'

I should have figured.

THREE

I put Patrick off by telling him we'd discuss his problem (Cynthia's problem) later and that I had to get back to work. He agreed to leave the courtroom after I pretty much made that a condition of my talking to him, and I got back to questioning Sergeant LeRoy, with the judge only a little grumpier than he'd been before the commotion. You'd think he'd be grateful to me for calming the courtroom down. You'd be wrong.

'Did the defendant ever bring up the subject of payment?' I asked LeRoy when we'd started the proceedings up again.

'Yes, she did,' LeRoy answered.

No, she hadn't. 'I've read the transcript of your conversations with Ms Forsythe, Sergeant,' I said. 'Can you point out the section where she says that she will require payment in exchange for sexual acts?'

Maddie grimaced just a bit. Her children were thankfully nowhere near the courtroom, but they were in the custody of their father at the moment and that didn't seem better. I was glad they couldn't hear the things being said about their mom, but I had to remind myself that I was arguing not just for her freedom but for any chance she might have to return to a normal relationship with them.

'She said I'd have to pay the price,' LeRoy said.

'Where in the transcript can I find those words, Sergeant?'

LeRoy looked at the judge. 'May I see the document, Your Honor?' she asked.

Coffey nodded and gestured to Longabaugh, who produced the printout of the transcript from a file on his table and handed it to me.

'Are you satisfied that is the correct document, Ms Moss?' Coffey asked.

I scanned the pages and saw what I had seen before, but I couldn't read it closely line for line. 'I believe it is, Your Honor.' Matt handed the document to LeRoy, who scanned it intently. 'I'll repeat the question. Sergeant LeRoy, where in this document do you see the words from Ms Forsythe, "you'll have to pay the price" in regards to sex?'

LeRoy, who had put on a pair of half-glasses, looked downright professorial. 'On page fourteen,' she said.

She took off the half-glasses.

Calm down; I knew Maddie had used that phrase. 'Sergeant, could you read the exchange on that page that begins with you, as Randy, saying, "It's gonna be a long night", please?'

LeRoy was not crazy about having to read the words she'd typed when trying to convince a suspected call girl (call woman?) to incriminate herself. But she did not even glance at Coffey for confirmation that this would be necessary. 'It's gonna be a long night,' she read, her voice instinctively dropping into a lower register. That must have been the voice she imagined when she was playing 'Randy'. In a town full of actors, even the cops knew how to get into character. 'What do you say we meet at your place?'

'What was the response?' I asked.

'Not here,' LeRoy read from the document. 'We can meet at a hotel in town. I'll book the room but you'll have to pay the price.' She looked up, vindicated in her own mind. Yes, Madelyn Forsythe had typed those words.

'Is that when you told Ms Forsythe that she had been identified as a prostitute and was facing arrest and possible imprisonment?' I asked.

'No. That came after the IT experts could verify the address and location of the computer being used to communicate on the chat room,' LeRoy said.

'How did you know that Madelyn Forsythe was the person typing those words in that house?' I said. 'How did you know it wasn't her husband Edward?'

'Mr Forsythe was not present in the house at the time of the conversation,' LeRoy said.

'But you weren't aware of that at the time of the incident,' I answered. 'It could have been him. It could have been a visitor.

It could have been a babysitter. The fact is, when you requested the arrest warrant for Madelyn Forsythe, you had no idea if she was the person you'd been trying to entrap.'

Longabaugh half-stood. It was the best he could do. 'Objection,' he said.

'Sustained. There has been no suggestion of entrapment in this case and you know it, Ms Moss.'

I nodded. 'Sorry, Your Honor.' I turned my attention back to LeRoy. 'So you felt that the phrase, "pay the price" meant money for sex?'

'Yes.' The professional witness was back.

'Did it not occur to you that she was suggesting "Randy" had to pay for the hotel room? So that this wouldn't take place in the house with her children present?'

Still LeRoy would not allow for anything but the testimony she had practiced, probably with a quick reminder from Longabaugh. 'No.'

'Why not? The exchange came immediately after you and she were discussing where to hook up. Wouldn't a real prostitute have a place picked out that she operated from regularly?'

'Yes,' LeRoy said, 'and quite often it will be a hotel. So her suggesting that "Randy" go to a hotel actually made me more certain she was soliciting.'

I think to this day that Longabaugh cringed a little when she said that.

'Did you discuss price?' I asked. 'Because I didn't see any negotiating in the transcript.'

'We did not,' LeRoy said.

'So on what are you basing your claim that Ms Forsythe was soliciting money for sex? On the suggestion that you pay for the hotel room?'

'That and the tone of the previous conversations, all of which are in the transcript,' LeRoy answered, a veritable filibuster coming from her.

'So just to be clear, you're saying that the previous conversations, which took place over a two-week period, point to Ms Forsythe being a prostitute despite the fact that she never mentioned money once?' I asked.

'Asked and answered,' Longabaugh said from his chair.

'Overruled,' Judge Coffey said. 'I don't believe the answer regarding the previous conversations was adequate. The witness will answer the question.' He nodded toward the court reporter. 'Will you read it back, please?'

She did, and LeRoy, who had surely heard it the first time, said, 'A professional would not have mentioned payment directly in an internet chat room. It is too likely to be monitored.'

'So I'll ask again,' I said, ignoring the fact that LeRoy had indeed been trolling around the chat room looking for prostitutes while Edward the husband was in his apartment with the dental hygienist and not paying a dime. 'What made you think Ms Forsythe's behavior warranted an arrest for prostitution?'

'Her tone made it clear she wanted to have sex with "Randy" and that she expected him to pay for the privilege,' LeRoy answered.

'In whose mind, Sergeant, Ms Forsythe's or yours?'

'Objection.'

'Withdrawn. No more questions.'

'Mr Longabaugh,' the judge said. 'Cross-examination?'

'Thank you, Your Honor,' like he was being introduced by the emcee at a celebrity roast. Longabaugh rose from his perch and approached Sergeant LeRoy. 'Sergeant, despite what the defense attorney is alleging, does the dialogue between yourself and Mrs Forsythe as related in the transcript fit the definition of prostitution under the laws of this state?'

'Yes it does.'

It was my turn to stand. 'Objection, Your Honor. It is not the witness's place to determine what does and does not fit the definition as the law states. That is up to the court.'

'Sustained. Please don't ask the witness for legal advice, Counselor.'

There was a small titter around the room, which was far from full. There were four more cases on the docket just for today and the spectators probably weren't here for this one. I saw two people in the back kissing up a storm and another eating a burrito just a few rows back.

'Yes, Your Honor,' Longabaugh replied. Then, back to LeRoy: 'As a police officer, have you made arrests before based on this kind of experience and this kind of behavior?'

'A number of times, yes.'

'So you know a prostitute when you see one,' Longabaugh said. I considered objecting on the behalf of all women everywhere that a style of dress or attitude does not immediately make one a prostitute but somehow this just didn't seem the time to stand up for the sisterhood.

'I believe so, yes.'

'Sergeant LeRoy, were you attempting to entrap an innocent woman by enticing her to solicit sex with a fictional man so you could boost your arrest total?'

'No, sir.'

'So you could advance in the department?'

'No, sir.'

'So you could feel better about yourself at night?' Clearly that question was meant to be taken as sarcasm but LeRoy clearly didn't get the nuance; her expression showed a touch of disgust with the prosecutor.

'*No.*'

'Sergeant, why did you write out an arrest warrant for Madelyn Forsythe?'

LeRoy was clearly a lot more comfortable with that question. 'Because she violated the law.'

'Thank you, Sergeant.'

Honest to goodness, I'll never understand how I lost that case.

FOUR

I talked to Maddie for a few minutes and made sure not to promise my client anything I wasn't sure I could deliver, but I definitely said I'd be filing for an appeal immediately on returning to my office. How any jury could find her guilty on that evidence was baffling.

Patrick tried his best to ambush me (he'd consider it an enthusiastic welcome) at the door to the courtroom, but I insisted we delay our conversation until I could find a quiet spot where we could talk. Matt the bailiff told me there was a small conference room free and unlocked the door for me. Matt the bailiff immediately became one of my favorite people in the world. Today.

Despite Patrick's best efforts to engage me in whatever strange plot he was cooking up, I was steadfast in waiting until we were inside, the door was closed and we were seated at the small conference table. The door was closed because my experience with Patrick, whom I'd considered a friend, indicated to me that I would soon be shouting at him, and I had a hard-earned, very small reputation in this courthouse that I wanted to maintain.

'OK,' I said once we were settled. 'What are we talking about?'

Cynthia, the woman who supposedly had the problem I was being asked to address, remained silent, as she had inside the courtroom and the whole trip down the hallway. Patrick took the opportunity to look mildly surprised.

'Didn't Angie explain?' he asked. 'I called her this morning.'

'Yes, and I went out of my way not to let her tell me what you'd called about. I'd appreciate it if you'd talk to *me* when you want me to do something,' I answered. 'Using Angie is beneath you, Patrick.'

He frowned. Acting. He was pretending to feel ashamed of himself. 'You're right about that,' Patrick said. 'I was . . . reluctant to call you cold. I didn't know if you'd take the call.'

'You had every reason to wonder,' I told him. 'I probably wouldn't have.'

Patrick shook his head like a dog trying to dry himself. 'But isn't it enough that we're back here together again? Sandy, we have a cause, and you can be part of it!' There's a reason actors become politicians; the skill sets are similar. Communicate, inspire!

I couldn't really reconcile why I was so angry with Patrick. He had no obligation to me. I was his lawyer, the case was finished, and there was no reason to be in touch with me again. And here he was, ostensibly offering me another case, not that my firm needed the business. Patrick was one of its biggest clients and had us on retainer. Maybe I could get this business done quickly and he could disappear again.

'What's the case, Patrick?' There didn't seem much point in asking Cynthia, who Patrick had said needed my help, since she never seemed to speak. She also didn't stray far from Patrick, although she was restrained enough not to drape herself over his arm.

'Ah!' Patrick appeared to believe he had won that round, whatever that meant. 'It's very serious. Cynthia here . . .'

'Suppose we let Cynthia tell me herself,' I suggested. If this was going to be a case for my firm and, more to the point, me, I wanted to hear the story direct from the client. And the client was going to be Cynthia, no matter how much Patrick wanted to be the center of attention.

'Of course,' he said, turning toward the obvious blonde to his left. 'It's OK, Cynthia. You can tell Sandy anything. She's amazing.'

Rather than dispute his statement I turned my attention to Cynthia, who before my eyes transformed from a scared kitten hoping Patrick would make the dog stop barking to a lioness on the hunt protecting her young against a herd of elephants. Her eyes narrowed and her lips thinned. Somehow I liked her better this way.

'My ex is trying to take my house,' she said. 'He can't do that.' Cynthia's voice, but not her accent (which I couldn't place), reminded me of home in New Jersey. She wasn't going to take anything from anybody. But she wasn't really telling me that much, and since I had already failed to save one woman from losing custody of her *children* and her freedom today, my mind immediately started trying to come up with reasons I couldn't take this case.

'Do you have a divorce agreement in place?' I asked. 'Don't you have an attorney handling your divorce . . .'

'Not that quack,' Cynthia said. I ignored the fact that *quack* is generally used to describe an inept doctor, while *shyster* was more accepted for unscrupulous lawyers. 'That guy gave away the store and left me in this crap.'

OK, so I couldn't slough the case off on her current attorney, whom Cynthia was clearly firing, as she spoke of him in the past tense. 'Was there an agreement in your divorce settlement?'

'Yeah.' Cynthia nodded enthusiastically, wanting me to know she wasn't the kind of idiot who'd go through a divorce and not have a provision to protect her home. 'I was supposed to keep the house, which I bought with my money, and he got the three cars and the vacation home in Aspen. Now he's trying to change it and the quack is saying I should sign off on it but I won't.'

Clearly this woman was not a poverty-stricken naïf being thrown out of her one-room shack by a cruel legal system. I really wanted to see any paperwork involved in this divorce because that, at least, would be written in language I could understand.

'What about your divorce settlement?' I asked her. 'Is there a copy I can see?' *And then could the two of you go away for a while?*

'I will have it emailed to you immediately.' Patrick had been trying so hard to stay in the background, but there was nothing he loved better than solving people's problems for them whether they asked him to or not. He was already pressing buttons on his phone. I nodded at him to avoid saying I thought he should let Cynthia handle her own divorce issues.

'What is your ex-husband using as a reason to change the agreement?' I asked Cynthia, making sure to maintain eye contact with her so she wouldn't look to Patrick for her answers.

'He says I'm bringing an undesirable element into my home,' she said, and to her credit she didn't stumble over the words. 'He says it's lowering the property value. Can you imagine?'

I looked briefly at Patrick, still engrossed in his screen so as to avoid looking back. He was a man who had been acquitted of murdering his estranged wife, but a lot of uninformed people still thought he'd been guilty. Maybe Cynthia's ex-husband was one of them. Patrick was unquestionably an eccentric character. But I didn't think that in itself would constitute a reason to change the divorce agreement. She was an adult and free to socialize – as it were – with anyone she chose.

'I understand that's very hard to hear,' I told Cynthia. 'But before we go any further I want you to understand that Seaton, Taylor is a very reputable law firm and our services are not going to be inexpensive. This kind of action with us could cost you a lot of money.'

Cynthia looked at me with something approaching contempt. 'I can afford it,' she said. 'I'm a star.'

Of course she was. 'Do you work on *Torn* with Patrick?' I asked.

Cynthia turned toward Patrick with exasperation on her face. 'Do you hear that?' she demanded. 'She doesn't even know who I am!'

'It doesn't matter,' Patrick said. To me. 'I have your firm on retainer and I will be paying Cynthia's legal fees.'

'Why?' Cynthia asked. But Patrick was heading in another direction and didn't answer.

He patted her hand. 'Sandy is very engrossed in the law,' he said, with an almost pitying tone. 'She doesn't pay attention to entertainment because she's so focused. It's what makes her so . . .' He stopped before he could say *brilliant*, a word I had banned from our conversations. Patrick had assumed I was, and I'm not. It was a fit of pique, I'll admit, but I couldn't go back on it now.

'I'm afraid I'm not familiar,' I told her. 'If you'd prefer another attorney . . .'

'No!' Patrick stood up as quickly as Longabaugh had launched himself for his many objections. 'You're our lawyer, Sandy.'

Our lawyer?

Cynthia looked a little skeptical as she assessed Patrick's face. 'OK,' she said.

'I'm sorry,' I said to her. 'Ms . . .'

'Sutton. *Cynthia Sutton*.' She looked at me, assuming that the name would jog whatever strange deficiency there was in my mind. But I'd never heard of Cynthia Sutton.

'Ms Sutton,' I continued, before she could express her shock at not being recognized. Again. 'If you're not comfortable with me representing you, it's not something you should do because of Patrick's opinion. *You* are the person who needs to be comfortable with me.'

Patrick, being Patrick, stepped in then, grinning with congeniality. 'You see?' he said to Sutton. 'She's so ethical!'

Cynthia nodded. 'Yeah.' She turned toward me. 'You're my lawyer.' She held out her hand but I didn't take it. I'm still doing the no-touching methods of greeting. Call me new-fashioned. I nodded significantly, almost a bow. I've been practicing.

'You're sure.' Literally any chance to get out of this case would have been welcomed, but I felt like the door was closing on that possibility.

'Sure,' she said.

I sighed a little. I hoped Cynthia Sutton hadn't heard me. 'OK, then,' I said. 'Let's hear the story.'

FIVE

'I can't believe you lost!' Angie said.

'It's nice to see you too.' I put down my laptop case on the table near the door and flung myself onto the sofa, kicking off the instruments of torture that men have imposed upon us (my shoes) at the same time. 'And thanks a heap for sending Patrick to the courtroom. That helped a huge amount.' I needed to change my clothes. That would be better.

'I *told* you he called and you wouldn't listen to me about it,' she pointed out.

Yup, different clothes. I got up, reluctantly, from the couch, and walked into my bedroom where I could find suitably grungy things to wear. Angie, of course, followed.

'So he brought his new girlfriend to the conference?' she asked.

I threw on a T-shirt with a picture of Claude Chabrol on it that I'd bought at the IFC Center in New York, and a pair of sweatpants because they were sweatpants and that was what I needed. We sat at the 'kitchen table', a tiny thing we'd found on the street one day and furnished with two barstools from IKEA. It was like we were sitting at an overpriced, pretentious café, but in our apartment. Angie had ordered bad Los Angeles pizza (they never get the crust right and they ask if you want *pineapple*) and we each took a piece out of the box.

'Well, they didn't actually touch while I was there but it was pretty clear,' I answered. 'His wife hasn't even been dead a year yet.'

'Patsy wasn't really his wife so much when she died,' Angie reminded me. 'But it still seems kinda quick. I thought if he was going to rebound with anybody it would have been you.'

'Patrick and I are *friends*,' I reminded her. 'Always have been. He can date anybody he wants. He's a grown man.'

'Uh-huh.' Angie is a woman of few syllables.

'Anyway, this is about her case. When I got back to my office there were all her divorce records waiting on my desktop. And the agreement she was being asked to sign was a travesty. This woman was supposed to give away all her rights if she so much as went to dinner more than once with another man.'

'Really?' Angie washed down her pizza with some red wine. I wasn't in that kind of mood so I was drinking beer.

'No, not really. I'm exaggerating. But the terms Cynthia Sutton agreed to . . .'

Angie's eyes widened and her mouth formed a perfect 'o'. 'Cynthia Sutton? Patrick's going out with *Cynthia Sutton?*'

I had googled the name once I left the meeting and discovered that Cynthia Sutton was an actress of some reputation. She did not work on Patrick's series *Torn* but was currently employed on an HBO prestige drama called *Tiny Panes of Glass*, which apparently was about a woman who murders people in the name of justice. What the panes of glass had to do with it was not clear.

'Yeah. Is she a big deal?' For LA the pizza was good. For Jersey it was average. After a year here, average still wasn't quite good enough, but it was getting better.

'Are you kidding? She got snubbed for an Oscar nom two years ago because she played a sympathetic superhero. And she *won* a TeeVee for best actress in a series.' Angie swirled the wine around in her glass, which would have been more impressive had it been a wine glass, but all of those were in the dishwasher. She was drinking out of a plastic cup I'd bought at Rite Aid.

I didn't pretend to understand all the words she'd just said, but decided the details of Cynthia's career weren't relevant to the part of her life I'd been hired to fix. 'So how does she know Patrick?' I wondered aloud.

Angie, of course, knew the answer. Angie is to pop culture what Neil deGrasse Tyson is to astrophysics. She knows everything and isn't afraid to tell you about it. 'They worked together once on a BBC miniseries before Patrick came over here for *Legality*,' she said. 'It was called *Silents*, about the silent movie era in the UK.'

'The UK? Cynthia didn't sound British.'

'She's not. She's from Pensacola, Florida.'

'How do you know that stuff off the top of your head?' I marveled.

'You know that part of your brain that has all the law stuff in it? I use it for this.'

I shook my head, not to tell Angie 'no', but to get that thought out of it. 'The point is, I need to talk to the lawyer who negotiated this travesty and find out why. Cynthia's just going to give me attitude because I'm not genuflecting when she enters the room. I don't know why she accepted me as her lawyer, except that Patrick told her to.'

'You should show her some respect,' Angie said. 'Oscar snub and all.'

'I'll try to keep that in mind.'

We finished dinner and Angie went into the living room to watch television on the giant screen she'd insisted we (I) buy when she moved in permanently. She *can* watch shows on her phone or her laptop, but she's a purist.

I went into my bedroom so I could shut the door and think about work. The issue at hand right now was Maddie Forsythe's appeal, not Cynthia Sutton's divorce. I had to figure out what – among the many issues with the trial – would be best on which to base an appeal.

That evening was spent digging into all the paperwork (now mostly PDFs) on the case in the vain hope that I'd spot something I hadn't seen before. The way I saw it, I had to punch holes in the ridiculous accusation that Maddie had been soliciting when she innocently went online in the hope of finding someone to fill the gap her husband was in the process of leaving.

I could call in Maddie's children to make it clear they'd never seen anyone coming into the house to sleep over with Mommy, but it always looked cruel to force children to testify, and Longabaugh would undoubtedly complain that I shouldn't be retrying the case in appeal, and he would be right. Besides, Maddie had specifically said she didn't want to do that.

So I spent three hours writing four different drafts of a brief in the hope that I could somehow convince the appeals court that Maddie wasn't a whore. That belief, however misguided, was the only thing I could see that would cause any judge to rule against Maddie.

Then I went in and watched three episodes of some sitcom I can't possibly remember with Angie. She wanted to watch *Torn* but I felt like I'd had enough Patrick McNabb for one day. She put it on the DVR for later.

There were three messages from Patrick on my phone when I woke up the next morning. Two were texts asking me if I was awake, which I had obviously not been, and the third was a voice mail: *Sandy.* (He did not identify himself because of course my phone knew him and besides, didn't everybody?) *I'm so excited that you'll be handling Cynthia's case! Can we meet for lunch today to discuss it? Please call me as soon as you can because I have a seven a.m. call.*

Lunch with Patrick? I'll admit I was tempted just to get him to myself for a while, but then I thought it through and realized that lunch with Patrick on a day he was filming his series would probably include a pretty serious entourage. I decided to ignore the message and get back to him after I'd given Cynthia Sutton's file a thorough reading. And after I'd called Cynthia Sutton to discuss it with her. Patrick was not the client.

When I told Angie at breakfast that I wasn't going to call Patrick back, she looked positively aghast. 'Come *on!*' she wailed. 'He wants to make it up to you. What are you waiting for?'

'Make *what* up to me?' I asked. 'Patrick doesn't owe me anything. He brought me a client and I'm sort of grateful for that, even if it's not a case I'd normally want to take. They should have gone to the firm, if Patrick is paying the bills – and knowing Patrick I'm betting he is – and let them assign an attorney. Now I'm walking in telling my boss that the client demanded me when I'm not even sure she wants me to represent her. Everything about this is wrong.'

'Patrick brought it to you because he wants to see you again,' Angie said. 'He feels bad about how things ended between you.'

'There were no *things* to end,' I said, and even as the words came out of my mouth I knew they were pointless. 'Patrick thinks I'm the greatest lawyer since Oliver Wendell Holmes and he wants to show his new girlfriend how well connected he is.'

'You don't know that.' Angie pulled out a bag of some kind of granola and poured some into a small bowl. Then she went to the refrigerator and got out some almond milk, which isn't milk but that's another story. 'You don't know Cynthia Sutton is Patrick's girlfriend. You don't know that he *has* a girlfriend.'

I pulled the remnants of a BLT out of the fridge and unwrapped the aluminum foil. It had been a pretty good sandwich when I'd bought it, but now the temperature was an issue. The lettuce and tomato should be fairly cold, but the toast and the bacon? No. This was a difficult problem to solve. 'You weren't there,' I told Angie.

'No. That was a mistake on my part. After I talked to Patrick yesterday, I should have insisted on coming with you, but I didn't know he was going to show up at your trial.' She poured the almond milk on the granola and started crunching away. I don't get granola. I'm from New Jersey. Sure, Angie is too, but she actually has respect for her body.

I took the sandwich apart. It was the only possible solution. The toast and bacon went on a paper plate and into the microwave. The tricky part was heating it just enough to be at room temperature. I settled on ten seconds and could do more if necessary. Never overheat. You're welcome.

'The absolute last thing you should do is follow me to work,' I said. 'I'm just barely managing to create a businesslike, professional reputation in the firm. After Patrick's case I was basically a curiosity for months.' Patrick's murder trial had generated, for lack of a better term, some unwanted publicity just when I was starting at Seaton, Taylor. It had taken months of work to get my colleagues to think of me as a competent attorney and not a very strange visitor from another planet. Which New Jersey, it should be noted, really is.

The microwave beeped and I took out the toast, now limp, and the bacon, see previous comment. My own fault. I stuck them back in their respective places and started biting. I have no shame.

'Fine,' Angie said. She was apparently perfecting her impression of my mother.

I had to leave for the office. I picked up what was left of the sandwich to eat on the drive, and my laptop case. 'You still offer fine advice,' I assured Angie.

'Good. Then go to lunch with Patrick.'

I opened the door and turned back for my exit line. 'There's no way I'm having lunch with Patrick McNabb,' I said.

So I had lunch with Patrick McNabb. And then I got shot at. So, Tuesday.

SIX

'**Y**ou are the most altruistic person I know,' Patrick McNabb said to me. Patrick, who had once bought me a Ferrari because my 2009 Hyundai was in the shop, was laying it on a little thick. He'd insisted on taking me to a chic Hungarian restaurant in Santa Monica for lunch when he knew my tastes ran more toward exotic frankfurters at a place called Destination Dogs (which is in New Brunswick, New Jersey). I was dressed for a day at the office, so it was OK to be in slightly fancier surroundings, but eating plant-based goulash was not what I'd expected when I woke up this morning.

'Tell me what you want, Patrick,' I said. 'You should know better than almost anyone that flattery is not only going to get you nowhere, but it'll just annoy me.'

'That is true,' he said. 'But please call me "Pat".'

That was new and different. 'Since when? I always called you . . .' Then it dawned on me. 'This is about playing someone with multiple personality disorder, isn't it? You want to try on having more than one persona.'

'It's called "research", love, and I need to experience what it's like if I'm to perform adequately in the role.' Patrick, eating vegetable soup although he'd considered the chicken paprikash, had to make sure his waist did not expand. The wardrobe on *Torn* was often quite unforgiving. What? Angie makes me watch it.

'Adequately?' I said. 'If your best friend Angie were here, she'd say you were nothing short of brilliant in the role.'

'Oh, you're allowed to say that word?' Patrick had mischief in his eyes. It was better for me to look away.

'Them's the rules, buddy. Take 'em or leave 'em. Besides, you've made yourself into an even bigger star on this show than you were on *Legality*. So much so that you don't even call old friends anymore.' Might as well get it right out there, if that's what this lunch was about.

He grimaced a little. 'You know how to hit me where it hurts, Sandy.'

'What are friends for?'

Patrick rarely breaks out his serious face in public. He likes to be the life of the party, the magic man who can make anything happen and would do literally anything for someone he likes. So, seeing him straighten out his mouth and let some sadness into his eyes left me with two feelings: one, that I'd made him feel bad, and two, that he might very well be acting.

'Sandy, right after my trial I was emotionally exhausted. You could see that. I was so grateful to you for helping me out of that awful situation and we'd gotten really close in a very short period of time.' He put down his soup spoon, another sign that this was sincere. 'But you have to remember that it was only a matter of a few months since my wife had died. I was still grieving for Patsy and then I had a role in a film that I had to shoot in Tunisia. I didn't call you because I was in a kind of turmoil I didn't understand and then I had to focus on being a two-fisted scientist fighting against neo-Nazis in the desert, for reasons I'm not certain I understand to this day. But the movie will come out in a few months and perhaps I'll find out then.'

'You were grieving for Patsy? You were in the midst of divorcing Patsy when she died.' I wasn't going to let Patrick off the hook that easy. I still had to figure out if he was playing the role of a disconsolate ex- what? Friend? Boyfriend? Client?

'You were there, Sandy. You know I still had feelings for her, even though I knew we couldn't stay together.' He had also been accused of her murder, and not without some at least circumstantial evidence.

'Nonetheless.' The goulash was far tastier than it had any right to be without meat in it. 'You asked me to lunch for a reason, Patrick, and it wasn't to explain why you ghosted me after your trial. So, out with it. What's on the agenda for today?'

Two young women three tables away were showing some signs of recognizing him. That's not very typical in LA, where actors of all types are out walking around all the time; people get used to it. And this restaurant was hardly a tourist trap. Patrick had fans everywhere and some were more, let's say passionate, than others. Patrick didn't look in their direction, but I knew he'd noticed them staring and asking each other if that was in fact him.

It was him, but I wasn't about to tell them that.

'I'm just glad to see you again,' he said to me. 'Isn't that enough?'

'For a normal person, sure. Not for you. So what's up? I'm already taking your new girlfriend's case. What else is there?'

Patrick actually snuck a glance at the two onlookers, whose faces darkened at the very suggestion. He didn't acknowledge them – not yet – but they knew he was aware of their presence. That by itself was a story to tell their friends back at the very expensive sorority house.

'Girlfriend?' When Patrick turned his attention back to me, he was wearing his innocent face. It was the one that had almost gotten him convicted. 'Cynthia is a friend, a colleague. She's in a dire situation and I'm trying to help her out. That's all it is, Sandy.'

'It doesn't matter,' I said, wondering if I meant it. 'My question is, why did you ask me to come to lunch today? Seems like you already got what you wanted.'

The two young women, having paid their check, stood up from their table and walked in the opposite direction of the door to the street. Instead, they headed directly to our table.

While they were walking over, Patrick sighed and said to me, 'Fine. I was going to ask you to draft a pre-nuptial agreement for me.'

Before I could answer, the smaller of the young women, the one with dark straight hair and a shy smile (as opposed to the taller one, who had blonde hair and a shy smile) approached Patrick, phone at the ready. 'Excuse me,' she said, almost mumbling from her terror that her idol might turn out to be an ogre, 'Mr McNabb, would you take a selfie with my friend and me?'

Patrick's public smile, the one that threatened to meet at the back of his neck and make his head fall off, shone in all its klieg light brilliance. 'Of course,' he said. 'I think perhaps we can impose upon my friend here to take it for us.' He gestured for the woman to hand me her phone.

It was a newer, more expensive model than mine, so I naturally gave some thought to the idea of taking it and running for the door, but it was probably traceable and I'd just end up having to plead myself down from grand larceny to simple robbery. 'Sure,' I said.

The taller woman looked closely at me as if trying to see if the pores in my nose were larger than those in my forehead. 'Are you . . . anybody?' she asked.

I motioned them into position, leaning behind Patrick and grinning their tanned, lean faces at me as I focused the lens.

'No,' I said. 'I'm nobody at all.'

Patrick and I were out on the street in front of the restaurant before I could gather my thoughts together to have a coherent conversation. The two young women, who had turned out to be college students ('UCLA') named Heather and Amy, had done their best to strike up a conversation with Patrick, who was being charming and accommodating because he truly loves his fans and also because he knew I'd be less irate with him if I had time to digest what he'd told me.

So he'd walked them to the restaurant exit, deliberately *not* taken any contact information from them and then waved as they headed toward the valet parking station. My ancient Hyundai was parked at the courthouse, where Patrick had insisted on driving me in his brand-spanking-new Tesla, currently charging itself in the restaurant parking lot. In Los Angeles it's easier to charge an electric car than it is to find a dentist who takes my insurance. Not that I'm bitter.

'So you're getting married but Cynthia is not your girlfriend?' I said once we were at a discreet distance from as much of humanity as was possible. The COVID-19 period had left us all with a natural ability to calculate how to remain six feet away from anyone on the street. Or anywhere else. 'How does that work? Who *are* you marrying?'

Patrick had his dark sunglasses on now and a baseball cap (Dodgers, of course) pulled down over his forehead; this was his way of avoiding fans on the street. He didn't like doing it because secretly he adored the attention, but he knew it was at best inconvenient to have people swarming him wherever he went. He had employed security in the past and I was not sure he had completely given up the practice. There was a large man with a shaved head leaning against the building and watching us while trying very hard to appear nonchalant but actually being pretty chalant.

'You don't know her,' Patrick said. 'She's not in the industry. Of course, you would be less likely to know her if she *was* in show business, wouldn't you, Sandy?' He thought he could charm me.

The look I gave him convinced him otherwise.

He stage-coughed. 'Right, well I met her when I was buying my new house. You know I moved out of that place I was living in after the divorce.' The 'place' he referred to was a twenty-two-room mansion in which every family member I have ever met could live and never run into each other, which was probably their fondest wish. 'She was the broker in charge of the listing and walked me through it personally. Things just took off from there, I suppose.' Patrick wasn't looking into my eyes probably because he thought I'd let him have it.

I only sort of did. 'You're marrying your realtor?' I asked.

'Real-estate professional, please.' I wasn't sure if Patrick was being sardonic or not.

'Patrick.' I was starting to worry about the man I had considered a friend, and maybe still did. 'Isn't it just a little bit possible you're doing this on the rebound?'

Patrick didn't answer right away, giving me the impression he was thinking about this for the first time. 'No, not this time,' he said. 'Emmie is the woman for me. It's so cute: yesterday she was angry at me because I forgot it was our four-month anniversary. Isn't that precious? I thought she was going to throw a coffee mug at me.'

I really had no answer for that.

We gave Heather and Amy time to get their car, give Patrick one last longing wave and drive off to count the likes their photo with him was no doubt getting this moment on Instagram. Then Patrick headed toward the valet working the parking lot and handed him his ticket. The young man, who was definitely hoping to make it as an actor, rewarded Patrick with his most ingratiating smile, chose not to offer to email Patrick his head shot and went for the car.

'I'm just saying this is very similar to the way you told me you married Patsy,' I continued. 'You tend to dive into things headfirst and worry about the consequences later. I'm worried you could be taking things too fast. Again.'

Patrick smiled. There was a time that would have had a serious effect on my nervous system, but now it just looked a trifle sad and maybe a little bit regretful.

'I'm very touched that you're concerned about me, Sandy, but you needn't worry. I know exactly what I'm doing and nobody is going to hurt me this time. Not even myself.'

I wanted to ask him about his new fiancée and more about how they met, why he was so smitten (if indeed he was, but I had my suspicions), and for one thing whether I would be invited to the wedding (because Angie, my plus-one, would have been ecstatic). But I didn't really know how to ask without sounding like I was jealous, which I was not.

Then I noticed the large man with the shaved head stop leaning against the side of the building, his eyes turned toward the street. He stood up straight, his eyes tracking something in front of him, then started running directly at Patrick and me.

Mostly Patrick.

'Gun!' he shouted. 'Gun!'

I didn't have a gun so I couldn't give him mine. Seriously, that was my first thought. Patrick looked equally puzzled by the sudden mood change and looked toward the bald man. 'Philip?' he said.

Philip (as I now assumed the bald man was named) rushed all the way to us and before I knew it had pretty much tackled Patrick to the pavement. Clearly I was not the one paying the security man's salary, because he didn't try very hard to take me down, which I considered slightly insulting.

'Gun!' he shouted again, in my direction. Then he pointed at the street. And I immediately dove for the sidewalk myself.

There was indeed a car driving up the street directly toward us and in the back seat behind the driver sat a man wearing sunglasses and a fedora (approximating Patrick's civilian disguise but for the choice of headwear), as well as – and this was the part I thought was weird – a denim jacket. And that man was aiming a handgun at us.

He fired and I actually heard the bullet whiz over my head,

then another shot which clearly missed us by some distance to my right as the car kept traveling up the street and gathered speed. I tried to look up to get a license-plate number, but the car was too far away already. The best I could do was see that the first letter of the plate was T.

It took me a long moment to exhale. My neck was stiff, not with pain but with fear. I couldn't feel my toes, but then I really didn't want to feel my toes. On the other hand, they would probably help me in standing up, which seemed the thing to do right now.

'What was that about?' I said from my sitting position (I'd managed to achieve sitting by now). I was hoping the security man could provide some clarity.

'That vehicle was trying to shoot Mr McNabb,' the bald guy said. Thanks, bald guy. That much I could figure out on my own.

Patrick stood up with a strange expression on his face, as if he were somehow pleased about what had happened. 'Excellent job, Philip,' he said to the bald man.

'Thank you, sir.'

Patrick reached down to offer me a hand and I took it. He helped me reach a standing position and looked me directly in the eye, still with that odd smile on his face.

'Rather like old times, isn't it?' he said.

SEVEN

'It's refreshing that this time you're actually reporting the shooting immediately after it occurred.'

Detective Lieutenant K.C. Trench of the Los Angeles Police Department was, actually, a homicide cop. The fact that he was showing some interest in the incident outside the restaurant where Patrick and I had finished lunch indicated there was some larger issue at hand. But Trench would sooner dance the tarantella naked in public than let on anything he didn't want me to know.

We had, of course, crossed paths before because Trench was the lead investigator on Patrick's case. He had testified at trial and probably did as much for me as he did the prosecution. Trench didn't play sides. So we had a strange cooperative relationship which Trench liked to present as irritation. Whatever worked.

He was ticked off at me (during Patrick's trial) because we – Patrick and I – had been shot at and, for various reasons, I had chosen not to report the incident until I had to. Cops don't like not being consulted when people are firing guns.

'The last time you were the enemy,' I explained. I was sitting in Trench's office, which was essentially a glass-encased room, spotless and neat as everything Trench did (and probably everything he owned) was. Through the window to my left I could see across the hallway, where Patrick was being questioned by another detective I recognized as Sergeant Roberts. Patrick looked delighted, Roberts not as much.

I didn't know where Philip was, but it could be reasonably assumed he was being asked all the same questions and giving all the same answers as we were. We had nothing to hide.

Trench raised an eyebrow, the equivalent of a screaming rage in another man. 'The enemy,' he said. It was question-adjacent.

'Patrick was accused of murder and you were on the side of the accusers while I was defending him,' I explained. 'Now we're just two people who got shot at for no reason and you are here to help us, I'm guessing. Why is a homicide detective interested in a shooting where no one was injured?'

Trench didn't so much as blink. I'm pretty sure he only blinked when no one was watching. It's possible Trench was a robot the LAPD was trying out as a detective in case people just stopped showing up to work. 'In the mandate of the robbery-homicide division of the department, Ms Moss, it is noted that the homicide division is involved at any time a special investigation is ordered by the chief of detectives.'

'Yes, and the Declaration of Independence says all men are created equal but I'm here to tell you they're not, Lieutenant.' I wasn't about to elaborate. 'Wait. Are you saying the chief of detectives ordered an investigation into a shooting that happened forty minutes ago?'

'Not specifically, no.' Trench laced his fingers behind his head and leaned back in his chair, yet still somehow projected as a man who was as formal and precise as a general during inspection. 'But I believe *you* are here to answer the questions, Ms Moss. Now, all you can remember of the license plate on the car that shot at you is that the first digit was a T?'

'Yeah. Oddly, I was somehow preoccupied when I had to dive to the ground and try not to get killed.'

'Do you remember what make and model car it was?' Trench asked.

Now, Jersey girls notice cars. Don't let anybody tell you otherwise. We know the difference between a guy who comes to pick you up for dinner in a late model Lexus LS and one who shows up in a 2011 Dodge Dart. He's probably come to take you bowling, and if the truth is told, he's likely to be more fun. All men are, in fact, not created equal.

But I was about to be forced to admit I hadn't taken note of the car itself, focused as I was on the barrel of the gun pointed out its back window on the passenger side. And that, for someone like me, was humiliating, particularly when I had to tell Trench, a man whose respect I secretly craved.

'I can't be sure, Lieutenant,' I said. 'It might have been a Nissan Sentra or a Honda Accord, silver, probably two years old. I mean, who can tell the difference at forty miles an hour?'

I couldn't look Trench in the eye. Having to confess a failing like that? I wanted to drop through a hole in the impeccably clean floor and vanish.

'Well, that gives us something to work with.' What? Trench was letting me off the hook? And they said LA had a car culture. Back home a cop would have done a tight ten minutes on me after an admission like the one I'd just made. 'And I am assuming until I see evidence to the contrary that the target here was Mr McNabb and not you. Am I incorrect?'

'I honestly couldn't say, Lieutenant. I know Patrick had hired some private security, but I don't know if that was just a continuation of the service he had while he was on trial. I take it a lot of actors do that.'

Trench stood up. That's it. He just stood up. He didn't stand up and pace, or stroke his immaculately shaved chin, or sit on the edge of his desk to establish a more mutual rapport with me. He just stood up. Maybe he was doing slow aerobics.

'Are you working on any especially sensitive cases right now, Counselor? Anything that might have someone angry at you beyond the usual limits?' This, from Trench, was amusing jocular banter. It was like getting trash talk from Sir Anthony Hopkins. I shook my head. 'The usual. A couple of divorces, one child custody matter and a pre-nuptial agreement.' I guessed I was writing up a pre-nup for Patrick now, although we hadn't actually formalized the agreement and I suspected his asking me was just his backdoor way of telling me he was getting married again.

'And also the criminal appeal of the woman accused of soliciting an undercover police officer?' Trench watched me closely to see if I was shaken to the core by his awareness of Madelyn Forsythe's legal issues.

To be honest, I *was* pretty amazed, but Trench and I had an unspoken agreement to be respectful but wary of each other. I tried very hard not to make an outward sign. 'How did you know about that?' I asked as casually as I could muster.

'I'm the police, Ms Moss. I know everything.' Trench was giving a master class in not telling someone anything they wanted to know.

I let off a little sigh to communicate that his game was a bore. 'Yes, Lieutenant. Madelyn Forsythe is a client of mine. What's your point?'

Trench actually allowed me to see a facial expression, and it was one of genuine concern. He glanced at the office door, which was shut. This was as close to a panic attack as I was likely to ever see from the man.

'Ms Moss,' he said in a hushed tone, 'I cannot say this definitively because I honestly don't know all the facts yet. But if I were you I would consider the very real possibility that it was not Mr McNabb who was being targeted in this shooting.'

My brain wasn't really operating at its true capacity right now because I thought I was hearing Trench, 1. Express concern about my wellbeing and, 2. Suggest that someone in Los Angeles might have actually gone to the trouble to shoot at Patrick and me without really wanting to hurt Patrick.

'You believe that they were trying to kill me, Lieutenant?' I asked.

'I believe that there are a number of people with considerable influence who are angry at you, Ms Moss, and I can't say for a complete certainty that they would stop short of murder if they thought it was a means to their ends.'

'That was a yes, wasn't it?' I said.

'I suppose it was,' Trench answered.

'Okey-dokey,' I said. 'Do you mind if I just sit here a minute or two longer?'

'It's fine,' Trench said, sitting back down behind his desk. 'But just for a minute or two.'

EIGHT

'This is a very serious situation,' Patrick said.

We were sitting at a conference table in the offices of Seaton, Taylor, Evans and Wentworth and the group assembled was not a logical one. I was there because I was the attorney handling the case. That made sense. Cynthia Sutton was there because she was the client. Also to be expected. Patrick was there because he was paying Cynthia's legal fees for reasons that had nothing to do with the real world as far as I could tell. And Angie was there because she is a force of nature and would not be denied. She adored Patrick and hadn't seen him in some months. Angie was going to show up. Period. Welcome to my life.

My boss Holiday Wentworth, the newest addition to the firm's masthead, had popped her head in out of deference to Patrick's money. She didn't want to intrude on my work and I appreciated it. Holly is a professional but she also has a heart, and I am always quick to seek out her advice when I need it.

I didn't think I'd require any help today, given that the divorce we were negotiating was a fairly straightforward one, just with a couple of extra zeroes at the end of every number involved. Take those away and this could have been a case from Linden, New Jersey, a place where I'd never in my life negotiated a divorce. I kept reminding myself I'd moved out here to LA because I didn't want to do criminal law anymore and family law had seemed so much less seedy and unpleasant. Until I'd started to do it.

In the ensuing months I'd defended Patrick against a murder charge stemming from his divorce from Patsy and then discovered in the real family law cases since then that people in the midst of breaking up what had once been a romantic relationship can be as vicious and petty as any drug dealer on the streets of New Brunswick. More, to be honest. The drug dealers just shoot you and put you out of your misery.

Speaking of shooting: I hadn't told Patrick about Trench's low-key warning. Patrick would undoubtedly have hired the 101st Airborne Division to act as personal security for me and that was the last thing I wanted. I *had* told Angie, largely because she would have simply picked up the vibe from me and hounded me until I came clean. Angie has powers beyond that of ordinary humans. It was one of . . . no. It was *the* reason she had insisted on coming with me to this conference.

'Patrick,' I said patiently (no, really), 'you have to remember that this is *not* your divorce. This is Cynthia's divorce from Michael Bryan and you're just here because . . . wait. It'll come to me.'

'He's here because he's looking out for me,' Cynthia said. 'Patrick's a loyal friend and he wants to make sure I'm not getting screwed here.'

Angie's mouth twisted a little; she didn't like the way Cynthia was treating me. 'Sandy's not going to screw her own client,' she said through lightly clenched teeth. 'You don't need *protection* from her.'

I took a quick glance at the ceiling for perspective and looked at Patrick, then at Angie. 'OK. So our seconds have agreed upon the location and the weapons of our duel. Should we move on to the rules of engagement?'

Well, *I* thought it was funny.

'Huh?' Cynthia said.

'The issue at hand, which as Patrick said is serious, concerns the terms of your divorce, Cynthia,' I said. 'I've read what you brought from your previous attorney and frankly, I don't understand what he was trying to accomplish.' (Perhaps this is the moment to note that Cynthia's previous attorney had ducked my call, but I'd find him even if I had to stake out his office. I didn't want this case and it was his fault I had it.)

'He was trying to bill me for as much money as he could and not get me what I'm entitled to,' Cynthia said. 'Look, I was crazy about Michael when we got married and in some ways I still love him, but the idea that I should pay *him* alimony and give him my house? I don't get that at all.'

Cynthia had a valid point. I had read over the draft agreement her previous attorney, David Dennison, had tried to get her to sign, and it did not appear to be written with his own client's interests in mind. He hadn't so much conceded every point as come up with new ones to surrender. If Cynthia had signed the agreement he'd drafted, she would have lost millions of dollars she'd already earned and probably would have continued to pay out to her soon-to-be-ex-husband for many years to come. It was hard to fathom.

'You were already a major earner in the entertainment field when you married Mr Bryan,' I said, 'but your husband was already a very well-off man. I take it he works for a brokerage house?'

'Yeah,' Cynthia said. 'He moves numbers around and people get rich. I mean, it's all legal and everything, but I can't say I understand exactly what he does that makes anything better for anybody.'

'Nonetheless,' I continued, 'he was easily capable of supporting himself and remains so to this day, yes?'

'Oh sure,' she answered. 'He's loaded. He doesn't need my money. He doesn't *need* the house. He doesn't need any of this stuff.'

People get weird when they're divorcing. I didn't know how much of Cynthia's story to believe, but I had no reason to think she was lying, either. Her husband might very well have gone off the deep end with his demands out of pure spite. I'd seen it happen and I'd been a family law attorney for less than a year.

'Can you understand why Michael is making all these demands if he doesn't need anything he's asking for?' I said.

'He's a guy,' Angie muttered. I would have silenced her with a look, but who are we kidding? I couldn't silence Angie with a sledgehammer.

'Because he's vindictive,' Patrick piped up. 'He sees a woman being more successful and powerful than he is and he can't stand the competition in his own home.' Patrick McNabb, feminist.

I looked over at Cynthia in an attempt to command her attention, while the two extra people in the meeting offered their opinions. 'Why do *you* think?' I asked.

Cynthia did glance at Patrick for a split second but then she made eye contact with me. 'I think it was his mother,' she said.

I thought that one over but, given the information I had in my possession, it still didn't seem like a relevant response. 'His mother?' I parroted back.

'Yes,' Patrick began.

I pointed a finger at him. 'Patrick,' I said, 'I need answers from Cynthia and I need them to be un-coached and unprompted. So either stay quiet or go wait in the extremely luxurious hallway.'

Patrick put his thumb and forefinger together and ran them across his mouth to indicate his lips were sealed. I'd believe that when I didn't hear it.

'Michael barely makes a move without asking his mother,' Cynthia said. 'It took months for her to consent to our getting married and we'd been living together for two years. Hell, it took a year for her to tell him it was OK for us to live together. The stuff in that paper' – she pointed at the proposed settlement in front of me – 'that stuff is straight out of his mother's mouth. Wendy Bryan isn't going to let me get away with a dollar in my pocket if she can do anything about it. I'm telling you. We could probably stay married if she'd leave us alone.'

'So would it be possible to talk to your husband without his mother around?' I asked. 'Maybe he could be convinced that this isn't the way to go.' I waved the settlement document in front of me, just to make it clear I was referring to that, something the average baby giraffe would have been able to infer.

'It used to be possible,' Cynthia answered with a little catch in her throat. 'I could talk to Michael when we were alone or when Wendy wasn't on the phone or coming over. But she started talking trash about me in his ear maybe a year ago, and for some reason he started listening. He became this . . . I don't know . . . this *thing* that I couldn't stand to be around. I was almost afraid of him.'

I'd heard some of these terms before and they weren't making me relaxed. 'Did he ever hit you, Cynthia?' I asked. Then I turned and pointed again to stop Patrick, who I was certain would be trying to answer the question himself. He held up his hands, palms forward, to show me he was staying quiet.

'Oh no,' she answered. 'Michael wouldn't ever. I mean, that's just not in him. But the emotional toll his mother's influence was having on him was just suffocating, you know? I knew anything I said to him was going straight to her, and anything she said about me would stick in his mind. She poisoned my marriage, that woman.'

'So one of my first strategies will be to try and remove Mrs Bryan from the negotiations,' I said. 'That's not something I can do blatantly, but it is possible to insist I speak only with Michael's attorney. Your mother-in-law won't have any influence over him, Cynthia.'

'So you'll take the case?' Cynthia seemed to think we were having this conference just to convince me I should represent her. Patrick was paying the legal bills, since a sizable retainer had already been paid, and *he* certainly wanted me to take the case. I wondered if his new fiancée the realtor had any idea he was doing that for Cynthia.

'Yes, I'm your attorney if you want me to be,' I told Cynthia.

Angie shot me a look that asked me if I knew what I was getting myself into. I gave her one back that was less eloquent but to the point.

'Thank you.' Cynthia actually started to tear up. 'I didn't know where to turn until Patrick told me about you.'

I looked over at Patrick, who was grinning but pinched his lips together with his fingers.

'It's OK, Patrick,' I said. 'The gag order is lifted.'

'I just wanted to say I'm glad to bring two of my favorite women together with a singular purpose,' he said. He'd been working on that one for a while, I could tell.

I stood up and the others followed. 'OK,' I said. 'I will set up a conference on the phone or in person with Joseph Dombrowski, your husband's attorney. Once we've had that discussion, I'm hoping I'll have better news to give you, Cynthia.'

We all stood up from the table with those grim professional smiles (except Patrick's, which was of course charming and didn't seem at all forced. Actors.) and nodded at each other. Patrick, ever the center of attention, insisted on taking me aside while Cynthia walked out looking slightly less terrified than when she arrived (people are afraid of lawyers). Angie, after I sent her the right look, walked out, but she clearly wasn't happy about being left out of the loop. Like that would last.

'About my pre-nup,' Patrick began.

'We should schedule a separate conference for you and me to discuss that, Patrick,' I said, cutting him off. 'Until I have all your financial records and let one of the money guys here in the firm see them, I won't be able to give you any useful advice.'

'I don't know if that will be necessary,' he answered. 'I'm calling off the wedding.'

That was quick! 'Really,' I said. 'Why?'

'Largely because of you, Sandy.'

NINE

'**P**atrick is in love with you,' Angie said.

I reached into the fridge and pulled out a beer because wine wasn't going to make me burp and, after the day I'd had, I really wanted to burp. They say in some societies letting a good *grepse* go is considered a compliment to the chef. In New Jersey, it's a form of self-expression.

My weariness as I took in the first swallow of Corona was palpable. I mean, I'd started the day being shot at, and now a major television star was telling me I was the reason he'd decided to tell a woman he wasn't going to marry her. And there'd been stuff *in the middle*! I wanted a nap.

'Patrick is *not* in love with me.' I sat down on a barstool we'd set up next to the pass-through in our kitchen. I figured if you were drinking a beer you should be sitting on a barstool. 'Patrick thinks I'm a genius, so the second I suggested he was rushing into marriage again, he figured he was getting it straight from Albert Einstein and should immediately change his entire life.'

'And yet here you are drinking at only six in the evening.'

Angie likes to tease me. Angie thinks she's witty. Angie isn't always right. 'You know he's in love with you.' See?

Angie was lying on the floor in sweats doing bicycle legs because I was drinking a beer. Show-off.

'I don't even want to discuss this,' I told her. 'Tell me something else. Anything else.'

'I interviewed for a job today,' Angie said. Her grin indicated there was a really good story behind what she'd told me.

I sat up a little straighter. 'No kidding! What kind of a job?'

The grin got bigger. 'I'm not gonna tell you.' In a singsong voice. The world was conspiring to annoy me as much as possible and my best friend was leading the opposition.

'Come on,' I whined. 'I had a real bad day. People shot at me.'

'OK. It's an assistant position.' I waited, but that was it.

'With whom?' Let it be known that stress brings out the best in my grammar.

'I don't want to jinx it,' Angie said. 'I'll tell you when I hear if I got it.'

Who had the energy to argue? Well, probably Patrick did because he never seemed to lose his verve. Whoever shot at me? They probably had tons of pep and were arranging to bump me off in some other way even as I pondered the question. I mean, Trench had said he'd have police cruisers pass by my apartment building more often than usual, but what were the odds they'd be there at the exact moment someone decided to off me? Luckily, I had Angie, who would blow up anyone who tried to harm me, no matter what. She never slept, so it was basically a 24/7 kind of arrangement. She was an amazing friend. I had to give her the benefit of the doubt.

I told her OK, she didn't have to explain anything until she got/didn't get the job, which she estimated would take a few days. I got up off the barstool and headed to the couch to close my eyes just as Angie, who had switched to raised-leg crunches, flipped over for push-ups. I got more tired just watching her. So I stopped watching, put my head back, and examined the insides of my eyelids, which I found rewarding.

Joseph Dombrowski, the attorney for Michael Bryan, had taken my phone call on the third ring.

'Michael isn't asking for anything unreasonable,' he'd insisted after I explained that I was Cynthia's new attorney. 'They both have adequate resources but Mrs Bryan is an established celebrity in the entertainment business and her income is more substantial than Michael's at this point. Why shouldn't she bear the heavier load, especially since it was Michael who filed to end the marriage?'

'Exactly for those reasons,' I countered, having anticipated this plan of attack and not bothering to correct him about my client's name. There'd be time for that. 'Cynthia's income is very high right now but careers in the movie and TV business are short. She can't be expected to maintain this level of financial stability forever. And since her husband did file for the divorce, it's clear he has a more urgent need to end the marriage. I won't speculate on why.'

I could hear the smile in Dombrowski's voice. 'Oh, speculate away, Ms Moss,' he said. 'There was no infidelity on Michael Bryan's part.'

'No,' I agreed. 'And there wasn't any on Cynthia's, either. I would have guessed that Michael filed for divorce because his mother told him to. How far off am I?'

There was a momentary silence. 'I don't comment on the mother,' Dombrowski said.

I'd struck a nerve. Maybe what Cynthia had told me wasn't that far off the mark. Not about the couple reconciling without the mother hovering over her son, because that wasn't any of my business, but if Michael really was that far under Wendy's thumb, it might explain why he was being so uncharacteristically (according to Cynthia) unreasonable about the terms of their divorce.

'OK,' I said, although Dombrowski hardly needed my permission to not talk about Michael Bryan's mother. 'So when can we get together and talk about some compromise that doesn't actually take everything my client owns for no reason at all?'

'We can't.' The answer came immediately and it sounded definitive. 'Michael will not budge off one single request in that agreement. If you turn it down, I promise you we'll come back with something even more favorable to Michael, go to court and take our chances with a judge, probably one who's a man and, in this county, one who's been divorced and feels fleeced. Do you want to go that route?'

You don't often get a declaration of war sent quite so clearly these days. And they would, I'd assume, usually sound angrier than the one from Dombrowski. He was just confident, or was trying to sound confident. It was working. I was a little unnerved.

But you don't win cases by letting your opponent know their tactics are effective against you. 'I guess we'll see you in court, then,' I said. 'Because Cynthia Sutton is not going to let you pick her pockets and then tell her how nice she looks in those jeans.'

Let's just say we'd left it at that.

Angie stood up, having done more exercise in the past half-hour than I'd done in the previous year and yes, I do actually run down to the tiendita every now and again. She didn't even have the good grace to be excessively sweaty. 'What do you want to order for dinner?' she asked.

Now, I need to be careful here because otherwise my behavior in this situation might be seen as petty or mean, neither of which was intended. But the fact was that Angie had refused to touch her savings account and was now living in what was essentially my apartment since she was paying no rent. And she was eating whatever food I bought. So the idea of ordering delivery and then paying for it myself was not a new one; it was the fact that she just *expected* it that hit my last nerve on this incredibly long and trying day.

'Why don't you spend your time during the day when you're not working and learn to cook?' I asked. 'We could save *me* some money if we didn't order in every single night.'

Again, I feel some explanation is in order. We didn't, in fact, order in every night. It just felt that way because we did it more than I hoped we would. And I did think Angie should take the time now to learn some new skills while she was looking for a job. She'd had this interview today and that was good, but she'd had a lot of interviews in the past six months and not one had panned out, so there was no reason to expect this one would be any different.

She didn't seem terribly offended. Angie is great at deflecting the things she doesn't want to deal with. 'Good idea,' she said. 'Because, you know, I can't cook at all, can I?' (In the interest of full disclosure, Angie is a really good cook, particularly of Italian food, and I am, you know, not.)

I let out a long sigh. 'You know what kind of day I've had,' I said, as if that gave me a pass for being a jerk.

'Yeah. And *you* know that I've been actively searching for a source of income so I could pay my half out here. Remember that when you decided to move to LA you did it because you'd been offered a really good job. I did it because I wanted to save your life.'

And I couldn't even accuse her of exaggeration.

I honestly felt like I didn't have the strength to open my eyes. 'I'm sorry,' I said, and it didn't even sound convincing to me. 'You are a good cook. And you are looking for work, and I hope you get the job you interviewed for today. But sometimes things pile up on me and you're the only person around for me to unload on.'

'See? If you'd admit that Patrick is in love with you, then you could be with him and I wouldn't get unloaded on so often.' I couldn't see her but I knew she was smiling so joyfully I'd want to pummel her. And Angie, if she wanted to, could kill me in at least eight different ways.

'Patrick. Is. *Not*. In Love. With. Me.'

'Think what you want.'

It was just as well that my phone rang just then because I didn't have a sharp, witty comeback to use. The Caller ID indicated the call was coming from my office, but not from Holly Wentworth or any of the other attorneys. It was from the front desk, which was only a little odd. That's who you get when the message is not from a partner or a specific colleague.

'Ms Moss, this is Janine at the front desk.' OK, so I knew Janine. 'I wanted you to know there was a call about one of your clients from the Santa Monica Police.'

Maddie Forsythe? Just out of the blue at the end of the day? How was that possible?

'What did they want with Ms Forsythe?' I asked Janine.

'Forsythe?' She sounded confused. 'They called about Ms Sutton.'

Cynthia? 'What about her?' Since when do the cops call about a divorce?

'She was arrested for murder.'

Having my eyes closed had been so good. I rubbed them but it just wasn't the same. For a moment I forgot I was talking to Janine, or for that matter anyone else. Angie looked at me as if I might need a quick trip to the ER.

'She offed the husband, didn't she?'

'Oh no,' Janine said. 'They're charging her with killing his mother.'

TEN

Cynthia Sutton didn't look like the first time I'd met her in Judge Coffey's courtroom. She wasn't about to get unhinged because someone didn't know who she was. She wasn't waving her posture around in everyone's face. She didn't even seem as confident as she'd been in the conference room at Seaton, Taylor, and that hadn't been terribly confident.

Right now, she was scared.

Without makeup, her hair uncombed, wearing sweats, Cynthia was almost unrecognizable. She was so dowdy she could have been me.

I sat down next to her in the interrogation room of the Santa Monica police station. I'd let the arresting officers know I was Cynthia's attorney and that she would be answering a grand total of no questions tonight. They'd just have to go and watch *Law & Order* reruns if they wanted something that quick.

The room was as nondescript as you'd imagine, with linoleum tile floors and a plain white ceiling. The walls were painted in something resembling a color, probably beige. Or off-white. Or something that nobody had ever thought about in history and would continue to not think about until they got painted again, at which time no doubt it would take a meeting of the city council to approve the new color, which would probably be beige. Or off-white.

From the outside, the Santa Monica police department is exactly what would be expected from a town with an amusement pier and a desperate need to be liked, mostly by rich people. It was modern and dynamic and pleasing to the eye, which is a strange thing for a police station to be. Inside, on the other hand, it was just a police station.

Cynthia had not been brought in from the jail section, which is larger than in most city precincts. She hadn't been arraigned yet and would not be until the next morning. I might be able to get into night court to ask for her release, but first I had to determine if I had a chance of convincing a judge to do that.

I'd picked up the police report on the death of Wendy Bryan (legal name) and it was a doozy. This was just the preliminary findings, by the way, not the full report that would be issued after the medical examiner's autopsy and any further indications from the investigating detective, who I saw was named Edward Brisbane and not K.C. Trench. More to my disadvantage if I was going to defend Cynthia, which I hoped I was not.

'It says here that they found you in the room next to where the body was found, in your mother-in-law's home, and that you were curled up on the floor and crying,' I told Cynthia. 'Is that true?' I wanted to see if the cops who had first arrived on the scene had exaggerated the facts and made too quick an arrest.

'Pretty much.' Cynthia's voice wavered. She was fighting back tears now, too. 'I couldn't talk. I couldn't even stand. They practically had to pick me up to take me to the police car.'

My first priority was to calm Cynthia down. My second was to try and get her released on her own recognizance (California is among the states that have ended the practice of cash bail). My third, but perhaps most important, was to find her another lawyer. I'd done one murder trial in LA; it had involved a television star and it had been perhaps – no, not perhaps – the most harrowing experience of my life. I had no desire to relive *that* ordeal.

'First things first,' I told her. 'Tell me what happened. Don't leave anything out and don't lie to me. I'm your lawyer, for right now, and I can't be blindsided with things the police will say and I won't know. Why were you in Wendy's house?'

'Michael texted me.' Cynthia was still in some sort of shock but I was forcing her to focus. I'd recommend her attorney have her examined by a doctor as soon as possible. It could have some bearing on her defense, assuming she didn't want to plead guilty and hope for the best in negotiations with the prosecutor. 'He said he wanted to talk about the divorce and it should be on neutral ground. He said his mother's place was neutral ground, can you believe it?'

I had so many questions, most of which were *why didn't you say no?* But I let her talk. There would be time to fill in the gaps when I had the general framework of the case.

'So you got there and Michael wasn't in the house?' There had been no mention of Cynthia's husband in the police report.

'That's right. I walked in and the place seemed deserted. I called a few times but nobody answered. And then . . .'

I waited, but nothing followed. 'And then what?' I asked.

'And then . . .' Another long pause, then Cynthia took a deep breath and the words came out in a torrent. 'I went into the center hall and I found her on the floor. She was bleeding, like, all over the place and I didn't scream, I just ran over to her, but she was already dead, I *swear*, Sandy!'

I put my hand on her forearm. 'OK. OK. So why didn't you call the police? They said the nine-one-one call came in from a cell phone that Wendy owned.'

Cynthia sniffed. 'I was just so shocked. I guess I ran into the den, you know, the next room, and I just sat there and cried. The next thing I knew there were cops standing there with me.'

I glanced at the report again so Cynthia could compose herself. You learn as an attorney not to try and play psychotherapist, but you're not devoid of feelings. The woman had indeed gone through an incredibly rough night, whether she'd killed Wendy Bryan or not.

When I felt a reasonable interval had gone by, I asked, 'The report says she was stabbed with a statuette? How is that possible? Was it a really sharp one?'

Cynthia's face took on a small fraction of the haughtiness she'd shown at our first meeting. 'It was a TeeVee award,' she said, something she clearly thought I should have known. 'The figure on the statue has wings that are very pointy. That's what Wendy was stabbed with.'

OK, so it was a TeeVee award. Now, who in that family might own a TeeVee award?

'Was Wendy at all involved in the television business?' I asked hopefully.

Cynthia once again regarded me as if I had just asked her what I should be breathing, that I'd heard air was good but wanted the straight story from her. 'Of course not,' she answered. 'She was in the art business. The TeeVee was mine.'

'And the police report said you were found holding it in the adjacent room, but the globe the statue was holding had been bent down. Did that make it easier to stab her?' There was no point in beating around the bush. If Cynthia killed Wendy, it was time to start planning for the plea bargain.

'How would I know?' Cynthia said.

I felt it was best not to answer that question. 'Why were you holding the award when the police found you?' If the answer was, *so it would be easier to find the murder weapon with my fingerprints on it*, that would make things easier. For me.

Cynthia shook her head. 'I really don't remember,' she said. 'I saw her on the floor and I saw the TeeVee next to it, all bent like that, and the next thing I knew I was crying in the den, on the floor, not even the sofa.'

'And you were holding the TeeVee,' I pointed out.

Cynthia didn't have the time to respond because the door opened and Patrick McNabb walked in. That would have been surreal enough, but Patrick being Patrick there had to be added an air of theatricality. He was wearing a wig of curly hair and a pencil mustache that his makeup artist had clearly glued on sometime that day.

'Cynthia, dear, I got in the car as soon as I heard!' Patrick flew to her side and knelt by Cynthia's chair.

'How . . . how . . .' That was me. Cynthia seemed completely at ease with Patrick just showing up out of nowhere in an outlandish costume. 'How did you get in here?'

Patrick looked up, seemingly noticing for the first time that I was there. 'Sandy, thank goodness!' He turned toward Cynthia again. 'If anyone can get you out of this, Sandy can, love. She's the best ever. Don't you worry about a thing.'

Cynthia, beaming at Patrick with something nauseatingly approaching adoration, turned her attention back to me because

Patrick had told her she should. I spent the time trying to get myself back into a professional state of mind.

'Patrick,' I said finally, 'how did you get into this room? There are I don't know how many cops out there whose job it is specifically not to let you in.'

Patrick took a seat next to Cynthia, which in itself was an accomplishment. He'd had to take the one on my side of the table that had been left in case two detectives would want to interrogate a suspect at the same time. He smiled at me as well, confident in me at the exact moment I didn't want him to be.

'There are a good many police officers out there,' he said. 'You're right. And they were adamant about my not being in here until I told them who I am.'

The multiple personality thing again. Oy. 'And who is it you think you are today?' I asked.

His eyes registered puzzlement. 'Why, Patrick McNabb. And a few of the officers are fans of *Torn*, while a few more enjoyed *Legality* when I was on it.' He grinned a smug grin and affected a confidential tone. 'They're on the bubble for cancellation, you know. Ratings plummeted when I left.' The fact that he'd been fired from the show after his trial for murder had morphed in Patrick's mind into his leaving voluntarily in favor of his current program. 'So I was able to gain entry when I told them I had hired you to represent Cynthia here.'

Have you ever felt like the walls were closing in around you? Here I was in a place built for the express purpose of keeping unwilling occupants inside, and the point was being driven home by a delusional actor. 'Nobody has been hired to represent Cynthia,' I said slowly. 'I am here just to assess the situation, maybe get you through night court and hope for arraignment, Cynthia, and then I will recommend a criminal attorney if one is needed for the rest of the way. And I'm pretty sure you *will* need an experienced criminal attorney.'

The whole proceeding was going so well that I'd completely given up on asking Patrick exactly why he was made up like someone's weird idea of Harpo Marx if he were a waiter at a cheap café on the Left Bank.

He shook his head. 'Nonsense. You handled my case beautifully and you were a prosecutor for years. You *are* the experienced criminal attorney, Sandy. You really must work on your problem with self-esteem.'

I didn't have a problem with self-esteem. I mean, I *do* have a problem with self-esteem, but it wasn't the issue in this case at this moment. I felt my teeth clench. My whole purpose here was to convince Patrick, and by extension Cynthia, that she should hire someone else specifically because I didn't want to be a criminal attorney anymore, or else I'd be back home in New Jersey where nobody killed anyone else with a TeeVee award.

This case was a loser, and that wasn't something I wanted any part of right now. My job at Seaton, Taylor was just getting its legs under it, I'd started making a small reputation as a family law attorney and I'd already been roped into one criminal case I didn't want. So it wasn't just because I was being petty; it was that I would be a bad fit for Cynthia's interests going forward.

And let's be real, this case was going forward. The prosecutor in me could just feel the excitement in such a slam dunk. I mean, the victim's adversarial daughter-in-law, in the process of a contested divorce against the victim's son, a television actress discovered in the room next to the body holding the murder weapon, which just happened to be *her* award for being a television actress? A gibbon in a tailored suit could try this case to a victory.

'Cynthia,' I said. Going through Patrick, who thought I was Oliver Wendall Holmes, was a losing proposition. 'Listen to me. Patrick is sweet and I did help him get acquitted, but he had the advantage of not having killed his wife and we got lucky in a number of key elements. I'm not the best lawyer for your case. I can recommend better ones and you can afford them. So please, let me find out if there's a night court we can apply to for release on your own recognizance and then you can move on with a new lawyer, OK?'

Cynthia Sutton must have been a very good actress. I'd never seen any of her films or her HBO series, but I was convinced she was very skilled at her profession. Because she sat there, looked up at me slowly, widened her eyes just a little (don't want to overplay it) and said, in a husky voice, 'Please.'

And that is how I became Cynthia's criminal attorney.

ELEVEN

I got Cynthia through a hastily arranged arraignment at night court, and although the deputy DA assigned at the last minute gave it her best, the judge decided Cynthia was not a great flight risk and allowed her release pending trial. I very carefully laid out the rules of the situation, noted that Cynthia would have to wear an ankle monitor and technically be placed under 'house arrest', although she would be allowed to travel back and forth to work and to conferences with her lawyer, who unfortunately was me, until her trial began, which would probably be a matter of months. I dropped her off at her house and arranged for her car, which was much newer and more expensive than my rejuvenated Hyundai, to be brought to her home in the morning.

Patrick offered to follow me back to my apartment to 'plot strategy', but I demurred, saying that strategy was something I preferred to plot on my own, which wasn't true. The fact is I just wanted to eat some Thai food and go to bed, which is what I did. Angie cleaned up.

The next morning I was in my office with Holiday Wentworth asking for help.

'You know, we did offer you the chance to head up a criminal law division in the firm,' Holly reminded me. 'If you want to take on cases and cut back on the family stuff . . .'

'That's exactly what I *don't* want to do,' I said. 'I backed myself into a corner on Forsythe but the Sutton case was foisted upon me by our most frequent client.'

Holly smiled. 'Patrick McNabb.' I've seen many women smile like that when Patrick's name comes up. It makes me worry that I look like that when I talk about him, then I remember it's Patrick and that seems unlikely. He's a good man and a friend, of sorts, but Patrick doesn't make me go all moony in my eyes. I'm pretty sure. I'd ask Angie, but she'd lie.

'Yes. And in order to keep Patrick happy I have to defend

Cynthia Sutton, who appears to be a friend of his. But that's it. After Sutton, no more criminal cases, Holly. I promise.'

Holly smiled on the right side of her mouth. She was so chic it was hard to tell, but I'd known her a while now. She was being California sarcastic. It's different from New Jersey sarcastic in that it's not California's national language and therefore practiced less frequently, less loudly and less effectively. It's not their fault; they just have never experienced the real thing. Like bagels.

'So what do you need?' Holly said. I reported directly to Holly, who reported to the partners, of whom she was the most junior. When I required assistance, Holly was the one I'd ask, and she had never not come through. Holly and I never socialized, but in the office she was undoubtedly my closest friend.

'I could use a full-time assistant, an actual attorney who can be second chair, on the Sutton case,' I began. 'We know from past experience that's going to be a publicity bear and there will be tons of witnesses. I'll need at least one investigator on that case, too. The cops found Cynthia holding the murder weapon and they've pretty much closed the case on the basis of that alone.'

Holly frowned. 'What do you think?'

'About what?'

She leaned on the edge of my desk. 'Do you think Cynthia Sutton killed her mother-in-law with a TeeVee award?'

I had given this considerable thought overnight, and after serious consultation with Angie (who had announced that she had a follow-up interview for the mysterious assistant job today or probably would have insisted on coming to work with me) I had an answer ready. 'No. I don't,' I said.

Holly narrowed her eyes a bit. 'Really. Why not? I mean, from all you've told me it seems like those two women detested each other.'

'They did, no question,' I agreed. 'But the one thing on this earth that Cynthia Sutton would never have used as a weapon is her best actress award. She would kill her mother-in-law with anything else at all, but not that.'

Holly smiled. 'I doubt you'll be able to use that in court,' she said.

I shook my head. 'That's why I need the investigator and a second chair.'

'I don't see why those will be a problem,' Holly said. 'I'll
approve it and you should just proceed as if it's policy. You
worked with Nate Garrigan on Patrick McNabb's case. Do
you have any objection to going with him again?'

'No, he'd be great. But I'll need a different second chair this
time.' Holly and I shared a smile. The person who had been
assigned to help me in court on Patrick's case no longer worked
at Seaton, Taylor and let's leave it at that.

Holly nodded. 'I'll see who we have. This is going to be fairly
long term. I'll assign someone who has a fairly low cascload
right now. Maybe Jon Irvin.'

Jon was good. 'Thanks.'

She stood up. 'Things will be different this time, Sandy. You
let me know what you need and you'll get it, as long as it's
within reason.' She turned and walked out of my office just as
Patrick McNabb, nodding to the adoring staff as he walked
through the office, arrived in my doorway.

'Patrick.' My voice reflected a little more of the weariness in
my head than I wanted it to. 'I promise you I'll let you know
when there are developments in Cynthia's case. Immediately after
I let *Cynthia* know. OK? I have to prepare for all my other cases.
So I don't have tons of time to talk right now.'

'Oh, I completely understand,' said Patrick. Then he walked
in and sat down in the client chair I have in front of my desk.
'You work so hard, love, and I think you need to have all the
information on this case. I can be of help to you.'

No, Patrick, please. You can't be of help to me. Go back to
work, pretend to be a guy with multiple personalities who solves
crimes. Don't try to help me. We both know how that works out.
Well, I know, anyway.

I found what I thought was a more diplomatic way of saying
that. 'I appreciate the offer, but try and see it from my perspective, Patrick. Cynthia's court date is likely to be at least four
months from now. Probably more. I have a number of other cases,
most of them in family court, and they will *all* be in the courtroom before Cynthia. So you can see how I might have to
concentrate on those first, right?'

'Of course.' I waited, but Patrick did not stand up. He was
being reasonable, but I knew he wouldn't be placated unless it

looked as if I was doing something that he wanted me to do. 'Will you be using the same investigator who worked on my trial?' he asked.

'As a matter of fact, I think we will,' I said. 'You remember Nate Garrigan.' What he probably didn't remember was how Nate had wanted to kill Patrick on any number of occasions for interfering in his work and jeopardizing our case. And our case was meant to keep Patrick out of jail. It was an interesting conundrum, really.

'I do.' Patrick was nodding enthusiastically. 'He was brilliant. So he's looking into Cynthia's problem right now?'

Where was this going? 'Not exactly right now, no. I was just given the clearance to get his help on the case before you walked in, so I haven't had time to contact him yet.'

The thing about Patrick McNabb's attention was that, when it was on you, it was on nothing else. The man could focus like no one I had ever met before. But right now his glance was darting around the room, taking in whatever details he thought were relevant or could help him in his work. Of course, now Patrick was no longer playing an attorney on television so I was spared the endless questions about procedure and my inner thoughts and his asking if he could 'use' anything I happened to do in the course of trying to get him acquitted. So his curiosity about my office, a place he'd been a number of times before, was a little baffling.

'You haven't, eh? Was I keeping you from doing that?' So that's what this was about; Patrick wanted to see me getting Nate Garrigan on the phone to start his work. That would make him feel like Cynthia's case was proceeding in the right direction. And passive aggressive though it was, I felt that calling Nate right now would solve a lot of problems for me, not the least of which was getting Patrick to go home, or back to the soundstage.

'It wasn't your fault at all,' I answered, 'but I can certainly get the ball rolling with Nate.'

'The sooner the better, before the trail goes cold, don't you think?' Patrick's accent was always a bit more pronounced when he was excited. I thought because he so often had to adopt an 'American' accent for work he became more British when he was simply being himself.

I didn't answer him but picked up the phone and dialed Nate Garrigan's number.

'I was wondering when I'd hear from you.' Nate doesn't only observe Caller ID. He also knows exactly when to be smug without crossing the line to obnoxious. 'I saw the headline about the actress offing her mother-in-law with a TeeVee and immediately thought of you. This is right up your alley, isn't it?'

'You're hilarious, Nate,' I said. 'Are you thinking of dropping in at the Comedy Store this week, because I'd want to make sure I was there to heckle.'

'OK, you're right.' Nate actually sounded a little regretful, worried that he'd offended me. 'So what *are* you calling about?'

'The actress offing her mother-in-law with a TeeVee,' I admitted.

To his credit, Nate didn't break into triumphant laughter. Too much. After the moment passed he asked, 'What do we have to work with?'

'Not a lot. Cynthia Sutton had motive because she was divorcing Wendy Bryan's son and thought that Wendy had a hand in breaking up her marriage.'

'Kinky,' Nate said.

Patrick was looking like a third-grader who wanted the teacher to acknowledge him so he could ask to use the restroom. He was a millisecond short of raising his hand.

'Not like that,' I told Nate. 'Wendy just didn't like Cynthia for some reason and apparently has an undue amount of influence with her son.'

By now Patrick could not contain himself any longer. 'Excuse me,' he said. 'Might I speak to Mr Garrigan for a moment?'

Now, I had been down this road before and knew it led to madness. I pretended not to hear Patrick, knowing it would only exacerbate his behavior but that it would buy me the few scant seconds I needed to set up the situation for Nate. 'She was sitting in the next room holding the murder weapon in her hand and barely communicating with the cops,' I told him.

'Sandy,' Patrick said. It wasn't within his spectrum of experience to be ignored, or at least hadn't been for the past few years. Young Patrick Dunwoody, who had come to Hollywood after having a few minor roles in British films and a recurring guest spot on an Australian TV series, was accustomed to a lack of attention. Patrick McNabb, star of *Legality* and *Torn*, hadn't been out of the spotlight for more than a bathroom break this decade.

I held up a hand to indicate I'd let him speak shortly. 'Wow,' Nate said through the phone. 'That ain't good. What's on our side?'

'Well, she says she didn't do it,' I noted.

'Oh, case closed, then. Why are they even bothering taking this one to trial? Do you want me to investigate, or are you going to bargain this one down to ten years and out in four with good behavior?'

I coughed. And I felt perfectly fine. It was a reaction to the situation I was finding myself in. 'Cynthia pled not guilty at arraignment last night and is out on her own recognizance,' I told Nate. 'She intends to take this to trial and clear her name.'

'Great. Let me know if I should be out looking for the one-armed man.'

'Uh, Sandy.' Patrick was a touch more adamant now. 'May I?'

There would be no denying him. 'Nate,' I said. 'There's someone here who wants to talk to you about the investigation.'

Nate was silent a moment. 'You're kidding,' he said.

'No. Patrick McNabb is very insistent on talking to you directly.' Patrick reached over but I didn't give him the phone yet because I didn't want him to hear Nate's immediate reaction.

'I mean, you've really *got* to be kidding,' the investigator said. 'How is he even involved in it this time?'

'That's a really good question,' I said, and handed the phone to Patrick.

'Mr Garrigan!' Patrick was already in his most charming, ingratiating mode. 'I am hoping you might have a few minutes. I have some knowledge of the situation in which my friend Cynthia finds herself and I think I can be of help to you in your investigations.'

I couldn't hear Nate's response but I could predict it. Patrick listened for a few seconds and said, 'No, I believe I have invaluable insight into the dynamic of the marriage and the mother-in-law's role in it. And I can suggest people to inter-view who can attest to Cynthia's patience in the situation that would . . . what?'

There was a slightly longer pause this time. 'No, I do *not* intend to go out and interview witnesses on my own, Mr Garrigan.' Patrick looked less annoyed than surprised such a suggestion might have been made. 'I would have every expectation that you would come along.'

I wanted to look away and I couldn't even see Nate.

Patrick waited and listened while I pretended to be looking for something in the top drawer of my desk. There was nothing in there except paper clips, Post-it notes and emergency peanut M&Ms. Could I make-believe I needed a paper clip (when what I really wanted was the candy)?

'No,' Patrick went on after Nate had responded, probably with less profanity than he'd actually wanted to use. 'I do not consider myself a professional investigator. But you have to admit we made a pretty good team the last time, didn't we?'

In order to prevent Nate from suffocating himself by swallowing his phone, I reached over to Patrick. 'Let me talk to him,' I said.

He looked startled. 'What?'

'Let me talk to Nate. Right now. This is my office, Patrick. If you don't want me to come to your soundstage and start telling the director where the camera should be set up, you're going to give me that phone.'

Patrick, no doubt aware that I would do just what I said, mumbled something about how I'd probably be an improvement over the director they had this week, but he handed me my phone. 'Nate,' I said.

'I think he just appointed himself my assistant,' he said.

'I'm not sure,' I told him. 'I think it might be the other way around.'

TWELVE

Patrick had to leave for a lunch meeting (he apparently had the day off from shooting *Torn* because they were filming with the guest star) so I got a chance to actually work on Madelyn Forsythe's appeal. Which was on the one hand a relief and on the other hand a terror. I had to get Maddie acquitted so she could both stay out of jail and have a chance at retaining custody of her children.

What seemed most likely was that I could prove to the judge (because an appeal is not a retrial, so there would be no jury) that Sergeant LeRoy had been, to abuse a word, overzealous in her pursuit of Maddie Forsythe because she was hoping to find out who Maddie's pimp was and therefore move up the chain of command. Problem was that Maddie actually wasn't a prostitute so there was no pimp and now LeRoy was facing the prospect of looking incredibly foolish in front of a judge, something I sincerely hoped to encourage.

I called in Jon Irvin, the attorney who had started at Seaton, Taylor a year or so before me and who Holly had appointed my second chair for Cynthia's case. Jon had a background as a public defender, something he'd done for exactly six months before the frustration had sent him looking for a more lucrative, if not nobler, branch of the law to practice. He was the only other lawyer in the firm with this kind of criminal law experience and, now that I was being forced back into that area, I figured Jon could provide some critical help, noting weaknesses in my case and helping me to bolster the arguments I'd be making. Luckily, he didn't seem to be upset that he was essentially my right-hand man despite his longer tenure at the firm. When parents wanted to explain the word *easygoing* to their children, they showed the kids a video of Jon doing anything.

He sat down in the client chair, which was considerably cushier than mine. Jon was in his early forties, a few years older than me (he'd come to the law later in life than I had, having first tried to make it as a screenwriter – this was LA after all) and probably eight to ten pounds heavier than he'd been in law school. He said he'd only started eating well when he had gotten married. His wife was a graphic designer, I thought.

We discussed Maddie's case for a few minutes and then Jon looked over my notes for an opening statement. 'I think you're going the wrong way trying to tear down the cop,' he said after a moment to consider. 'People don't like cops, but they are afraid to see them disrespected. It makes juries uncomfortable.'

That shot a big fat hole right through my main line of defense and I wasn't about to give up without a fight. 'But that's the crux of the case,' I said. 'The fact is that LeRoy really did want to raise her profile in the department by making a few busts of suburban prostitutes, of which I'm sure there are some.'

'There are.' Jon sounded quite convincing. I felt it was best not to ask how he'd come by this information.

'She had been working mostly traffic control and was trying to get some attention. She couldn't stumble into a big murder case or supersede an actual detective, so this was one step up. She coerced Maddie into some online shenanigans and then entrapped her without Maddie even knowing it. How can I argue anything else when the facts are so clear?'

Jon took a long pause. 'Shenanigans?'

'You know what I mean.'

'I think you need to find another way around it. You can discredit the evidence without discrediting the officer. Particularly a female officer trying to make a vice bust. It's going to make you look mean and juries hate that.'

I moaned. Another man telling me how women should treat each other. Worse, he was probably right. 'Madelyn Forsythe isn't a prostitute,' I said.

'No, she isn't. But Sergeant LeRoy isn't a dirty cop, either, and you can't make that stick.'

I closed my eyes. He had a point and I hated that. 'This is going to take a long time,' I said finally. 'You want to get some lunch?'

'What? And give up my planned excursion to the Seaton, Taylor cafeteria?'

We decided to go to a Japanese restaurant two blocks from

the office, where I could get sushi and Jon could get something that wasn't sushi. He hates fish. To each one's own, as long as I can get sushi.

But we hadn't gotten more than fifty feet from the revolving doors of the Seaton, Taylor building when I noticed a man in a denim jacket walking toward us. It wasn't the man so much as the jacket. The temperature was well over eighty degrees Fahrenheit that day (welcome to fall in Southern California), so the jacket seemed like a strange thing to be wearing when everyone else on the street, including me, was sleeveless. Even the businessmen in suits had long since abandoned their jackets inside their air-conditioned offices and rolled up their shirtsleeves. Scandalous.

So the denim jacket caught my eye and so did the way this guy was walking directly toward me, as if I were his destination. At the last possible second, I remembered Lieutenant Trench's warning about people in high places being angry with me.

Instinctively I veered away from the guy as he approached, but in doing so I stumbled all over Jon's feet and that made *him* stumble as we headed for the street. Then I wasn't sure what was happening but I heard a loud report like a tire hitting a really sharp nail at eighty miles an hour on the New Jersey Turnpike and don't ask me how I know what that sounds like. People shouted and some ran. My ankles gave out from the stumbling and I ended up on the concrete, more embarrassed than injured. I had scraped my left knee a little and rendered the pants from this suit unusable but that was about it.

I sat up and turned toward Jon, who had also sat down on the pavement. 'What happened?' I asked, because I figured he'd had a better vantage point before I'd basically tripped over him.

Jon stuck out his right hand and pointed, but his mouth just opened and closed without any sound coming out. And then I saw the red stain on the lower part of his shirt, just on the left side. Jon, having used up his energy, fell back on the pavement and I just managed to cushion the blow the back of his skull would have sustained by catching him and lowering his head slowly.

'He's been shot!' a woman shouted, as if that hadn't been obvious enough.

Just to make sure I was included in the festival of redundant clichés, I screamed, 'Call nine-one-one!' despite the fact that at least four people already had their phones out.

I leaned over Jon. 'You're gonna be OK,' I promised him. And I'll admit to being a jerk and saying it quietly, so that if he died no one would know I'd assured him of that except me. 'They'll take care of you. Hang on.'

He looked at me but I wasn't sure whether he could actually see my face or not. He closed his eyes and very deliberately, with great effort, said, 'Why?'

I wished I had an answer to that. I had already scanned the crowd for the guy in the denim jacket but he was nowhere to be seen. Probably three blocks away by now. He'd probably taken the jacket off, too.

I removed my own jacket and rolled it up to put under Jon's head. His midsection wasn't exactly gushing blood but it was definitely not living the good life at the moment. He was breathing but his respiration was shallow and where the *hell* was the ambulance already?

Actually, it was pulling up at that moment, and two people, a man and a woman, pretty much exploded out of it. The man immediately began extracting a gurney from the back of the van and the woman rushed over to Jon and me.

'When was he shot?' she asked me. No fooling around with details.

'Like, two minutes ago.' Or a half-hour. Like I knew.

She examined the wound and noted its location. 'Missed his heart by a mile but he could still be in trouble,' she said mostly to herself.

'Trouble?' Was I going to have to call Jon's wife? Could I remember her name? Did they have kids? Why couldn't I remember anything?

'We're not going to worry about that now,' the EMT said. 'We're going to get him to where they can help.'

Holy shit. That meant Jon could die.

'Can I go with him?' I asked.

'Not in the ambulance,' she said definitively. 'We're going to take him to SoCal. That's right near here. You can follow. But you know the cops will be here any second and they're going to need you to answer questions.'

'Yeah,' I said. 'And I know exactly which detective is going to show up.'

THIRTEEN

Detective Lieutenant K.C. Trench was not a gleeful man. Nor was he an unfeeling one. But I decided three minutes after he arrived (when the EMTs had already driven Jon away and I had in fact put in a call to his wife, whose name was Diane, and imparted the bad news) that Trench was in a perverse way enjoying this terrifying situation.

'Two shooting attempts in two days,' he said after Sergeant Roberts had thoroughly grilled me on everything I'd seen, mostly the man in the denim jacket, whose face I had not seen clearly. I hadn't actually gotten a look at the gun either, largely because I didn't know it was there until after the shot was fired. 'That's a new record even for you, isn't it, Ms Moss?'

'It's not funny, Trench.' I wasn't in the mood. A friend and colleague had just been shot because of me (probably) and carted off to the hospital. Witty banter wasn't really at the top of my priority list.

'I wasn't suggesting for a single second that it was,' Trench responded. 'I was commenting on the fact that I'd warned you about this just yesterday and yet there you were, without Patrick McNabb, walking out of a building in the middle of a major city and not employing any security at all. Does that strike you as wise?'

'If you're trying to get to the point that my friend was shot and could die and it's my fault, I'm a mile ahead of you, Lieutenant.' I was noticing my breathing. I was taking deep breaths. Not rapid ones. I wasn't hyperventilating. That was worth knowing.

Trench watched me sit down on the steps to the building again.

Standing just seemed a little too much effort right at the moment. 'I was not trying to ascribe blame,' he said quietly. 'The only person responsible here is the one who fired the gun. And the more you can tell us about him, the closer we can get to making him pay for his actions. No, Ms Moss, my intended purpose here was to impress you with the seriousness of the situation you're in.'

He was saying something without saying it or, more to the point, saying only enough that I would be frightened without actually being informed. 'Lieutenant, if you think I'm not taking it seriously that a friend of mine just got shot a foot and a half from where I was standing, and that it's more than likely the shooter was coming for me, I think *you're* not reading the situation very well. And since I know you're very good at reading situations, I'm willing to bet that's just a way to warn me to be careful. And it would really help if I knew what I was being careful about. So are you going to tell me what's going on or not?'

Trench didn't look at me and that was unusual. He was a man who made eye contact because he wanted to observe you and make judgments. Instead he stared away from me, toward the street where the guy in the denim jacket had been walking toward me with the intention of shooting me. If the lieutenant wanted me to be aware of my apparent danger, he was having a bang-up day.

So to speak.

'The man who shot Mr Irvin: was he tall or short?'

What was Trench up to, other than not answering my question? 'I've already done my best describing him to Sergeant Roberts,' I reminded him.

'Yes, but you were still in shock from the events that had happened. Was he tall or short?'

'He was a little taller than average. But since I don't really know what average height is for a man, I can't give you numbers. You want me to guess his weight as well?' I was getting tired. After all, I'd been involved in my second shooting in two days and I was trying to pull teeth out of the police detective obviously vying for the Lieutenant Coy of the Year award. In Los Angeles they like nothing better than giving out awards.

'If you could that would be helpful.' Not just coy. Trench was approaching cute, which was an unusually long drive for him.

'I'm going to go with average,' I said. 'Now how about you tell me who I should be afraid of and then I can take the necessary steps to protect myself, since it seems the LAPD might be among the suspects.'

That got him, just as I'd intended it to. Trench turned back in my direction and, if he had been capable of an expression of rage, I'm sure this would have been it. His face was two degrees angrier than normal. 'If you're insinuating that the Los Angeles Police Department is trying to kill you, Ms Moss, I'd advise you to turn your attention elsewhere.'

I stood up to look him as close to in-the-eyes as I could get. 'You were the one who spoke in hushed tones about people in high places being upset with me and you suggested it might have something to do with a trial I'm working on,' I shot back. 'So if you *don't* want me to assume that the cops are at least involved in something that involves me possibly getting killed, why not tell me what you were talking about?'

Again his expression went to his standby, which was impassive but knowledgeable. 'I am not at liberty to tell you any more than I already have,' Trench said. He turned as if he was going to walk away and then pivoted on his heel and faced me again. 'But rest assured that the LAPD has at least one member who will do his best to see to it that you remain alive.'

I slow-clapped him to show his planned exit line had not landed as he intended. 'Thanks for caring, Lieutenant.'

'I was referring to Sergeant Roberts. He hates an incomplete suspect description.'

'Uh-huh. This is bothering you, Trench. There's something you want to tell me and, for whatever reasons, you feel like you can't. That's odd for you. I think maybe you need to unburden yourself or at least advise me on the kind of protection you think I need right now.'

From behind me I heard the familiar voice that couldn't be there but it seemed always was. 'Protection!'

Trench looked past me and his mouth tightened a little. 'Mr McNabb,' he said.

'Lieutenant! So good to see you again. Has something happened here? I know you are assigned to the homicide division, aren't you?'

Patrick walked up to my right and shook Trench's hand, which was something Trench clearly found less than desirable. Patrick was old school, when people used to shake hands a lot. Trench probably didn't like it since he was seven years old because it would assume a level of familiarity that would make it impossible for him to be impartial and deductive, so was therefore something to avoid.

'We also investigate attempted homicides,' the detective said, disengaging from Patrick's hand as soon as he conceivably could. 'And I am finished investigating this crime scene so I will be on my way.'

He turned and strode off, discreetly using hand sanitizer, before Patrick could question his statement, which meant Patrick would immediately begin questioning me.

My best battle plan was a preemptive strike. 'Why are you here?' I asked Patrick before he could ask me anything.

'Why is *he* here?' The other ever-present voice. Sure enough, Angie appeared just behind Patrick, her eyes darting around until she saw the bloodstain on the concrete. 'Sand! What happened?'

There was nothing else to do; I told them the whole story, left out nothing because Angie would know, and sat back down on the concrete steps. The area had been cordoned off with yellow police tape so people were walking around it but I, privileged as I was, could stay inside. It was a way of keeping people away. Except Angie and Patrick, who just showed up whenever they decided I needed them. Whether I did or not.

Patrick's usual buoyant smile flattened itself into concern. 'Someone shot at you and I wasn't here?' He's an intelligent man despite his desperate attempts to prove otherwise, and he was putting two and two together and coming up with the right solution. 'Does that mean they weren't aiming for me yesterday?'

'That seems to be what Lieutenant Trench thinks,' I said. 'He's hinting at something but he's being very Lieutenant Trench about it.'

'What do you want from a man who won't tell you his first name?' Angie pointed out.

Patrick reached a hand down to me and I took it. He pulled me to my feet a little bit more fervently than I might have expected. Patrick was worried about me. 'You are not going to argue with me, Sandy. I am hiring security personnel to stay with you and you will do what they tell you to do, right? I will not allow any resistance.'

'I'm not going to offer any,' I told him. 'I'm scared enough. Thank you, Patrick. Will Angie and I be seeing your pal Philip at our apartment soon?'

'Oh good lord, no,' Patrick answered. 'Philip is on my personal detail. No, we'll be getting you an entirely new group. In fact, I'll get my assistant on that immediately.'

Then he did what I should have expected and totally didn't. He turned toward Angie and said, 'Would you please call Executive Security and tell them I want a full team on Sandy ASAP?'

Angie nodded. 'I'm way ahead of you.' She had already pulled a much more up-to-date cell phone than the one I knew she owned and was pushing its screen furiously. She put it to her ear. 'I'm calling Mr Anthony. This is Patrick McNabb's executive assistant.'

I looked at Patrick, who was trying to suppress his smile. 'She told me she had a lunch meeting today that was a second interview for an assistant position,' I said. 'Why didn't I see this coming?'

'Because you see Angie as your friend the ice-cream manager from New Jersey,' Patrick said. 'I see her as someone who has a great deal of knowledge, terrific instincts and unlimited potential.'

Angie was still talking on the phone behind me. I regarded Patrick very seriously. 'Just promise me you won't sleep with her.' Because I knew Angie and I knew how men saw her.

Patrick looked lightly offended. 'Never,' he said solemnly. 'That would be unspeakably unprofessional.'

'Not to mention it would piss me off.' Patrick, without intending to do so, tended to leave women crying in his wake. That was *not* going to happen to Angie.

'Message received. You need not worry. I just got out of a painful breakup.'

Angie disconnected the phone call. 'They'll be here in twenty minutes,' she told Patrick. Not me. Patrick. We were discussing someone who would be trying to keep me from being murdered and she was reporting to Patrick. My world was becoming very odd. And it hadn't exactly been normal before.

'Excellent. You are already paying great dividends, Angie.' Patrick turned his attention from her to me. 'You should go back to your apartment as soon as the security personnel arrive.'

'I can't. I have a murder trial to prepare and a prostitution case that doesn't make any sense as well as a bunch of divorces. I've got to prepare, and I have to keep up with how Jon is doing in the hospital.'

'You can do all those things from home,' Patrick said. 'Surely we've learned that if nothing else.'

I looked at him. 'Are you going to be running my life now?' I asked.

'No,' Angie told me. 'I am.'

FOURTEEN

'I was trying to get Jon's opinion on this appeal and he was telling me things I didn't want to hear,' I told Angie.

We were sitting in the common area of our apartment. Angie was still dressed for work because Patrick was here, having ridden back to the apartment with me and letting Angie drive his car, which she must have absolutely loved. I, on the other hand, had immediately changed out of my work clothes so I could feel comfortable sitting on the sofa with my files and my laptop in front of me. And so I could wear clothes that didn't have blood all over them; that was also a consideration.

I'd called Holly and let her know I'd be working from home. She had heard from other employees of the firm about Jon's shooting and must have known I'd somehow been involved because she'd asked no questions. I had asked her what she'd found out about Jon's condition and she said he was currently in surgery.

It was possible for me to feel more awful, I supposed, but I was reserving that for when things got worse.

Right now, the focus was on Maddie Forsythe. I was hoping that perhaps while I was doing my best to win her appeal, I could figure out why bigwigs in some area of the city were concerned enough about this petty crime (which hadn't really been a crime at all) to order me shot. Twice. So far.

'So what did he tell you that you didn't want to hear?' Angie said. 'That's usually a good place to start.'

'He said I shouldn't make my case around the idea that the arresting officer was trumping up charges to advance herself in the department,' I told her. 'That seems the only motive she'd have for entrapping Maddie into what Sergeant LeRoy could call soliciting.'

'He's right,' Patrick said. 'It's a mistake to go after a police officer, especially a female one, in a bench case. Judges know the cops and they don't like you casting aspersions on officers.'

I searched my mind for the time when I had asked Patrick's opinion on the case and came up with none. But it wouldn't have helped to mention that to the man who was footing the bill for Judy, the six-foot security guard standing at my window and trying not to make it obvious she was watching for any assailants who might be approaching the building. I knew Angie had asked for a woman to guard me just because she was Angie. Patrick would not have thought of that.

'But it goes directly to the bogus nature of the charges.'

'You don't have to prove the sergeant wanted to trap Maddie,' Angie said after a moment. 'You just have to prove that Maddie's not a hooker. What's the proof they're using besides the cop's testimony?'

Patrick, who'd spent years playing a lawyer on television – to the point that he sometimes thinks he used to be a lawyer – clapped his hands like a small boy delighted with a cupcake. 'Precisely!' he crowed. 'It's not about intent; it's about innocent until proven guilty. Yes, Angie, you're brilliant.' He looked at me. 'It's OK if I say that about Angie, isn't it?'

'Sure.' Who had the time to argue that one? 'To answer your question, Ang, the prosecutor's discovery has consisted of the transcript of the online chat between Maddie and Sergeant LeRoy, who was pretending to be a man calling himself Randy. That and the signed copy of Maddie's divorce settlement, which doesn't show anything besides her allegation that her husband was fooling around and some financial records.'

That was when it hit me. *Financial records!* The exact sort of thing that could hide the kind of corruption a highly placed official in the city – like in the police department – would not want to be disclosed. Why didn't I take any accounting courses in college?

'I've got to get our financial people to take another look at the divorce settlement,' I said out loud to myself. 'There's probably something there.'

Patrick and Angie exchanged puzzled glances. 'You don't think the problem is in the transcript of the chat?' Angie asked. 'I mean, isn't that where they think Maddie agreed to being a hooker?'

'She isn't accused of being a hooker,' Patrick mansplained. 'A hooker works a street corner. They think Madelyn was either a call girl or an upscale escort.'

Angie and I stared at him for a moment. Then independently each of us shook her head slightly and decided to ignore the comment.

'It's about why there's so much interest in this tiny little case,' I said. 'I'm starting to see it now. There was no reason to prosecute this. It looked like a loser and they knew it. They should have listened to Maddie's explanation at the beginning, read over the chat and realized this was a load of crap masquerading as a criminal charge. But the DA went ahead with it. And amazingly they got a conviction. Somebody in high places wants to see that woman destroyed, and I think the financial records will help us find out why.'

Angie walked over to the woman who was intimidating everyone simply by standing next to my front window. 'Judy,' she said. 'You're an ex-police officer, aren't you?'

Judy looked down at Angie, which is not easy to do (Angie's quite tall) and said, 'That's an affirmative.' Because she was incapable of not acting like a clichéd idea of a security guard. I can't help it; that's how she behaved.

'So have you ever seen anyone brought up on charges of soliciting based just on an internet chat?' Angie could have asked me, of course, since I'd had years of experience as an assistant county prosecutor, but no, she felt it was more credible to ask the question of a woman she had met ninety minutes earlier.

'That's an affirmative, ma'am.' Judy added in the 'ma'am' for variety, I guess.

'You have?' Angie had committed the lawyer's sin of asking a question to which she did not know the answer. Worse, she had anticipated one answer and gotten the opposite. Luckily Angie was now an 'executive assistant' and had never gone to law school. Largely because she had never wanted to go to law school.

'Affirmative. Many a sting operation will involve officers going undercover online to find sexual predators and human traffickers. They might pose as young people or people of the opposite sex to lure pedophiles or predators into making an inappropriate illegal suggestion and that leads to the possibility that past records would indicate a pattern. It has worked at times.'

That had gotten me interested. I stood up and walked toward Judy, trying to seem more like a friend than an attorney. But as I approached Judy tensed up her body, held out a hand toward me and said, 'Stay away from the window, ma'am.' You heard Judy's tone and you would pretty much do whatever Judy said to do.

I stopped frozen in my tracks and put up my hands, palms out. 'OK,' I said. 'But those operations usually culminate with the officer arranging an in-person meet with the suspect and making the arrest there.'

'That has been my experience, yes, ma'am.'

'Judy, I have a question,' I said. I must have made another step forward because her face tensed up more, if such a thing was possible.

'I can hear you perfectly from here, ma'am.'

'I have no doubt that you can. But what you just described was an operation intended to flush out sexual predators and pedophiles. Are you aware of any that were aimed at finding suburban moms who were prostitutes on the side?'

There was no hesitation. 'No, ma'am.'

I nodded and retreated quickly to my post on the sofa, which seemed to make Judy feel much more relaxed. She stood straight as a board but she at least let her arm drop to her side. 'What branch?' Patrick asked.

Judy barely glanced at him; her concentration was first on me, then on the view from my window. 'Sir?'

'What branch of the service were you a member of?'

Judy's mouth twitched just a tad. 'Marines, sir.'

'Thank you for your service. Where were you?'

'Afghanistan, sir.' Not so much as a blink. If an army of termites was planning an invasion of my building, Judy would have seen it forty feet up from the sidewalk. Her expression did not change in reaction to Patrick's question.

I was impressed by Judy's service but that wasn't the time of her life I found most relevant right now. 'How long were you a cop, Judy?'

'Thirteen years, ma'am.' There was absolutely no way of knowing whether Judy considered the questions too personal or annoying. She had not moved a single facial muscle since I'd met her and I doubted she would if I were to need her – please, no – for a year.

'Do you still have ties within the department?' I asked. 'Are there people you know who are still on the job, maybe higher up in the LAPD?'

Not a glance in my direction. Judy was focused. 'I have a few friends still on the job,' she said. Maybe the lack of a 'ma'am' was some indication that she was wearying of the questioning, or that we were now best friends forever.

'It would be a boon to my security if you could find out whether there are people in the department or the city government who are holding some grudge against me,' I told her.

This time Judy did take a quick look at me. Perhaps that registered alarm. But then she was back at the window. This followed her incredibly detailed examination of our apartment, which I sincerely wished we had cleaned before Judy arrived. She had found nothing suspicious, or at least didn't say she had found anything suspicious. I figured if she was being paid to protect me she'd let me know if something dangerous was in my home.

'A grudge?' she asked. 'I don't understand.'

'I've been told by a very reputable source that there are people in high places who are upset with me, possibly for taking on the case we've been discussing here this afternoon,' I explained. 'It's possible some or all of those people work for the LAPD. I can't ask anyone I know there but it might be helpful if you could without compromising yourself.'

'Who told you that?' Patrick asked.

'It's confidential,' I said.

'Was it—'

I cut him off. 'No. It wasn't.' The last thing I needed was Judy asking around about Trench (because surely that was who Patrick was going to name), especially when I couldn't be sure where her alliances fell either. I'd known Judy for an hour and a half.

'Would it be too uncomfortable for you to ask around?' I said to her. I wanted to offer her a bonus for doing so, but I figured that was bad in two ways: first, it might offend Judy to the point that she would break me in half and, second, I didn't have the extra money (and Patrick was paying for Judy anyway), although I was drawing a very nice salary from Taylor, Seaton. Paying for two halves of the rent had been a little bit too much. Now that Angie was Patrick's executive assistant, and I assumed making a decent amount on her own, perhaps that would change.

I'm sorry; what was I talking about?

'I could do that, ma'am,' Judy answered. Right. The LAPD and who wanted me dead. That was it.

'Thank you.'

'I'm not able to do it right now, though, because my shift isn't over for another three hours and I have to maintain my post.' Judy pointed out the window as if I did not understand what she meant by her post.

'Of course. Whenever you get the chance.'

Judy nodded, did one of her periodic sweeps of the apartment and then took up her post at another window. In case the termites were regrouping.

All I had to do now was figure out how to keep Maddie Forsythe's conviction from being upheld. And what I knew for sure was how *not* to do that. So now I had to tear up my planned strategy and devise something else entirely.

But luckily stress would keep me up all night so there'd be more time to work on it. Then I could try and figure out how to stop Cynthia Sutton from going to prison for the rest of her life.

And it was only Thursday.

FIFTEEN

'Wendy Bryan saved my life,' said Pierre Chirac.

Nate Garrigan had asked me to come along for his talk with Pierre, who was an artist associated with Wendy Bryan's gallery Rafael, which was exactly as swanky as you'd assume from that name. According to the Google articles I'd scanned as Nate drove to Pierre's home in (where else?) Santa Monica, he was an up-and-coming artist and sculptor whose anticipated (note: it was not *highly* anticipated, and apparently that makes a difference) show at Rafael had been expected to boost him up to the next level in art. If art has levels.

It should probably also be noted that Pierre Chirac's real name was (according to Google, since he didn't merit a Wikipedia page) Pete Conway and that he was from Muncie, Indiana. He was a muscular man with blond hair that hadn't started out that way, wearing (in the 93-degree heat) an ascot complementing the $140 T-shirt and $200 tan slacks he had on to look casual.

'She saved your life?' Nate asked. It wasn't really a question so much as a prompt for Pete to go on. I'm going to call him Pete. You can read Pierre if you want to.

'His *professional* life.' Pete's agent, Penelope Hannigan (whose real name was Penelope Hannigan, if you were wondering) had insisted on being present for the meeting and that was OK with Nate, who had wanted to talk to her anyway.

There had been some scuttlebutt around Rafael's patrons and fans regarding Pete's upcoming show. Some, Nate told me, had said Wendy had been going out on a limb showcasing an artist of Pete's relative obscurity. Others whispered that Rafael was actually in some financial trouble because Wendy had been overlooking more established artists with whom she has some history in favor of Pete. One had to consider what kind of relationship Wendy and Pete might have shared. She had a good thirty years on him, but I'm not one to judge.

'That woman did everything she could to save my works.'

Pete was doing his best to appear to be choking back tears. 'Her loss is a body blow to the Los Angeles art community.'

'OK, that's the quote for the obituary,' Nate told him. I was letting Nate do all the talking because, frankly, this was his part of the job. He had asked me along because he thought there might be some difficulty getting Pete to testify for the defense and I was here to scope him out and decide whether I wanted him on my witness list. If he testified, it would be to discuss the gallery and Wendy's state of mind. Nobody thought Pete was anywhere near Wendy's house the night she had died. Certainly Detective Edward Brisbane did not, according to his report, which was among the least informative documents I have ever been called upon to read.

'Pierre is going to be a force in the art scene in Southern California,' Penelope said. 'Wendy recognized that and devoted herself to showing the world his talent.' Which must be what the young people are calling it today.

'Yes, but what about Wendy's state of mind?' Patrick asked. You're surprised that Patrick was at the meeting with Pierre and Penelope. You shouldn't be. 'What kind of mood was she in right before she died?'

Nate shot a look at Patrick that indicated he should not have spoken at all, since we'd told Patrick that very thing right before ringing Penelope's expensive doorbell. Patrick was very careful not to look in Nate's direction because he'd heard us tell him that but didn't want to abide by it. Patrick really wants to help. He just mostly doesn't. Help.

'What mood?' Pete seemed puzzled by the question. 'She was Wendy.' Well, *that* was helpful.

'And what does that mean?' Nate asked before Patrick could insert himself into the situation again.

It seemed to be Penelope's turn to look confused. Maybe they were switching off so neither of them would especially tax the tiny lines around their eyes, which only Penelope had not yet treated with Botox. 'Wendy was an upbeat, kind person whose mission in life was to foster the careers of powerful artistic talents,' she said, not telling us anything at all or even answering Patrick's question, which we had – I can't say this enough – not encouraged him to ask.

'Yes, I'm certain of that,' Nate said. 'But what kind of mood was she in before this all happened? How did she strike you as she prepared for your show, Pierre?' Nate was calling Pete *Pierre* because he wanted to ingratiate himself with the witness. On the way home he'd refer to the guy as *Pete* or something considerably less friendly.

'She was excited. We all were.'

'Not worried? Not more concerned than usual?' Nate asked.

'Worried!' The very suggestion was enough to make Pete scan the ceiling for some sign that he should cooperate with this boor. Apparently the ceiling told him to go ahead. 'Wendy was *never* worried.'

'She knew Pierre's work was extraordinary and so she was completely confident in everything we were doing,' said Penelope, who probably hadn't been doing much about the show at all.

Patrick, never to be denied, leaned forward to achieve a sense of urgency and intimacy at the same time. I didn't think it worked, but then I'm immune to many of his tactics. You could ask Angie about that, but Patrick had dispatched her to Cynthia's house to make sure my client was holding up well under the strain in her absurdly expensive house.

'Did she ever mention Cynthia Sutton?' Patrick asked.

Pierre and Penelope, the Pretentious Twins, exchanged a knowing look. 'Oh yes,' Penelope practically crooned. 'She mentioned her daughter-in-law.'

'And what did she say about Ms Sutton?' Nate asked, trying in vain to take control of the conversation away from Patrick.

The ceiling fan, in addition to the very efficient air conditioning, was making me regret not wearing a jacket over my sleeveless shell. But I think the chilliness I felt from our two witnesses had something to do with the gooseflesh on my arms.

'Let's just say it wasn't complimentary,' Penelope attempted.

'She hated Cynthia Sutton,' Pete said. Pete hadn't yet acquired the filter an artist needs when talking to 'civilians', particularly those admitted to the bar. 'Wendy said her daughter-in-law wanted her to die.'

Well, that wasn't good.

'Those were her exact words?' Nate asked. '"She wants me to die"?'

'Verbatim,' Pete said, nodding.

It was fairly clear these two would not be on my witness list, but I could count on them testifying for the prosecution. Now all I had to do was figure out how to get them to shut up.

SIXTEEN

Nate asked me to come along to one other interview and I had to resist the impulse to run away and hide, but told him I would as long as it wasn't Cynthia Sutton's estranged husband and son of the victim, Michael Bryan. Nate assured me it would not be Michael, and he wasn't lying. He knew better than to dupe me into an extremely uncomfortable conversation that he didn't need me for in a legal capacity.

Instead, he, Patrick and I (because we couldn't convince Patrick we were just going back to our offices separately no matter how hard we tried) ended up at the door to the office of Leopold Kolensky, who Nate had found listed on the financial records of Rafael as 'executive manager', a title which didn't mean anything at all. I was along to see if there were issues with Leopold (*Leopold?*) possibly incriminating himself on the stand if the rumors about Wendy Bryan's business floundering turned out to be true. Men don't like to admit they screwed something up. It's why they invented GPS.

I'd called Jon Irvin's wife Diane, reluctantly because I felt the shooting was my fault and she'd probably yell at me. But even though she was clearly very shaken, she did not mention how I might have gotten her husband killed.

Instead she reported that Jon had tolerated the surgery well, had lost one kidney but could get by with the one he had left, and that now they were hoping no infections would set in and that the loss of blood would not continue to affect him badly. I'd told her to let me know if there was anything I could do, and the words sounded just as empty then as any other time anyone has ever said them. Diane had said Jon couldn't have visitors yet but that she'd let me know when he could.

'I'm not gonna knock,' I told Nate. 'You knock.' I wanted to blend into the wallpaper here, not because it was an especially scary place but because someone had shot at me and that tends to put one a little bit on edge. Trust me; I have experience in these areas.

'Knock?' Nate didn't exactly sneer, but you couldn't say he didn't, either. He pushed the door open and walked in. What do I know? In New Jersey we knock.

The offices were, in a word, bare. There was no receptionist's desk, no waiting area. There were no chairs. There was no rug. There was a corridor off the room just inside the entrance and three other doors off that hallway. The lights were on, so the place had utilities, but other than that it was . . .

'Abandoned,' Nate finished my thought. 'Or there was never anything here. Could be just a mailing address for someone.'

Patrick felt bold enough to walk down the corridor without any compunction and open each door. 'There's nothing in any of these rooms,' he reported back. But Judy, who had been silently dogging me from the time we'd left my office (and had done and said virtually nothing except stand and look concerned, in a professional, intimidating way) insisted on following behind him and confirming each empty room.

'If you were a front for something, would you leave the office door unlocked?' I asked Nate.

'I would if I had to leave in a hurry and didn't care what somebody found after I was gone,' he said. Nate walked the perimeter of the main room then called down the corridor. 'Any dust in there? Markings where there used to be furniture?'

'That's a negative.' Judy. Like I had to tell you.

Nate nodded to himself; that confirmed what he'd been thinking. 'Somebody left here in a hurry, and not long ago.'

Patrick emerged from the hallway, and from the sound of it, had used the restroom at the end of the hallway and then washed his hands, which he was wiping with a brown paper towel that would have had to have bulked up to be one-ply. 'The accommodations here are not lush,' he noted.

'Yeah, it doesn't seem like the kind of place that would be affiliated with a higher-end art gallery, does it?' I asked Nate. I wasn't basing the question on the thin paper towels in the bathroom so much as the dark fake-wood paneling on the walls.

'No. There's something very fishy going on and it's too big a coincidence that the one client we know this guy worked for got herself murdered with a TeeVee award.' Nate was doing his tough cop act. He had once *been* a tough cop, but now it was an act.

There was nothing to do but take a few pictures on Nate's phone in case we needed references about the office, look around without any success for any papers or other indicators of what Kolensky Associates did for a living, and then head back out. I made Nate drive me to the Seaton, Taylor office building, which I entered through the parking garage because I wasn't up to the front entrance again just yet.

Judy, now just outside my office but visible through the glass, stood in the hallway and looked for all the world like she was waiting for a general to come by and inspect her. Her hands were clasped behind her back and her posture was absolutely straight. She moved in such tiny increments that a casual passerby might think she was a mannequin for the least distinctive clothing imaginable.

I felt the only thing to do was call Angie, who had left Cynthia's house and was heading back to the studio to follow Patrick around. I reached her in Patrick's Tesla because of course.

'What does the empty office mean about Cynthia?' Angie said.

'Anybody's guess. I'm guessing it doesn't mean she was about to start issuing stock. What are you and your boss up to?'

'Patrick is out with Nate Garrigan talking to her husband and I'm sure that's going to be great fun for both of them.'

I groaned. I didn't hold back the groan, despite the fact that I was now officially talking to Angie about her boss. 'I *just left them*! He really doesn't have a clue that he's getting in Nate's way and messing up the investigation, does he?'

'He's Patrick.' That's Angie being diplomatic.

'On the incredibly unlikely chance that anything at all of interest comes from that meeting, I'm sure Nate will tell me about it when he reports back,' I said. 'But try to keep Patrick from calling me every ten minutes with his latest brilliant idea of how to defend this case, OK?'

'So you're allowed to say "brilliant" and he's not?' Angie's smile was audible.

'Hey. Whose side are you on?'

'I'm on company time. Right now Patrick is paying my half of our rent.'

'Between us,' I said. 'Do you have any idea why he was so gung-ho about me defending Cynthia? I mean, do they have a past or something? What's Patrick's stake in this?' I thought I knew Patrick pretty well and I had been wondering about this question since he'd first showed up in Judge Coffey's courtroom insisting I should handle Cynthia's divorce. Those were the days.

'All I can tell is that they're friends and Patrick is doing his knight-in-shining-armor bit,' Angie answered. 'You know how he gets when a friend is under siege.'

I glanced out at Judy, who had not visibly moved a muscle since the last time I'd checked. 'Yeah. I know how he gets.' Seriously, that woman needed to move around or her whole body would stiffen and she'd be a subject of much interest at Madame Tussaud's.

'So that's what I think is behind this. Why? Are you jealous?' Angie, the most Jersey of Jersey girls, is incapable of speaking without at least a hint of sarcasm, but that last word practically dripped irony off the phone and onto the carpet.

'No, I am not *jealous*,' I told her. Definitively. 'I'm skeptical. This is Hollywood. People don't often act out of altruism in the entertainment business. I'm trying to figure out what the upside is for Patrick in paying the bills for a woman who could easily afford her legal bills out of the craft services budget from her last movie.'

'That's "people", not Patrick,' Angie countered. 'And you are too jealous. But I'm here to tell you, there's nothing to worry about. Patrick's not in love with Cynthia.'

'No, he's in love with his real-estate agent,' I said. 'To the point that he was going to marry her about twenty minutes after meeting her until I gave him a talking-to.'

'Yeah, she was pissed at him even before he broke it off because he insisted on actually having friends who were women and not her. She's nuts,' Angie said.

'You've met the latest crush?'

Angie laughed. 'Good thing you're not jealous.'

'You're going to be impossible now that you're working for him,' I mused.

'I've always been impossible,' Angie said.

'True. Listen, try to find things for him to do so he's not dogging Nate's steps every second of every day, would you?' Patrick, in the guise of 'helping', could do more to damage a case than anyone I'd ever seen who was actually trying to mess things up.

'Sandy, the man's shooting a television series and working with a ghostwriter on a novelization of the series. He's got movie offers coming in every half-hour and a publisher is after him for a memoir. He *already* doesn't have time to do what he's doing right at this minute. The only way I could slow him down would be tie him to a chair.'

'It's an idea.' I hung up a minute later. I'd already lost Maddie Forsythe's case and now I had to work on appeal to undo that mistake (*how did I lose that case?*) while trying not to repeat the same process in Cynthia's murder trial.

I'd already filed for a preliminary hearing for Cynthia and it had been scheduled for the middle of the following week. She was out on her own recognizance so there was no urgency on my part. The more time I had before there was a trial, the better off Cynthia was, and she knew that. She was shell-shocked but not stupid.

The police report was just as helpful as you'd expect, especially given that it was the first to be filed and did not have the results of the medical examiner's investigation. Edward Brisbane, whom I had never met, had covered the place with video and photography so there were plenty of grisly photographs for me to see. His prose, however, left something to be desired. He was the very epitome of a drudge cop, less Lieutenant Trench and more Sergeant Joe Friday from *Dragnet*. Just the facts, ma'am, and not in a way that will lead to any insight. It was as if he'd sent a drone into the crime scene and it had written the report for him.

The bottom line was that Wendy Bryan had been killed with a TeeVee award, possibly the first time that had ever happened in TV Academy history. There were stab wounds in her chest and her back. She'd lost a lot of blood but the damage to her heart and lungs were probably enough to have killed her on their own. We'd know more when the ME issued a complete autopsy report, which probably wouldn't be for a couple of weeks at best.

What Brisbane had noted, as much as he could be said to have really noted anything, was that the body was in an unusual position but did not appear to have been moved after death. There was no trail of blood leading from anywhere else. The murder weapon, of course, had been discovered in the hands of my client, sitting practically in the fetal position in the adjoining room. It had been examined for fingerprints and guess what? Cynthia Sutton's were all over it. Big surprise.

At the moment the song stuck in my head was 'Walk of Life' by Dire Straits, which seemed incongruous given the circumstances under which I was operating. I barely even noticed it, except that when I was getting ready to scroll down to the next page on the crime-scene report, I was making sure to do so before Mark Knopfler hit the 'J' on 'Johnny' the second time. So I forced myself to slow down and concentrate on every word, or at least every phrase.

That was when I found something that seemed out of place in the report of Wendy Bryan's murder. In the photos, which Brisbane had included just to ruin my appetite for the entire month, were four aimed at the body but which also showed the floor of the center hall, where she'd been discovered, in plain view.

Then I checked on some of the video from when the uniformed officers first on the scene had found Cynthia in the den, sitting on the floor and clutching the award in question close to her chest. The first officer, who according to the label on the image was named Crawford, asked Cynthia her name and she just rocked back and forth on the floor like one of those crazy women in the movies who seem to revert to early childhood given any unusual level of stress. I was embarrassed that my client was adhering so closely to the insulting cliché.

From off camera I could hear the other officer, named Lyons if the transcript was correct (which wasn't as certain a bet as you might reasonably expect), say, 'That's Cynthia Sutton. I know her from *The Broken Mirror.*'

Crawford: *The Broken Mirror*? Is that like a support group for people with body-image problems?

Lyons (with an exasperated sigh): No. It's a movie. *The Broken Mirror.* You don't remember? It was about this woman who suffers a disfiguring accident and . . .

Crawford: I don't care.

Lyons (mumbling): She should have won an Oscar.

Crawford (to Cynthia): Ma'am? Are you Cynthia Sutton?

Cynthia kept rocking but might have nodded.

Crawford (encouraged): Do you know who that is in the next room?

No response from Cynthia.

Crawford: She's too far gone. What's the ETA on the ambulance?

Lyons: They'll be here in three. (To Cynthia): Um . . . Miss Sutton? What have you got in your hands there?

Cynthia (in fully normal conversational voice): It's a TeeVee award, idiot.

And that's when the questioning began. Cynthia, without her lawyer (who didn't even *know* she was Cynthia's criminal defender yet) present, didn't say much, thank goodness. She admitted to being herself, which was reasonable. She said she had recognized her mother-in-law and had 'probably' found her on the floor in the next room. And she said, much to her lawyer's dismay, that the pointy object in her hands, with blood still dripping off of it, was hers.

With blood still dripping off of it.

That was the key. I called the cops and asked for Brisbane, who answered with a surprisingly soothing voice. I identified myself and his voice didn't change tone, which it often does when cops (or prosecutors, like I used to be) talk to defense lawyers. 'What can I do for you, Ms Moss?'

'I'm representing Cynthia Sutton.'

'Yes.' No snarky comment. What was wrong with this guy?

'I've been looking over your report and I have a few questions,' I plowed on.

'OK.' I got the impression Brisbane was looking at his computer and thinking about something that wasn't what I was asking, but he'd go ahead anyway.

'How did you get the call about the murder at Wendy Bryan's house?' I asked.

'I got a call on my phone like always.' He sounded puzzled that I'd ask.

'I mean, is it a rotation and you just caught the case, or was there something about this homicide that made the dispatcher think of you?'

Brisbane didn't sigh but I knew he wanted to. 'I don't decide who calls me or why. I'm a homicide cop. I get called when there's a homicide.'

I wanted to ease into what I was asking him because if I ever got him on the stand – and that was a pretty sure bet – I didn't want him to think I was calling him just for that. Even though I was. 'I get that, but I'm wondering if you've dealt with a lot of cases that involve the entertainment industry.'

I could have written his response myself: 'This is Santa Monica. This is LA County.'

Great. Now I'd have Sheryl Crow in my head the rest of the day, and she makes me speed up. Maybe that wasn't a bad thing.

'That's true, Detective,' I said. 'So it didn't impress you one way or the other that the suspect was a movie star and the victim owned an art gallery.'

'No. What's that got to do with the facts of the case?'

He'd played right into the subject I wanted to discuss. 'About that, Detective.'

At that moment Brisbane decided (or it was simply a reflex) that he wanted to be friendly with me. 'Ed,' he said.

Luckily it wasn't a Zoom call so he couldn't see my eye roll. 'Ed. Of course. I wanted to ask about some of the photographs from the crime scene.'

'Pretty bloody, aren't they?' 'Ed' suggested.

'That's my question. There's blood all over the place except in one area.'

Suddenly my pal seemed to sit up and take notice. 'Where?' he asked.

'To the left of the body on the floor,' I told him.

There was a great clamor of clicking keys. He was calling up the pictures on his screen. It took a while. Municipal government computers. Then his voice came back, a little moony like he was mesmerized by what he was seeing. 'You're right.'

I *was* right. The defense attorney was right about me being right. I'd noticed something the crack homicide detective hadn't gotten despite being on the scene in addition to looking at these very photographs, I assumed, a number of times. 'How do you account for that?' I asked.

Brisbane sounded like I shouldn't have asked. 'I guess she didn't bleed that way,' he said.

'Thank you, Detective.' I ended the call as quickly as I could. He'd given me the weapon I'd need in court and didn't know it. I called Nate.

'Get this man out of here.' Some people start with 'hello', and others are Nate Garrigan.

'I will in a minute. But first I had something to ask you about.'

Nate's attention snapped into place. 'What?'

'I'm going to send you two pictures. Tell me what you notice.' I moved the one photograph of Wendy's body and the expensive carpet next to it onto my desktop, then added a still photograph of Cynthia on the floor in the den holding the dripping statuette. I sent those two photos to Nate and waited.

'OK, I've got the two pictures,' he said. 'What am I looking at?'

'Don't concentrate on the body so much,' I answered.

'If you insist.' Nate has a dry wit. You could use it for kindling.

'Pay attention to the floor next to the body, particularly to the left, which leads into the den,' I went on. 'See the area I'm talking about?'

There was a long pause while Nate looked it over. In the background I could hear Patrick asking if that was me on the phone. Nate didn't answer.

He did respond to me, though. 'It just looks like floor.'

'Exactly,' I said. 'Now look at the picture of Cynthia in the den. Look at the award statue she has in her hands.'

Nate is gruff and likes to play the part of the crusty old ex-cop who's exasperated with laypeople getting in his way, which he is. But he is also really smart and observant. 'There's no trail of blood from the scene of the murder to the place where they found her holding the bloody award statue,' he said finally. 'If she'd killed the woman in the one room and then walked into the other holding the murder weapon, there'd be blood all over the floor because it's still there in the picture in the den.'

'Exactly.'

I could practically hear the lightbulb going on over Nate's

head. 'So it's possible that either the body was moved or the object our client had in her hand wasn't the murder weapon, but was intended to look that way.'

I felt myself grinning. 'Welcome to the same case, Nate,' I said.

'We might not have a guilty defendant on our hands,' Nate said, mostly to himself.

'Wouldn't that be something?'

I could hear Patrick in the background. 'Haven't I been saying that all along?'

SEVENTEEN

'We need to mobilize.'

Patrick McNabb had invited me to his new home for dinner to 'plot strategy' in the upcoming Cynthia Sutton case. I was going to decline but Angie was of course going to be there, and she'd spend the evening answering questions about me if I wasn't in attendance.

Right now, at a magnificent dining table in Patrick's 'sitting room' (I couldn't imagine what might have been lurking in the dining room if this was the ancillary), Patrick was holding court as only someone with a really healthy ego can. Although Patrick's ego is far from the most massive one I've met in the entertainment business since I moved to LA.

'Mobilize?' Angie asked. Given that this was a gathering after business hours, she was not 'on duty', as she and Patrick had both assured me. Angie was a guest like me, and Richard Tolbin, the expert on blood spatter Patrick had met while on set on a movie called *Deadly Thoughts*, and one of the producers of *Torn*, Lee Browning ('like the poet').

Henderson Meadows, the butler I knew from Patrick's 'bachelor pad', had returned to his native London when Patrick's trial was over, and – given all that had come out in the courtroom – it was probably best. So now there was a 'skeleton staff' consisting of a cook named Luann and a butler called Jason who was considerably less stiff than Meadows. Luann had made us a lovely rack of lamb and Jason was a calm, almost invisible presence, who always seemed to be in the right place when something was needed, having anticipated the problem and already solved it.

The wild card in this merry group was Emily Webster, whose name didn't register with me until Patrick called her *Emmie*. That, I recalled, was the name of the real-estate agent to whom Patrick had been, until I'd stuck my nose in, engaged to be married. She had not glared at me with unmitigated malice. Yet.

'Yes, mobilize,' Patrick answered Angie. 'Cynthia' (who was oddly not present but being discussed at length) 'is in danger of a very long prison sentence for a murder she did not commit. The police want her to be guilty because that makes them look good and it makes their job easier. So they're not looking into other possibilities. That means we must find the real killer ourselves.'

'No it doesn't,' I said loudly. All the heads in the room turned in my direction. 'Patrick. You should have learned this the last time. We *don't look for the real killer*. That's not our job . . . *my* job! I mount the best possible defense for Cynthia, and I think we'll have a pretty good one by the time the case reaches a court-room. And if Nate turns up anything in his investigation that leads to the conclusion that someone else killed Wendy Bryan, he will be thrilled to give that information to the police, whose job it *is* to find the real killer. We – *I* – don't do that. It's not TV. The killer doesn't confess on the witness stand. OK?'

'Of course!' Patrick was a master of agreeing to something he had no intention of doing. But as a trained actor and a good one, he could convince himself he believed it at the time he said it and that, for Patrick, made all the difference. For the rest of us it was exhausting.

'I mean it, Patrick.'

'He knows.' Emily's eyes didn't bore holes in me. They weren't even really trying. I was probably projecting. For all I knew, Patrick hadn't even mentioned my name when he broke off the engagement. Right?

'Just want to make sure,' I said.

'So what *should* our next move be, Sandy?' Now Patrick was going to pretend to defer to my authority and expertise, while actually plotting, probably as someone with multiple personality disorder, to make my life sixteen times more difficult and be charming doing it. It's an art.

The trick now was to make it seem like I was including Patrick in whatever plans I had to defend Cynthia while really giving him nothing to do at all. But Lee wasn't going to make it easy.

'We could host a fund-raiser,' he said. 'Have something on television, maybe, to raise money for Cynthia's defense.'

'I *am* Cynthia's defense, and believe me, she can afford it,' I said, careful not to emphasize the *she* because I was almost certain Patrick was paying her legal bills. *Why?* 'No, what I think I'm going to have to do is in Richard's wheelhouse.'

Richard started at the mention of his name, probably lost in thought about patterns of spatter from the rack of lamb, or maybe he was thinking about who might win the Dodger game that night. Either one of those things was possible.

'Me?' he asked. It was like he was waking up. I realized we hadn't exactly been scintillating company, but a nap seemed somewhat out of place.

'Yes,' I answered. 'I'm interested in your analysis of these two pictures, if you don't mind taking a look.' I called up the two photographs from the scene of Wendy Bryan's murder on my phone.

'Busman's holiday,' Patrick chimed in from across the table.

'Are you showing off those gross pictures again?' Angie asked. She was teasing me but no one else at the table would know that.

'He's a professional,' I said of Richard, speaking of him as if he weren't actually there himself. 'He can bill me for the time.'

'It's perfectly fine,' Richard said, reaching out for the phone I was offering. 'I don't mind answering a question if it'll help.'

Richard turned the phone sideways to get a larger view. He did not react at all to the gruesome image, no doubt having seen a few even more vicious (I did not want to think about those) in his time. He simply looked studious and engrossed.

After swiping from one of the pictures to the other, he looked over at me and said, 'The TeeVee award is allegedly the murder weapon?'

I nodded. 'I'm impressed you knew by sight it was a TeeVee.'

He shook his head lightly from side to side, probably without knowing he had. 'I've lived in Los Angeles all my life,' Richard said. 'You get to know the hardware. And I can tell you that what's sitting in Cynthia's hands here is not a real TeeVee award.'

There was a strange silence around the table. Finally I managed to activate my vocal cords. 'What?' I sounded as if I'd just swallowed some ground glass.

'A TeeVee award is solid,' Richard explained. 'It's strong. There is no way an average, or even unusually strong, human being could bend the arms and the globe down like that to get to the wings that were used as weapons to stab the woman. That's a fake TeeVee.'

'What?' Emmie said.

I decided on the spot that I'd been right. Emily wasn't good enough for Patrick.

EIGHTEEN

Dinner wasn't really so much fun after that.

It wasn't that Richard's comment had been necessarily bad for Cynthia's defense; it was just that it was so unexpected I didn't know what to make of it, and I tend to think such things are bad until proven otherwise. But we'd had a lovely dessert that Luann had constructed of chocolate in a way that would make even Paul Hollywood smile; it was a cake and a piece of art all at the same time.

But I did notice that only Angie and I were really enjoying the amazing calorie-packed object. Everyone else seemed to be picking at it, to the point that I almost expected Angie to ask Lee, sitting next to her, if she could have some of his delicate buttercream frosting. In a remarkable demonstration of restraint, she did not, but she did agree to take some of the cake home. And was told we could, so since no one else asked we drove home in separate cars, each with enough rich chocolate cake for six people.

Life with Angie. I would have only taken one extra slice. But then I supposed donating an extravagant dessert to a Hollywood soup kitchen wouldn't have been sending the best message. Let them eat cake, indeed.

Angie got home first, so the lights were on and the door unlocked when I got to the apartment. She had filled our refrigerator with dessert for the next two weeks and I had an equal amount in a bag Jason had anticipated I would need and had already delineated with my name in flowing script. Jason was a keeper.

'You had to ask for dessert to take home?' I said the minute I closed the apartment door.

'What'd you want me to do?' Angie countered. 'Let all that chocolate go into the trash? It wasn't my fault nobody else there has eaten dessert since 2002.'

I put my enormous bag of confectionery on the counter in the kitchen. I'd push Angie's cake out of the way in the fridge later; this story was too good. 'So what's the deal with Emmie? Patrick broke off the engagement and she still showed up for dinner?'

'Well, Patrick didn't *exactly* break it off. He made his executive assistant do it.'

I stared at her. '*You* broke off Patrick's engagement?'

'Yeah. She was pissed. It's sort of her default emotion.'

'I bet. But she showed up for dinner.'

'I think she has hopes,' Angie said.

That was when there was a knock on our apartment door and I stiffened up. I'd already been shot at twice and Judy was off (although her 'relief', a woman named Carolyn, was stationed outside the apartment door – but what if an assailant had managed to overpower Carolyn?). I felt more secure when Judy was around.

Angie tensed up a little too, meaning that she grabbed a knife out of the block on the kitchen counter and wielded it like a weapon. I was spending my time cursing the landlord for not putting security cameras – which under any other circumstances I would consider a violation of my privacy – outside each apartment or at least in every hallway.

So I texted Carolyn: *Who's out there?*

Almost immediately came the answer: *It's OK*. That didn't tell me who it was, but it gave me the courage to walk to my apartment door, which I hadn't had before. Carolyn wasn't Judy, but she wouldn't sell me up the river. Assuming that the text really *had* come from Carolyn.

'I'm right behind you,' Angie said, and sure enough she was, carving knife in hand.

Somehow that didn't make me feel better.

Nonetheless I opened the door and there stood Detective Lieutenant K.C. Trench, in his impeccable suit, perfectly knotted tie and mirror-shined shoes. 'I hope I am not intruding, Ms Moss,' he said.

'Not at all, Lieutenant. Come in.' I relaxed my stomach muscles while Angie put away her lethal weapon and Trench apologized to *her* for the visit at this late hour.

'I want you to know I don't have a habit of dropping in unexpectedly at the homes of people involved in cases I'm investigating unless I consider them suspects,' Trench began. I gestured toward the sofa but he stayed on his feet. 'And I think it's obvious I do not consider you a suspect in any crime I'm investigating.'

'Please, Lieutenant, you'll make me blush.' From him that admission was an unprecedented flow of emotion. He looked uncomfortable.

'I assure you, Ms Moss, this is not a laughing matter. I was unable to talk to you in my office or at the crime scene out of concern that I might be overheard. I parked my car three miles from here and walked the rest of the way so I could be certain I was not being followed.' Trench's face was, as ever, unexpressive. Someone looking from behind a window would have thought he was trying to sell me insurance, except that salesmen are generally more congenial.

Angie took a seat on one of the barstools near the pass through to the kitchen and observed. Angie, when she's not being a true Jersey wiseass, is very good at seeing what's going on and interpreting it later. She's invaluable as a source of information that isn't related to the law.

'I don't want you to think I'm taking it lightly, Lieutenant,' I said. 'Please, tell me what you've been trying to say for the past few days. Who's after me, and why?'

Trench clasped his hands in front of him, as if he were afraid that left to their own devices they would each take up some mischievous task and humiliate him. 'I can't tell you that for certain, Ms Moss, and it's only because I don't know yet. But you can be certain I am doing some very quiet investigating on the subject and will act accordingly.'

'You sound like you did on the other two occasions you were trying to warn me,' I pointed out. 'Now that we're definitely not being watched or overheard, what can you tell me?'

'You must understand at the outset that this involved some business in the LAPD that I will not and cannot tell someone who is not employed by the department, and even then at its highest levels,' Trench said. 'What I have been able to piece together is based partially on unsubstantiated rumor and is therefore by definition not verified.'

'It must be killing you to have to deal with things you can't prove,' I said.

Angie put her hand lightly over her mouth to stifle a laugh, but I'd meant what I said. A man like Trench has to have everything be provable and objective. When he is required to act without knowing all the facts, I have no doubt he is extremely queasy about anything he has to do. And it gets worse when he has to tell a civilian – worse, a defense attorney, who can be seen as the enemy – like me.

'It is not my preference, no,' he said. 'But the unit I drove when I was a rookie cop used to have the slogan "To Protect and to Serve", and I still take that seriously. You need protection, Ms Moss, and I was glad to see you have a security officer outside your front door.'

'You weren't supposed to notice her,' Angie said. 'She's supposed to blend in.'

'A woman can only tie her shoes for so long and look natural,' Trench told her. 'I'm a cop.'

'Who do you *think* is trying to get me to stop being alive, Lieutenant?' This hilarious banter could only sustain so much of an evening, especially when I'd already been to a stressful dinner at Patrick McNabb's house.

'As I said, I cannot be certain about that yet,' Trench said. Before I could object, he raised his index finger and pointed to the ceiling like a political science professor about to puncture his poor students' notions of what Socialism was. 'But I can tell you that the Madelyn Forsythe case has aroused an undue amount of interest with the deputy chief of police.'

The deputy chief? On a trumped-up prostitution charge that wasn't worth six months in jail even if it were true? 'Why?' I asked.

'An excellent question. There are some possible ties that I could mention but, as I noted, they are unsubstantiated and you are not a member of the Los Angeles Police Department. Suffice it to say Ms Forsythe's husband has friends who have connections to the deputy chief and that might have some relevance.'

'So they want to kill the lawyer because somebody wants Maddie Forsythe to be convicted of a ridiculous prostitution rap?' I said. 'That doesn't make any sense.'

'Yeah,' Angie piped up. 'The way you've been handling that case, she'll probably go to prison anyway. Killing you would do them no good.' You can always count on Angie.

'It goes far beyond the charges on which Ms Forsythe was already convicted,' Trench said before I could tell my closest friend since high school to shut up. 'There have been whispers that something might happen to Ms Forsythe if she ever actually sees the inside of a correctional facility, even for just a few nights.'

That took a second to sink in. 'Somebody is going to kill Maddie Forsythe in prison?' I said, mostly just to the room. 'It's already been set up?' I would have to file that appeal as soon as possible and let the judge know there were questions about my client's safety if she were to be sentenced to anything other than house arrest.

'I'm not saying this is factual and I will not tell a judge that it is if you're already thinking about filing papers,' Trench said, possibly reading my mind. 'I felt you should be cognizant of what I've heard because you should take steps. Some of which you have.'

'Why, Lieutenant? I don't mean why won't you talk to a judge. I mean why are they doing this? Why would they be so afraid of Maddie Forsythe that they would actually plan to kill her in prison and kill her lawyer?' I tried not to remind myself who that attorney might be.

'Excellent questions, Ms Moss. And I promise you that I will do my very best to find the answers.' Trench broke his 'at ease' stance and turned toward the door, apparently thinking that was his best exit line.

'And when you do, you'll tell us?' I asked.

'I sincerely doubt it,' he answered.

Now *certain* that he'd put a cap on the scene (in LA, even the cops are aware of the mechanics of a good story), Trench reached for the doorknob.

'Lieutenant.' Angie got off the barstool and took a few steps toward Trench, which forced him against his will to turn back toward us.

'Yes?'

Angie gave me a long look. 'Would you like some chocolate cake to take home?'

NINETEEN

'I didn't kill anybody,' Cynthia Sutton said.

I was a prosecutor in New Jersey for years, so I had heard those words (and variations on 'kill' like 'steal', 'sell', 'run over' and, once, 'electrocute') many times from people who had been accused of crimes. I rarely believed them, and most of the time had been proven correct by the verdicts reached by juries and sentences carried out by the Department of Corrections. But this time, coming from Cynthia, I was fairly well convinced, although I couldn't exactly put my finger on why that was the case.

Sitting in her painfully tasteful living room with twenty-foot ceilings, an atrium, an actual indoor palm tree and not a bookshelf in sight, Cynthia actually looked out of place today. She was wearing no makeup, her hair was just brushed and not professionally styled, and her right pinkie nail actually had a chip in its polish. In the realm of entertainment royalty this was a desperate plea for help. I was reminded of staying home during lockdown, when everyone took to sweatpants and stayed in them. Cynthia's were probably silk.

'OK, but just saying that isn't going to be enough of a legal defense, so we need to go through some questions to get closer to something I'll be able to use in court when we get there,' I told her. 'Remember that we have attorney/client privilege, which means I am required to hold anything you say in the strictest confidence. So you can feel free to tell me anything.'

'She already told you she didn't kill anyone,' Patrick said. 'Cynthia has nothing to hold back from you.'

Yes, Patrick. I have no idea how Patrick had found out about the conference in Cynthia's house, why he was not required on the set of *Torn* or why Angie (who had already informed me she would not divulge anything about Patrick's workday to me because he had to trust her implicitly) was not present if Patrick was there. I guess he figured he wasn't going to need any assistance.

Patrick just shows up. That's what I've learned. It's not much, but it's all I have.

'I appreciate that, Patrick, but you'll recall I said you could stay for the meeting as long as you stayed quiet.' I still hold some mystical qualities for Patrick because I defended him in court, which he considers a magical power. And I was not about to disabuse him of that notion because it gave me the only modicum of control I had over our relationship.

Which was professional in every way.

Patrick mimed a key turning on his lips, which was cute in 1966. I'm guessing. But he folded his arms and sat back on the extremely cushy armchair. That would buy me maybe five minutes of silence on his part, so I immediately turned my attention back to Cynthia and tried my best to force eye contact with her. Patrick, her old friend (I guessed) was hard to ignore under the best of circumstances, which these were not.

'So tell me again why you went to Wendy's house that night,' I said.

'Like I said, Michael texted me about six.' I had told Cynthia that the time when things happened would be important, so it was a good sign she remembered that without prompting. 'He said he wanted to work out the divorce, that we could be civil about it and just decide between ourselves and that it would be easier and much less unpleasant. He sounded like the man I married, not the one I was trying to divorce.'

'And that's why you agreed to go to Wendy's house? I know Michael said that was neutral ground, but you didn't think so, and you could have said that. Why didn't you?'

'Stop victim blaming,' Patrick said. Five minutes had been an optimistic estimate.

'Patrick, please go into the kitchen or something,' I said. 'You're making this much more difficult than it should be and as Cynthia's lawyer I'm asking you to go wait in another room until I call you back in.'

Patrick put up his hands in a gesture of surrender. 'It won't happen again,' he said.

'Right, because you're going to be in another room. Now, go.'

To Cynthia's amazement but not mine, Patrick nodded and extricated himself from the armchair (which meant his abs were working far better than mine and that I should start running every day again), then walked out of the living room without speaking another word.

Cynthia watched with wide eyes. 'Wow. How'd you do that?' she asked when Patrick was out of earshot.

'He knows I mean it.'

'Amazing.' I had removed the distraction and gained some respect from my client. All to the good.

'So. Why not? Why didn't you tell Michael you wouldn't go to his mother's house? Why not meet in a Starbucks or something?'

'Michael was so insistent.' All of a sudden Cynthia didn't want to make eye contact. That's never a good sign. 'He kept telling me to trust him.'

I stood up to better take advantage of a superior (that is, taller) position to Cynthia's. 'Come on. You're in the middle of a divorce that hasn't exactly been amicable, if such a thing is possible. You knew perfectly well not to trust him. So why did you go to Wendy Bryan's house, Cynthia?' I used the same tone of voice I use in court to give the jury the impression that I don't believe what a witness is saying. Although sometimes I do, but that's not my job.

Cynthia was a fairly major star in Hollywood (which I knew because I had looked up her IMDb page) and she was not used to being treated with anything but deference. But she was also far from stupid and she knew I was her best chance to stay out of jail. So she was willing to take some lip from me, particularly because she'd just seen Patrick do the same. She seemed to take her emotional cues from him.

She looked me directly in the eye so I'd know it wasn't acting. 'I wanted my TeeVee back, OK?' she said. 'It had always annoyed me that Wendy had it and I made it a condition that if I showed up, she'd give it back.'

That was the opening I'd been looking for. 'You're sure it was your TeeVee?' I asked Cynthia.

The question seemed to mystify her. 'Of course it was. It has my name on it.'

'Yes, but was it the authentic one?' If Richard from Patrick's dinner party was right, that would be questionable.

Still Cynthia looked puzzled and I believed her. 'Authentic? Is there another kind?'

'Are there places you – anyone, a person – could buy a fake TeeVee?' I asked.

Her eyes narrowed, not to show irritation but because she was thinking. 'Why would someone want to do that?' she asked.

'It's a really good question.' I told her what Richard had told me about the TeeVee award. 'You must have held onto it at least a little, when they gave it to you certainly. Did you get the impression a person could bend it like that?'

'Like what?' Cynthia still didn't remember anything after she'd discovered Wendy's body.

'With the globe and the figure pointed down, forward, out of the way, so the wings could be used as blades.'

Cynthia's eyes seemed to remember why they were there and widened considerably. 'Oh, no. That's not possible. The statue is too solid and heavy.'

'Let's get back to the night it happened,' I said, taking the opportunity to sit back down. It was, after all, a very comfortable sofa. 'You walked into the house and you found Wendy right away? Is that what happened?'

She shook her head, indicating that she didn't *want* to remember. Cynthia was a woman of crossed signals. It must have driven her lovers crazy. 'Not exactly. I went in and looked first . . .'

'You went looking for the TeeVee.' It wasn't exactly a difficult guess.

Cynthia looked down at the floor, which was impeccably clean and sported a lovely Persian rug that was probably vacuumed every hour on the hour. 'Yes,' she said quietly.

'And you found it?' I was playing prosecutor now. I wanted to see how she would respond on the witness stand when it was suggested that she might indeed have killed her mother-in-law.

'Oh no,' she said. 'I knew she kept it in the den so I went straight there through the foyer, but it wasn't where it was supposed to be.' Cynthia got up and started wandering around the room, which was large enough to lend itself to wandering. If she didn't speak up, I soon wouldn't be able to hear her and might actually have to worry about her bolting out the side door never to be seen again. 'The space on the shelf was there, dusted and everything, but the TeeVee wasn't there. So I went into the center hall and that's when . . .' She didn't finish the sentence.

'That's when you found the body.' A good prosecutor wouldn't allow for that scenario, but as I kept reminding myself, I was working for the defense. And, by the way, shouldn't Holly replace Jon as second chair? I mean, it was a little cold but I needed the help. I made a note on my phone to ask her.

Cynthia just nodded. She started walking back in my direction, which was helpful. I wouldn't have to talk as loudly or listen as carefully.

'And you found the supposed TeeVee there too, or was that in the den when you went in?' Three answering options. Either of those was possible, or she'd found the statuette somewhere else. Not leading the witness, Your Honor.

And of course, the answer was, None of the Above. 'I really don't remember, Sandy. I can picture walking in through the library entrance to the center hall, I remember seeing something, but I didn't know what, on the floor, and then it's a blank.'

Blanks, I should inform you, play very badly in a court of law. Juries *always* think a person who says they have memory lapses is lying.

Cynthia had told me this juicy tidbit before so I knew to move on. 'Now, tell me how you got from the center hall to the den.' This was key. The trail of blood (or lack thereof) made her moving from one room to another questionable if Cynthia was not the killer, which – let's face it – was our contention in court.

She shook her head. 'I don't remember. I told you, Sandy.'

'Well, here's the thing,' I answered. 'It's important that we establish this. There's no physical evidence of you getting from Wendy's body to the place where the police found you, and you had the TeeVee in your hands. No footprints, no trail, nothing.' I thought it was wise to leave out the whole 'of blood' reference. 'So if we can figure out how you got there, we might be able to prove that you weren't the one who stabbed Wendy with the wings from the TeeVee.'

Cynthia stopped in her pacing and stared off into the middle distance for a second as if this scene were being blocked by a really hacky director. Then she looked at me and said, 'There's only one way that makes sense, really.'

She didn't follow up so I delivered the straight line. 'What's that?'

'Someone must have carried me.'

Patrick stuck his head in from the kitchen. 'Is it safe for me to come back in yet?'

TWENTY

'I've made some inquiries.'

Judy the intimidating guard was walking to my left, on the curb side, and a hair behind me as we walked from Cynthia's front door to my prehistoric Hyundai half a block up and across the street. Patrick, who had wanted to stay at Cynthia's for lunch and would have been better off doing so in my estimation, had instead insisted on coming with us, so he was to my right. But it was Judy doing the talking.

I'd asked her to check around with her friends in the LAPD so I knew what she was talking about. 'What have you heard?' I asked. I got the impression Judy was walking especially slowly (for her) to allow for my typical human gait, while she could have been to the car, driven to Burbank, picked up a sandwich, eaten it, driven back and found another parking space in the time it was taking me to walk perhaps a hundred and fifty yards. (That's 137.16 meters, rest of the world.)

'Your name has not been mentioned specifically, ma'am,' Judy said in a measured but low-volume tone. 'But the case of the alleged prostitute is apparently of keen interest to people in the department, specifically in the chief's office.'

That didn't make any sense even given what Trench had said. 'The chief's office? What do Maddie Forsythe's divorce and the deputy chief have to do with the chief's office?'

'That is an excellent question, ma'am.' Not a missed step, but you knew she wanted to break free, like a racehorse being walked out to the track.

'Any idea who's been shooting at us, Judy?' I asked.

'Not yet, ma'am. Sorry.'

I could have told Judy she had no reason to apologize, but I'd done that about thirty-five times since I'd met Judy and I'd only known her for a couple of days. Patrick, keeping pace but also more fit than I was (I really did have to start that running again!) wasn't even breathing heavily. 'You say Lieutenant Trench thought it had to do with the deputy chief of police?' He could barely hide his excitement. For Patrick, being hated by one of the top cops in a huge city would be a weird sort of validation, that he was important enough to merit such a high level of attention. For me, it was more a source of unmitigated terror. Each to their own, I say.

'That was confidential, Patrick. I shouldn't have told you at all.' A couple walking on the other side of the street (which was odd, because nobody in LA walks anywhere – that cliché is actually true because the city is set up for cars) seemed to recognize Patrick, which was not very unusual at all. The woman pointed a phone in our general direction and probably was working with her zoom lens to verify the Celebrity Sighting. Tourists. 'But yes, that's what the lieutenant said.'

'And you believe it to be tied to the prostitution case I heard you argue in court?'

The one you lost, Sandy? 'Yeah.'

Patrick didn't speak for a while, which was not his practice. 'So shouldn't that case be your priority right now?' That was unexpected; usually Patrick's tunnel vision on what he cares about is almost absolute. His asking about Maddie's case took me by surprise.

'I'm working on the appeal and that won't be in court for weeks if not months.'

We reached the car and Judy unlocked it, but I walked to the driver's door. Patrick had come by car service and was in need of a ride, which was his way of monopolizing my time on the way home. And that was fine with me. I actually enjoy Patrick's company.

'Please don't get in just yet, ma'am.' Judy walked to the door, opened it, and hit the hood release.

'Is this necessary, Judy?' I asked. 'I have a meeting coming up in an hour.'

'Better to be safe, ma'am.'

Judy had been checking under my hood and occasionally under the car itself for any evidence of an explosive device since she'd been seeing to my safety. I'd actually had a car blow up in my vicinity before, and still I considered this something of a drag.

She looked carefully through the engine compartment and then dropped down to her knees briefly to check the undercarriage. She stood up and put the hood down, nodding. 'All clear, ma'am.'

I resisted the impulse to roll my eyes because Judy was in fact doing her job and doing it well. 'Thank you,' I said, and got into the car. Patrick sat in the back because Judy insisted on riding shotgun and I don't think she meant that to be a metaphorical term.

'Angie said you and Nate went to see Cynthia's husband,' I said to Patrick once the GPS told me where I should be going. I could negotiate New Jersey roads practically in my sleep (and had almost done so a couple of times) but Los Angeles's highway and road systems had all the logic of a Salvador Dalí painting. Besides, I didn't have experience driving in LA for more than twenty years. 'What did you find out?'

'Not very much,' Patrick answered. He didn't seem to mind riding in the back because that was where he always rode in a limo. 'Michael Bryan is about as average a man as one could meet, frankly. I have never understood what Cynthia saw in him, but she saw it, so I am conceding the idea that it's there. She is a woman of considerable insight.'

That, in my opinion, was yet to be seen, but I let it go. 'What did Nate ask him about when you let him get a word in edgewise?'

Patrick half-smiled, an acknowledgement that what I was implying was true. 'It's not my fault that the man doesn't ask the right questions.'

'He does,' I countered. 'The problem is you think our job is to solve the crime when in fact our job is to prove that Cynthia didn't do it.'

'Isn't that the same thing?'

There was no use explaining it. Again. 'What did Nate ask Michael Bryan about?' I repeated.

'Mostly about his whereabouts on the night of the murder. Michael said he had been called to a meeting at his office, which I assume Mr Garrigan is attempting to verify.'

He already had, according to a recent text message. 'Is that why he texted Cynthia to come to his mother's house but never showed up?' I asked.

Patrick looked at the back of my head (I could see him in the rearview mirror) for some time. 'He texted Cynthia?'

'Yes. You'll recall. Cynthia said she went to Wendy's house because Michael texted her and offered to negotiate a reasonable settlement to their divorce without involving people like me who actually know what they're talking about in such matters.' Most of the time.

'It can be . . . distracting to hear other people discuss one's marriage,' Patrick said. I had sat in on one conference about his impending divorce before his wife was murdered and it had not been a love-in. Whatever those were.

'Anyway, what did Michael say about texting Cynthia? Did you forget?' Then I remembered Cynthia had told me about Michael texting her before Patrick had arrived at the police station, but Patrick had not been exiled from the room today when she'd said it again.

'Michael said specifically that he had not communicated with Cynthia that day or for a week before, on his attorney's advice.' I caught a quick glimpse of Patrick smiling after he said that, thinking he had somehow scored a point on me for mentioning attorneys in a manner that wasn't derogatory.

'Does Cynthia have an assistant?' I asked. 'Maybe Michael texted to a number that doesn't get through to Cynthia.' There had to be *some* reason she'd gone to her mother-in-law's home that night. Unless the reason was to kill Wendy Bryan, which would put a major crimp in my case.

'Cynthia has three assistants,' Patrick answered. 'But to my knowledge she always keeps her personal matters to herself and does not have her assistants answer on any texts that aren't going to be about business.'

I hadn't heard the last part of that. *Three assistants?* I worked for a high-end law firm and had to share a secretary with two other lawyers, but the actress had three assistants all by herself? There needed to be major changes made to employment laws in this country.

'So why did Cynthia go to Wendy's house if Michael didn't ask her to?' I pondered out loud.

I should have known better. 'Seems like a hole in her story,' Judy said. Thanks a heap, Judy.

'She must be confused,' Patrick offered. 'Or Michael is lying. I'd vote for the latter. The man's a cobra.' The blandest man in the world was a cobra. Make up your mind, Patrick.

I pulled the car over and stopped it. 'Maybe we have to go back and ask Cynthia why she told me a lie about Michael texting her.'

Patrick waved a hand. 'Nonsense,' he said. He pulled his phone out of his pocket and was talking to Cynthia before I had a chance to turn around in my seat and look at him. 'Cynthia, love,' he began. I knew he was just being Patrick, but I thought he was slathering it on a little thick. 'We have a question.' He waited, then put his phone on speaker so we could hear. 'When I went to see Michael yesterday—'

Cynthia interrupted him immediately. 'You went to see Michael?' It wasn't panic in her voice. It was annoyance bordering on anger.

'Yes, love. I told you I went there with the investigator, Mr Garrigan. And when we were there, a question about the night . . . it all happened came up.'

'What did Michael tell you?' That was years of anger, all in five words.

'He said that he was at a business meeting that night, which Mr Garrigan is trying to verify.'

'I bet he won't be able to,' Cynthia answered. 'I bet he was off with some woman he thinks is the next love of his life.'

I decided that if this was the way we were going to play it, I might as well assert myself as the lawyer once again. 'Cynthia, it's Sandy. Here's the thing: Michael said he never texted you and asked you to come to his mother's house that night.'

'So he's lying.' Well, problem solved!

'Can you prove that? Did you save the texts on your phone?' If she had, we could easily show that Michael had indeed called his wife that night. The content of the conversation might not be admissible – her word versus his – but the text itself, given that Michael had lied about it, would be a useful weapon in court. I'd have to get Michael deposed.

'No. I deleted them.'

Of course she did. 'You deleted the texts from your phone?' I said. It wasn't so much clarification I was after as some sense of why someone who *hadn't* committed a murder would do something that stupid.

'Yeah, before I went there. I delete all his stuff. I don't want to be reminded of them.' It wasn't quite enough to make the Flimsy Excuse Hall of Fame, but it would certainly be in the conversation.

I'd have to check with Nate and see if he could check with Cynthia's service provider for her account records. There might be a tech marvel who could retrieve deleted texts from Cynthia's phone, but I was starting to worry that I was on the wrong side in this case. Cynthia was suddenly doing her best to act like someone who had indeed killed her mother-in-law with a television acting award.

'Do you remember what the exact words he used were?' Ask for details and you can sometimes get a stronger sense of how confident the person is in their story. Confidence doesn't always equal truth but it doesn't hurt.

'I don't know. Why are you taking his side?'

'She's not taking his side,' Patrick butted in. 'You have to understand that Sandy needs to be able to prove anything she says in court. Evidence is very important.' That's what he learned from playing a lawyer on TV. That evidence is important.

'Patrick's . . . right,' I said, overlooking my impulse to say he was *sort of* right. 'The more verifiable evidence we can get, like a record of the texts, the better we can prove that you didn't kill Wendy Bryan.'

'Well, I didn't.' Cynthia might have been on some anti-anxiety medication or she might have been on sedatives. But even in this short period of time she had lost some of the intelligent edge she'd had when I'd talked to her in her house only minutes ago.

'We know that, love,' Patrick said, trying to modulate his voice into a soothing tone. Patrick doesn't like people to be upset and he wants to solve all their problems for them. It's a sweet impulse, but as with everything else he takes it too far. 'We'll get back to you when we hear from Mr Garrigan.' And he disconnected the call. I was too overwhelmed to take him to task for ending my client meeting.

'She sounds guilty,' Judy said, as ever with no inflection at all.

'She's *not* guilty!' Patrick doesn't often shout or show anything but charm, which as an actor is very unusual. But now he was practically vibrating with rage. 'She's not guilty and you shouldn't ever say something like that!'

'Sorry,' Judy intoned.

From the front seat it was hard to make eye contact, but I turned in my seat to attract Patrick's attention. 'OK, Patrick,' I said. 'You've got to come clean with me. I get that Cynthia is a friend of yours and you're upset that she's in really bad trouble. But you're paying her bills when she doesn't need you to and you're picking out attorneys for her. You're defending her when her case seems difficult to defend. You swear you've never had a romantic relationship. Fine. So what's the deal with you and Cynthia Sutton?'

'Cynthia is my sister,' was the reply.

TWENTY-ONE

A coffee shop is not the best place in the world to figure out a puzzle that makes your head hurt. For one thing, caffeine feeds the pain. For another, there are people around who might, just on the off chance that one of your companions is an extremely famous TV actor, tend to stare and potentially interrupt. But it was close, and I couldn't hold this conversation and drive in Los Angeles at the same time.

'Your *sister*?' I said. 'You have never mentioned having a sister and you didn't bring up this juicy little tidbit when you introduced Cynthia to me. Or, for that matter, in any of the many conversations that you and I have had about her since then. What do you mean, she's your sister?'

'It's very simple,' Patrick said.

'Why do I doubt that?'

Heads were already turning and the waitress (this place wasn't trendy enough to have baristas) had made a point of lingering a little too long at the table when she'd taken our orders. I'd gotten a bottle of spring water because see above re caffeine.

'All right, so Cynthia is actually my half-sister,' Patrick went on, without acknowledging my remark. 'After my parents divorced my dad moved to the States, got remarried and they had a daughter. So Cynthia, if you look it up anywhere but IMDb, where she didn't tell them, is a Dunwoody.' Dunwoody is Patrick's real name, although not his legal one. He became Patrick McNabb officially to the city of Los Angeles, the state of California and the United States of America less than two years ago.

'And you both came here as actors and became great big stars?' I asked. 'That seems awfully unlikely.'

'Ask Warren Beatty and Shirley MacLaine,' he countered.

'Oddly I've lost their phone numbers. And if you have to go back sixty years to prove your point, it might not be as obvious as you think. How did you both manage that when you admit yourself you barely had a test reel when you came to LA?'

'Cynthia was already a bigger name than me even when I was still in London,' Patrick said. 'She didn't exactly pull any strings for me when I got here, but mentioning her name in a couple of interviews certainly didn't hurt. I think the producers on *Legality* looked at my reel, thought I was OK, and then found out I was Cynthia Sutton's brother and hired me. But Cynthia made sure it was written into both our contracts that the connection would never be used to publicize any project either one of us was connected to.'

'Why not?' Judy could stare at the door with the concentration of a Doberman whose owner had not come home yet and still manage to join the conversation.

'We both, but Cynthia especially, didn't want it to look like we were remarkably close or that we were involved in each other's career,' Patrick explained. 'The fact is we grew up in separate households in separate countries. We'd visit every year or so and that was about it. My mum didn't want me flying across the ocean to be at my dad's, and when I was really young I wasn't crazy about the idea myself.'

I shook my head, mostly to get the cobwebs and the confusion out. 'This is beside the point,' I told Patrick. 'You're paying for Cynthia's legal fees and pushing me on the case because you're her brother, or half-brother, and you never even mentioned it to me.'

He hung his head a little, but I saw it was meant to obscure his face from people at a nearby table and the waitress, who brought our drinks, saw how Patrick was positioning himself, and left, probably cursing the Hollywood big shot who couldn't be bothered to acknowledge his loyal fans. 'I am sorry about that, Sandy,' he said when she had left. 'I've just gotten so used to not telling that part of the story that it's become reflex. But no matter what, you must make sure that she is acquitted.'

I noticed Judy's neck tensing up in the back as she looked out the front window. 'Something?' I asked her.

'Man carrying a gun,' she said steadily. She might just as well have been mentioning that there was a blue jay nesting in a tree in front of the coffee shop.

Now I tensed up, but Judy shook her head. 'He's walking past. Didn't even look in.'

'You know the process, Patrick,' I said. 'This will take a few months at least to iron out. In the meantime, Cynthia can continue to work, to see friends, to have relationships. The only thing she absolutely has to do is answer the phone when I call and answer my questions honestly.'

'That's two things,' Judy noted. Her neck still wasn't a hundred percent relaxed. Even for her.

'Mr Garrigan is dragging his feet,' Patrick complained. His lips were pursed, a sign of impatience.

'Mr Garrigan is being thorough and professional and, like I *just told you*, we have a good few months to build a case. I know your thinking, Patrick. Stop expecting Nate to deliver the real killer all wrapped up with a bow on his head. That's not his job.'

'Lindsey Waverly would be able to do it.'

'Who's Lindsey Waverly?' I asked.

Patrick looked positively wounded and made eye contact for the first time in a couple of minutes. 'He's the character I play on *Torn*. One of them, anyway.' It bothers Patrick that I don't watch his show regularly. Angie, on the other hand, has devoured every project the man has ever come close to being involved with and can recite whole paragraphs of dialogue without so much as a prompt.

'Forgive me. But you must learn patience. Our job right now is to establish not who killed Wendy Bryan, but that it definitely wasn't Cynthia. And I'm not sure I'm certain of that.'

Patrick's head swiveled in my direction quickly, like it was being manipulated by very taut rubber bands attached to each temple. 'What?'

'You heard me. Cynthia is acting like a guilty party and I need to figure out if that's just part of what she does to inspire sympathy, or if it's because she actually took the TeeVee award – or something – to Wendy's chest herself.'

'Wow,' Judy said without any inflection whatsoever.

Patrick huffed. I drank some more water. Judy scanned the room again. 'Not crazy about that guy with the gun,' she said. 'LA's not a big "concealed carry" town. Not this part of town, anyway. Too big a coincidence.'

'Should we leave?' I said, not letting on that the hairs on my arms were standing up, which was not attractive in the Southern California heat. I reached for my jacket.

'I think so,' Judy answered.

We stood up, Patrick still with a grumble on his face, and headed for the door. And it was that exact moment, when I was worried about being shot, that my phone rang.

I thought to ignore it, but the ID indicated the call was coming from Maddie Forsythe. She was the client whose case I had bungled and I should have been working on her appeal right now. Yes, I'm that infused with guilt. Call my mother and ask her why.

We had just made it outside the coffee shop and were heading to my car, parked three spaces up the street, when I connected with Maddie. But I couldn't get a word in before Judy yelled, 'Down!'

She stayed on her feet and pulled her weapon from the hip holster she was wearing. Patrick and I dove for the pavement like we had (with help from Philip, who suddenly appeared from around the side of the coffee shop, gun in hand) at the restaurant the *first* time I'd been shot at (this year). You know, two days ago.

But I did hear shots ringing out and I did in fact hide my eyes because everyone knows you can't get hit with a bullet if you don't see it coming.

I heard a total of six shots. Then for a long moment it was quiet and I worried that Judy and/or Philip might have been hit. Or Patrick! I tore my hands off my eyes. Was Patrick all right? I forgave him for everything while I turned my head to the left to check on him.

He was fine. I could start blaming him for things again. He stood up and patted Philip on the arm. 'Well done,' he said.

'What the *hell*,' I said. 'This is getting really old.' I somehow managed to get myself to my feet without tearing any article of clothing. When I looked around I had some inkling of what must have happened.

The man who had passed the coffee shop before and attracted Judy's attention was on the pavement, face down, not moving, about thirty yards away. The handgun she'd seen weighing his pocket down was still in his right hand. Another man I'd not seen before was sitting on the grass bay (the strip of grass between the sidewalk and the curb), holding his arm, which was bleeding. Philip was standing next to him, pocketing a handgun he'd picked up off the ground next to the as-yet-unidentified man.

Patrick walked over, concern on his face. 'Are you all right?' he said. 'I heard all those shots and I thought something awful had happened.'

'Something awful *did* happen,' I told him. 'But I'm OK, and I'm glad you are, too.'

We fell into a hug on the sidewalk. It was all about terror and relief.

Then I remembered I was on the phone with Maddie just as Judy was calling 911 and letting the cops know what had happened. I still had my phone in my hand and oddly it was not damaged. I must have subconsciously protected it when I'd dived to the ground. A weird outgrowth of modern technology and its effect on the urban woman. I'd suggest it to a sociology major as soon as I met one.

Patrick and I separated and I brought the phone to my ear. 'I'm so sorry,' I said to Maddie. 'It's just that all of a sudden—'

'Someone just tried to kill me,' Maddie said.

TWENTY-TWO

As if I'd had him on retainer, Lieutenant Trench showed up at the scene of my latest devastation within ten minutes. Given LA traffic, it was a minor miracle he could arrive the same day as the shooting. I figured Trench had planted a homing device on me at some point and just cruised around Los Angeles waiting for someone to take another shot at me.

'This is becoming an unfortunate habit.' He had arrived only a few minutes after the first uniformed officers, who were taking statements from Philip and Judy largely because they actually knew what had happened. I had covered my eyes and done my best ostrich impression, so my account was going to have some serious gaps in it. 'Does this happen often in New Jersey,

Ms Moss? Did you bring this sort of mayhem with you when you immigrated?'

I ignored the banter; Trench was back to his needling mode and in the professional manner he'd abandoned only the night before in my apartment when he'd wanted to warn me that this might happen again. To be fair, he wasn't using any I-told-you-so points, so my admiration for him was not in any way diminished.

'Lieutenant, my client just called me and said someone had tried to kill her at almost exactly the same time this was happening,' I said. 'It sounds to me like these were coordinated attacks.'

'*Brava*, Ms Moss. You have mastered the art of the obvious. Yes. I am aware that Ms Forsythe was assaulted on the street outside her home by a man carrying a knife. Luckily she is uninjured but there are officers on the scene as we speak and they will report to me given that these are, as you have so aptly pointed out, related incidents. The real question remains, who exactly are the people who just opened fire on you?'

There were cops surrounding the man with the arm wound, since he could answer questions. The other one, whom Judy had told me she'd shot in the chest, was in no condition to answer questions and never would be again. I wasn't that upset about those circumstances, but then I didn't have to call his mother that night. Everybody is some mother's child.

On the other hand, I wasn't dead, and I considered that a major plus. It's all in how you look at things.

Judy was going to be questioned by the cops for quite some time, so she had already called for Carolyn to fill in for her. I couldn't argue since my need for a guard had been very recently confirmed in a rather graphic fashion. Carolyn would be here in twenty minutes, Judy said.

What was it Trench had asked me just now?

'Yeah,' I said, shaking the cobwebs out of my brain. 'It would be nice to know who is interested enough to put in all the time and money. Anyone in your sphere of influence leap to mind, Lieutenant?'

Trench is, I'm certain, capable of looking uncomfortable. He came close at that moment, but the best he could manage was to squint just a little and it was a sunny day in Southern California. You might have heard we have a few of those out here every year.

'If I knew that, arrests would be made,' he answered in his usual tone. 'The real question is: what can be done to keep you away from people with homicide on their minds?'

'Catching the bad guys is probably the most efficient way to do that,' I suggested.

'Another is for you to advise Ms Forsythe to accept her guilty verdict and negotiate a very short prison sentence for her,' Trench said. 'If the person or people behind this are truly only interested in you because of her case, you would have it done and Ms Forsythe would have served a relatively light penalty.'

That was as stunning a statement as I'd ever heard from him. I lowered my voice in case the uniformed officer questioning Patrick nearby was involved in the enormous police conspiracy against me that I'd created in my own mind. 'You told me yourself that something very bad might happen to her if she goes to jail,' I told him. 'That is not to mention the fact that she's not guilty of the ridiculous charges.'

'I might be able to arrange some form of protection for her, if you can talk a judge into putting her in a Los Angeles County jail,' Trench suggested. 'I can't guarantee it beyond any doubt, but I do have a bit of influence.'

Patrick looked as if he was having the time of his life being questioned about almost getting shot. People in the entertainment business like nothing more than attention, and the circumstances surrounding it are rarely a deterrent. He caught my eye and winked at me, which I'm sure the officer noticed. Now the cop was probably going to report to his superiors that he suspected Patrick and I had arranged to get ourselves shot at so we could become bigger deals in LA. Which was ridiculous because Patrick was already about as big a deal as you could be, and I was not any kind of deal.

Certainly not a plea deal for Maddie Forsythe, anyway. 'I don't think so, Lieutenant,' I said. 'I'm not going to tell a client that she needs to go to jail for something she didn't do just so I can sleep a little easier at night.'

'Your call, Ms Moss. I see your substitute protection has

arrived.' He nodded toward the street, where Carolyn was being dropped off by an Uber. She strode purposefully (they all strode purposefully) toward me, glancing at Judy as she approached.

'Lieutenant Trench,' Carolyn said when she reached us.

'Ms Townsend.' No hint of an opinion in Trench's voice. How did they know each other?

'Used to be Officer Townsend,' Carolyn reminded him.

'I recall.' Look up the word *inscrutable* in the dictionary. It might not be next to a picture of Trench, but you can bet he personally wrote the definition.

'I thought you might.' They were holding a contest in advanced emotional suppression. It was like watching Mr Spock look in a mirror.

'I'll leave you to your work, then.' Trench glanced toward me. 'Ms Moss.' He walked to one of the officers who was questioning the man with the bullet in his arm, which no one seemed especially concerned about. Except that the guy kept pointing at the bleeding wound and seemed to be suggesting that medical care should be forthcoming. The cop speaking to him nodded reassuringly but did nothing else.

Patrick, released from the interrogation he had so utterly enjoyed, walked over to us smiling his usual hundred-watt beamer. 'Are we all finished here?' he asked.

'We got shot at,' I reminded him.

'I'm aware, but I've told them everything I know about it, which isn't very much. What about you? Have you mentioned to the police that this is the third time you've been shot at in as many days?'

I knew it was his way of trying to lighten the moment, but I didn't need my moment lightened just now. 'No. I didn't see that as relevant,' I said. 'What do you think, Patrick?'

'So where are we off to?' Patrick asked, like we had just finished a refreshing beverage and were about to continue our day.

'I'm taking you back to wherever you need to be and then I'm going to see my client,' I answered. I was approaching Patrick overload and needed to park him somewhere as soon as possible.

He looked confused. 'We just came from Cynthia's house,' he said.

'My *other* client.' I actually had thirteen cases open at the moment, but most of them were divorces. Only two in the criminal system, and in my opinion that was two over my limit.

Patrick nodded. 'Of course. You need to work on the prostitute.' He caught himself and grinned naughtily. 'I suppose that was a rather unfortunate turn of phrase.'

'She was just assaulted with a knife right outside her home,' I said with a considerable amount of ice in my voice. 'I'm going to make sure she's all right. Now, where am I dropping you off?' I started to walk toward my car. If Trench or one of the uniforms wanted to stop and question me some more, this was their big chance. Nobody made any move toward me so I kept walking.

Patrick didn't answer right away. I was paying attention to the cops so I didn't notice immediately, always a mistake with Patrick. Even when you don't give him time to ruminate, he's going to come up with something that he thinks is wonderful and you will spend the rest of your day (if you're lucky) regretting.

'I think perhaps I should go with you,' he said when we reached the car and Carolyn, without scanning for bombs, did a quick check before allowing me to open the driver's side door and get in. 'This seems to be a situation that is tied to the people who shot at us, don't you think?'

He got in next to me, which Carolyn seemed to find annoying but didn't protest. She took a position in the back and gave me a look that indicated I should not tell Patrick to change seats with her.

'I think there is no question that they're related and no, you're not coming with us, Patrick. This is an attorney meeting with a client and there will be no intrusions. And you, my friend, are an intrusion.'

I started the car and set the GPS toward Patrick's office at his production company, which was where we'd been heading before the world had gone crazy, again. I pulled out of the space where the Hyundai had been parked, noting mentally that – despite Carolyn failing to drop to the ground and look under the car – it had not blown up. Luck, or a demonstration that perhaps Judy was overcautious? (I had snuck a glance under the car before I got in and didn't know what I was looking for. Apparently it hadn't been there.)

Somehow, driving away from having survived a murder attempt largely because of Judy, an abundance of caution didn't seem like such a bad thing.

'How about this?' Patrick went on undeterred. 'I will stay outside the room where you are conferring with your client so that I cannot make any comment or ask any questions that would embarrass you. I will not attempt to listen through the door, and you can post Carolyn here as a guard to ensure it. I just want to go along, say hello to the prost . . . to the woman – and offer my sincerest hopes that she was not injured and will not suffer such an indignity again. How's that?'

This would go on until we reached Dunwoody Inc. (Patrick had decided to use his birth name for his production company because 'it reminds me where I came from') and I had Carolyn physically remove him from the car and toss him to the pavement. But I couldn't do that. So I glanced quickly over at him.

'One condition,' I said.

'Name it.'

'Call your executive assistant and get her to meet us there.'

TWENTY-THREE

Naturally Madelyn Forsythe was upset. She'd been convicted of soliciting an undercover officer for sex and money online and had been threatened in front of her apartment building (her home since the divorce) with a knife, all in less than forty-eight hours. Anybody who wasn't upset after a period like that is on some serious anti-anxiety medication.

But Maddie was not the type to throw things or berate employees (like, for example, her increasingly unconfident attorney). She was more the sort who would sit very still and quiet when upset, chew over her own thoughts, reach a conclusion and then never in a million years let you know what it was. Maddie was a little scary, frankly.

We were sitting in her bedroom (the scene of her alleged crime), which was large enough for a king-sized bed, a small lamp table by the window, and two chairs in which we were seated at the moment. It was certainly upper-middle-class, but the lower end of upper, if you know what I mean. Tasteful without bragging about it.

'I was trying to get to my hairdresser,' she said. 'I was walking to the curb because my Uber driver Marvin was only two blocks away in his red Toyota Prius.' She coughed.

'Did you notice the man who approached you?' I asked. Immediately I was reminded of the day before, when a man with a gun had approached me and shot Jon, who was still in the ICU but expected to recover, according to the email from his wife.

'Not at first,' she said, which was exactly what I had told the cops on the scene outside my office. Maddie, to her credit, was answering the questions directly and thoughtfully. She was clearly very shaken but was not letting that get in the way of telling her attorney what had happened. 'I did notice he was wearing a jean jacket and that was weird because it was so hot today. Nobody else on the street was wearing any kind of jacket.'

A jean jacket! Could it have been the same man who'd come at me yesterday? He'd shot Jon and this guy had tried to stab Maddie. Maybe it wasn't the same man. Did they have a uniform?

'How did you manage to get away?' I asked.

Maddie looked surprised and maybe a little amused. 'Get away?' she said. 'I didn't get away. I took that jerk down in two moves and didn't even break a sweat. And it was ninety-eight degrees out.'

That shook me a little. 'How?'

'I've been taking martial arts training for years,' Maddie explained. 'I started with tae kwon do and then I switched to karate. Now I'm studying karate and traditional Chinese kung fu. I've been planning on starting kickboxing, but then all this happened.' At that point the emotions did seem to get hold of Maddie and her eyes welled up, but she didn't so much as sniffle, breathed in and seemed to swallow whatever had been about to escape through her mouth. 'Once I saw the knife I knew exactly how to disarm and take him down.'

I hadn't been able to get a police report yet simply because there hadn't been time, but I would ask someone from the office to pick it up as soon as I left here. I knew I had to keep the interview with Maddie short because Patrick was in the next room, probably with a glass to the outside of the door like in old movies, trying to hear what was going on. I really couldn't figure exactly what about Maddie's case was fascinating him so completely.

'So you called nine-one-one?' I asked. 'The cops came and arrested this man. Did he say anything to them when that happened?'

'He handed them a business card with the name of his attorney and refused to say another word,' Maddie told me. 'They hauled him away and I never once heard his voice at all. It was like he'd been ready to get arrested all along.'

He probably had. This sounded like some kind of coordinated effort and that meant the men with the weapons were hired hands, not the masterminds. The question was, who had hired the hands and whose minds were doing the mastering?

That's two questions.

'Why all the martial arts?' I asked, largely because I couldn't ask Maddie who had hired the assassins. That would just be too damn easy.

She raised her eyebrows a little. 'I'm back on the dating market, Sandy. I've got to stay in shape and I've got to be ready if someone tries to go a little too far.'

When we left the bedroom Patrick, as I had suspected, was sitting as close to the door as he possibly could. No glass in sight but there was probably an app on his phone that could hear through walls. I put nothing past Patrick.

'I do hope you weren't badly hurt, my dear lady,' he said to Maddie, taking her hand the way he had with Carolyn in the coffee shop. She, a fan of his current TV show, stared into Patrick's eyes and smiled.

'You have nothing to worry about,' she told him. 'It was the man who attacked me that they needed to take to the emergency room.'

'Oh, good for you.'

Carolyn was standing near the window, of course, but within range of the door to the den, where we were standing now. She was preparing for any form of attack, which should have made me feel more secure but actually had the opposite effect.

'Thanks for seeing me, Maddie. I'll get in touch with you very soon.' I extracted Patrick from the death grip he'd had on Maddie's hand and pointed him in the direction of the exit.

'Do you think what happened today will help with my case?' Maddie asked. That stopped me on the way to the door. 'I mean, if someone's trying to kill me that means they don't want the truth to get out, right?'

She was so naïve I wanted to give her a hug. 'We can hope,' I said. The fact was that an attempt on her life would probably be used by the prosecution to suggest that Maddie had ties to known criminals and was therefore more likely, not less, to be involved in illegal activities.

Patrick waited until we got outside – and Maddie had said goodbye to him a few more times – to say confidentially to me, 'Does she have a chance on appeal?' He knew enough about studying lawyers (mostly me) when he was playing one that he knew the right words to use when discussing criminal cases.

'Sure she does,' I answered. 'The charges were absurd and they have the least damning evidence I have ever seen.'

'I'd like to see the file,' Patrick said in his most lawyerly tone.

'I'd like to see six million dollars in my checking account,' I said. 'You don't always get to see what you want, with apologies to Mick Jagger.'

Patrick stopped walking. 'Why do you need six million dollars?' he asked. He reached into his pocket and I thought he was going to reach for his phone and Venmo it to me.

'I don't. It was a figure of speech. Hey, where's Angie? I thought she was going to meet us here.'

He took his hand out of his pocket, thankfully. 'She'll be around.'

'We're clear,' Carolyn said. Even that she didn't sound very happy about.

'We should wait for Angie,' Patrick said. 'She'll be here—'

That is, of course, when Angie pulled up in Patrick's snazzy Tesla, no doubt her very favorite perk of the new job. She stopped right behind where my Hyundai was parked, got out of the car and looked at us. 'Are you two all right?' she demanded. 'Philip said there was shooting.'

'Just another day in LA,' I told her.

'We're fine,' Patrick said. 'Are you ready to work?'

Angie, now smiling but clearly in business mode, nodded. 'Fire away, boss. Oops. Sorry. Too soon?'

Patrick ignored the remark, just as I did. Carolyn probably hadn't even heard it because she was busy looking back and forth on the street for any possible new assailants. Or she was trying to find a Krispy Kreme. What do I know?

'You're assigned to Sandy for the rest of the day,' Patrick said. 'I'm driving back to the studio for some night scenes later, so I need the car. You go with Sandy and assist her with both Cynthia's case and the woman who was running a prostitution service out of her house.'

'She wasn't . . .' Oh, what was the point?

Angie just glossed over it. 'Gotcha.' I got that she was Patrick's employee now, in a real job, but it was still a little weird. You should never visit your roommate/best friend at work.

We all walked over to my car, despite Patrick having insisted that he was driving his own car back to his job. I couldn't figure out why he was tagging along, but being an actor, Patrick was probably looking for the perfect exit line before he could separate from us.

Carolyn stood by the passenger door, not to be denied her vantage point again. Angie followed me, no doubt to take the back seat behind the driver. Patrick also stuck with me and spoke softly, perhaps trying not to be heard by Carolyn. He wasn't shying from Angie, so I guessed it was OK if she was in on the conversation.

'It's about the engagement,' he said in a perfect stage whisper.

'Or lack thereof,' Angie stuck in.

Patrick winced a bit at her volume but didn't comment on it. 'The reason I cancelled my forthcoming marriage,' he said.

'I thought it was because I pointed out that you were rushing into something the way you did with Patsy, and that it hadn't worked out so well the first time.'

Carolyn, who seemingly didn't notice our lagging around, was studying cars going by, no doubt wondering if one of them was carrying people carrying poisoned blow darts. Anything was possible these days.

'That wasn't it,' Patrick said. 'Well, yes, it is that, but the reason I found your argument so effective was completely about a side issue.'

Was this some sort of strange business meeting? I knew there wasn't a pre-nup in place because Patrick had ended the engagement before I could write one. 'A side issue?' I asked. There was a strange, somewhat unsettling smile on Angie's face. I braced myself without knowing why.

'Yes,' Patrick answered. 'I broke off my engagement because I realized that I'm actually in love with you.'

Then he continued on his way while I gaped at him, got into his Tesla and drove away.

I had to admit, it was a really good exit line.

PART TWO
'Lovers'

TWENTY-FOUR

Four months later, the nightmare trial was real.
Madelyn Forsythe's appeal hearing was possibly the most sloppily presided legal proceeding I'd ever seen. Judge Colin Klemperer sat at his bench and didn't even try to conceal the contempt he was obviously feeling for my client, who sat at the defense table looking like a kitten confronting a grizzly bear. It wasn't so much fear as total bewilderment.

'The defendant offered sexual favors to an unknown internet acquaintance she'd met on a site for people seeking such transactions and she made a reference to payment,' Longabaugh told the judge. 'I don't see how that's anything but the solicitation of sex for money.'

I was already on my feet. 'Your Honor, it's anything but clear that such a transaction was being discussed. My client thought she was on a simple dating site and – given her recent divorce – was seeking someone to meet and flirt with. Never was money even vaguely suggested as payment for sex and never did so much as one cent change hands. These charges never should have been brought, let alone a conviction handed down. We are requesting simple relief from what was clearly an unjust and unwarranted verdict.'

Klemperer looked at me and shook his head with something approaching disgust. 'Ms Moss, how long have you been an attorney?'

So this was going to get personal. Exactly what you never want. 'Eight years, Your Honor.' Don't try to defend yourself; just answer the question. You know a snide comment is coming and you'll just have to take the shot and rebound from it.

'In that time, did you never learn the meaning of the word *appeal*?' Oh good. He was going to school me on the basics of the law.

'I believe I understand the concept,' I said, hoping I could keep this little display short and get back to the absurd charges against my client.

'I'm not certain of that,' Klemperer responded. Judges aren't supposed to sneer but that wasn't stopping him. 'We are not here to consider the validity of the original charges or to once again argue the merits, as you see them, of the case. We're here because you filed a brief that suggested there were irregularities in the original trial. This is an appeal, not a retrial. So let's keep the proceeding focused on the problems you had with the trial that took place four months ago, please.'

My problem with the first trial was that the charges were stupid and the verdict a miscarriage of justice. The fact that the judge allowed testimony he shouldn't have or that the jury had seven divorced men, three of whom had slipped Maddie their business cards after a day in court, constituted icing on the cake here. But, hey. Tell the man what'll get you where you want to go.

'Of course, Your Honor.' I sat down and let Longabaugh rant on some more and waited for my turn.

Maddie leaned over to me at one point. 'This isn't going well.'

'Wait for our turn,' I told her, not in the least confident that it would go better.

'The prosecution rests,' Longabaugh said after his latest smug diatribe, and walked back to his table.

Klemperer looked at me. 'If you can put forward your case for appeal, Ms Moss, without trying to present new evidence.' Again, a dig suggesting I didn't know what an appeal was.

I had requested a panel of three judges to hear the appeal, which is indeed supposed to focus strictly on the way the original trial was conducted and any errors or misjudgments that could have swayed the verdict in the wrong direction. My reasoning was that all three judges couldn't be biased against a) women generally and b), for some reason, Maddie Forsythe specifically. I needed irregularities that had taken place at trial and I had plenty of those. But having sat through four hours of Judge Klemperer I was coming to the conclusion that a change in strategy might be in order.

'Your Honor, the defense's case is based on the premise that errors in the trial at the municipal level were deciding factors in the verdict, which we believe was clearly unjust. I have a long list of those errors and evidence to review, including taped testimony from the trial and the transcripts of the internet conversation that took place between the defendant and the arresting officer, who was operating under a false identity in a sting operation. We contend that the execution of that police exercise compromised the defendant and that the municipal trial did not adequately take that into account.'

What I was really saying was: *The cop was being a jerk and tried to trap Maddie, who was just out for a quick giggle, and the judge and jury in the first trial were obviously bought off by her enemies in the LAPD, which for reasons I still didn't understand were holding a grudge against her.* But you have to sound legal and intelligent when you say stuff like that in court.

'It's all in your brief, Ms Moss. What sort of evidence do you wish to offer that does not fall outside the bounds of this sort of proceeding?' Klemperer could have been lighting a pipe while saying that – it would have fit his tone and his image – but there is no smoking in Los Angeles courtrooms.

'My point here, Your Honor, is that the evidence we intend to present might take considerably longer than the time the court has to hear it today.'

'We can be here again tomorrow, Ms Moss. The courts are open on Thursdays, too.' That drew the desired titter from the small group of spectators, most of whom were there for upcoming cases on the court calendar and were probably not pleased to hear that I'd be taking so much time their presence here today was unnecessary. They'd have to ask for another day off from work.

Unless my plan worked.

'Of course the courts are open tomorrow, but if Your Honor will check the schedule, you'll see that I have already been granted time off in order to appear in Judge Hawthorne's court on another matter. I applied for that time two months ago.'

Klemperer was frantically pushing on the screen of his iPad. And he clearly didn't care much for what he found. 'That is noted on the schedule, Ms Moss, but I don't understand why you can't simply have another associate from your firm handle this case. In fact, I don't understand why you appeared here at all today.'

I had anticipated that question. 'Your Honor, my client has been adamant about having me represent her in this matter. And I did request a continuance in this matter to place it after my other trial, but it was denied.' *And you were the one who denied it, so you should have read all the documents pertinent to this case before you did, right?*

Klemperer looked sour but nodded. 'Yes, I see that,' he said, as if it weren't entirely his fault to begin with. He took off the reading glasses he used to view the tablet. 'How long did you say you are anticipating your case will continue, Ms Moss?'

'I would think about six hours, Your Honor.' If I spoke really slowly and asked for a bathroom break every fifteen minutes, it might go three hours. But he didn't need to know that.

He wasn't an idiot, though; he looked surprised. 'That long?'

'There are a lot of issues to discuss and I want to be thorough in the defense of my client,' I said. 'I believe it would be a serious miscarriage of justice if her conviction was upheld and I intend to make every possible argument to keep that from happening.' Klemperer was well known for wanting to get out on the links as soon as he could after court, even in this stifling weather. The longer I said it would take, the better.

He sat back in his cushy chair. It squeaked. The judge seemed to consider his options in some detail and then leaned forward again. 'Ms Moss, in the interest of efficiency in this court, I believe we are best served by continuing this case until such time as you can make yourself available here without reservation. And I would advise you to make it more clear when you have a conflict that another member of your firm is unable to handle the case.'

If he wanted it to be my fault, I was OK with that, as long as I got what I wanted. And it looked as if I was going to get exactly what I wanted. 'I'll be sure to do that. My apologies, Your Honor.' I sat down.

Wow. This was going to be even easier than I'd imagined.

The judge banged his gavel and Maddie looked at me, seeming confused. 'What just happened?' she asked.

'We were just granted a continuance. That means the trial won't continue until after I'm done with Cynthia Sutton's case.

'Why is that good?' Maddie asked me as we started up the aisle. Longabaugh glared at me, probably out of habit.

'It gives me time to get us a new judge,' I told her.

TWENTY-FIVE

'You're not in love with me, Patrick.' It was the third time I'd said it today and would probably not be the last. The man had been going on about this for four months. Four. Months.

Now, don't get me wrong: Patrick McNabb was a very attractive man and I knew I loved him as a friend. He could be kindhearted and generous very much to a fault. He had real feelings and didn't mind sharing them. He was also very good at his job and from everything I'd ever been told a joy to work with.

But he wasn't in love with me and he really needed to understand that.

We were sitting at lunch with Angie, now a fixture at Patrick's side, and Cynthia, plus Cynthia's 'spiritual advisor', a middle-aged woman named Chrys (short for Chrysanthemum), who wore a gray ponytail and was helping Cynthia get through this ordeal emotionally and, for reasons I have never understood, Emily the former fiancée, recently returned from an extended business trip during which she had studied for and passed her exam to be a real-estate broker rather than simply an agent. It had taken her months. I'm told it takes most people a few weeks, and they don't have to go away on a retreat to manage it. I'm just saying. She mostly scowled, not always at me.

I was trying to help Cynthia get through it legally, and prefer-ably to avoid being convicted of killing her mother-in-law Wendy Bryan. But the previous four months had not led us to the clearest legal path in the history of jurisprudence. The man who'd shot at Patrick and me outside the coffee shop had been arrested, identified as one Albert Pentergast (aka Al Romano, Abe Poston and Andy DeFelise) and then summarily released under justifica-tions that Trench would describe only as 'unusual'. So he'd been no help, which I had never expected him to be. Albert's *mishegas* seemed more bound to Maddie Forsythe's appeal than Cynthia's trial. But the attacks had stopped, and at least nobody had tried to kill me in four months. So that was certainly refreshing.

Circumstantial evidence – and that's all it was – had piled up that seemed to implicate Cynthia in the crime. We'd found very little to prove she *hadn't* killed Wendy with a TeeVee. Which never didn't sound weird.

The most pressing problem was that the trial was scheduled for the next day. I should have been at my office preparing an opening statement and hoping against hope that Nate Garrigan would call with game-changing information. (Granted, Nate could call me here too, but I really felt like I should have been in my office.)

But Patrick, being Patrick, had insisted we gather to commemorate the eve of our great victory (as he saw it). Patrick believes in the power of congeniality because it has gotten him quite far in life, but my faith in the concept was at best a little shaky.

'I understand if you're not in love with me,' Patrick responded, 'but I object – that's a legal term, you know – to your telling me how *I* feel.'

Under normal circumstances, having this conversation among other people would have been excruciating for me. But after the first six weeks or so of Patrick's current delusion it had become almost routine. He'd bring this up with Angie present, with Cynthia present, with Emily present (she didn't look pleased), with colleagues of mine (even Jon, who had returned to work only two weeks ago and was walking a little stiffly with a cane but was otherwise OK) present, once even when I was on a phone call with my mother, who'd told me to marry the man immediately. I'd grown a scab over my mortification and didn't even feel it anymore.

'I'm saying this fits the pattern you have established for yourself and you need to recognize it,' I told him for the four hundred and fifth time. 'You attribute any feeling you have toward a woman as romantic love and you stay fixated on it until it's reciprocated, at which time you get bored and decide to move on. You're too good a friend for me to let you do that, Patrick.'

Cynthia, having known Patrick longer than anyone at the table, pointed a breadstick at him. 'She's got you down,' she said, nodding toward me. 'That's exactly what you do, Pat.'

'So what do you think I should do about it?' Patrick asked his sister.

'Marry her.' Then she grinned at me and took a big bite of the breadstick. Cynthia, a woman in a business that had an unhealthy fixation on the physical looks of its women especially, didn't mind eating. It was one of the reasons I'd come to like her.

'You're not helping,' I told her. 'But the reason we're here, if I recall, is to work on the opening of the trial tomorrow.'

Angie, her eyes stuck on the iPad Patrick had given her and which she carried absolutely everywhere she went, nodded. 'Court is at ten in the morning,' she said, as if I wasn't aware of that. 'Judge Phyllis M. Hawthorne presiding.'

'Does it help that we have a female judge?' Cynthia asked.

'I think it's a wash,' I told her. I'd ordered the gnocchi and was now regretting it. That was a heavy lunch. I should have ordered a salad. I should have bought a salad from the place down the street from my office. I should be in my office now. 'I mean, it's good because you're a female defendant and the judge will hopefully not be biased against women, but on the other hand the victim was a woman too and, from what I know about Judge Hawthorne, she's going to be pretty fair-minded anyway.'

There was what I perceived as a slightly awkward silence at the table, which lasted only a moment. 'Actually, I was asking Chrys,' Cynthia said. 'She has certain abilities to understand vibrations coming from the universe.'

I went to college for four years and majored in political science because there was no such thing as 'pre-law'. Then I went to law school for another three years. I clerked for a state Supreme Court justice. I spent seven years as an assistant county prosecutor in New Jersey sending criminals to prison. Now I was employed by a prestigious law firm in a major city, drawing a nice but not extravagant salary and slowly building what I thought was a decent reputation in the Los Angeles legal community. And I was being shouted down by vibrations coming from the universe.

Sometimes it barely feels worthwhile getting out of bed in the morning.

'Of course,' I said. I tried not to clench my teeth, but they appeared to have a mind of their own. It was all I could do to keep my head from vibrating.

'I believe in the judge,' Chrys said. 'The judge has a kind and just heart and he will rule fairly.'

'The judge is a woman,' I pointed out again. Nobody seemed to notice except Angie, who gave me a light kick under the table. I was not supposed to sully the reputation of the spiritual advisor. I'd have to sit Angie down tonight and remind her where she was from.

'Since we all know that our dear Cynthia here did not commit the crime of which she was accused, we can rest assured that she will not be convicted, but there are dangers in the process that must be avoided,' Chrys went on.

'Dangers?' It was Patrick, and not the accused, who seemed most disturbed by the suggestion. 'What kind of dangers?'

Chrys, who was so slight a woman that she seemed more rumor than human, still commanded attention easily and with authority. 'Obstacles,' she intoned with serious gravitas. 'Hidden traps. A man with an agenda. A woman whose past threatens your future. And most insidious of all, a friend who is really an enemy.'

That was either the plot of the next *Star Wars* movie or literally every legal drama ever written. It was so general that you could honestly apply it to any situation and find ways that it fit. It was like an online daily horoscope. *Gemini: Things will go well until they take a turn.* No kidding.

So it was really disturbing to see my client, her brother, who was a good friend of mine, his onetime fiancée (her I didn't care about so much) and my closest friend in the world take what Chrys had said seriously. No. Gravely.

'That's frightening,' Cynthia said. 'A friend of mine will turn on me during the trial? Who could it be?' If we were at a long table and all pointed in the same direction for no reason, it could have been Leonardo's *The Last Supper*.

'It must be referring to your husband,' Patrick asserted. 'There's no doubt that he'll be a snake in the grass; he always has been.'

I had in fact scheduled a meeting with Michael Bryan for this very afternoon when I discovered his name was not on the prosecution's witness list. That was a serious omission, one that was either troubling or encouraging. Could Michael present evidence that would seriously boost my case? I should probably leave this lunch right now and go prep for that meeting, I thought.

I could handle anything that was going to come up in the courtroom if I had the confidence of my client and knew that she was going to trust me to do whatever it would take to ensure her freedom. If you have a client who doesn't believe in you . . . well, that's why I keep a file of business cards and contacts in my phone of other lawyers who might better serve the client. Because going into battle with a client who thinks you don't know what you're doing pretty much always ends in the verdict going the way you didn't want.

'I can't say I understand the vibrations,' I said. 'But what we'll be dealing with in that courtroom is the reality of the criminal justice system and, believe me, that's something I do understand. I won't let people turn on us on the witness stand. I'm not going to be taken by surprise. But right now I need to get back to my office so I can prepare for the beginning of the trial. Cynthia, I'd advise you to do the same, and call me if you have any questions or concerns you want to talk about. You know I'll always take your call.'

I stood and picked up my purse to indicate that the high-powered attorney Cynthia had hired (are there low-powered attorneys and, if so, can't they just plug themselves into a wall charger?) was moving into battle mode and couldn't be stopped. All the while, though, I was asking myself why I was auditioning for a client I hadn't wanted and had taken all the way to the eve of the trial.

'I don't know . . .' my client said.

If the trial were as much as a week away, I might have resigned the case on the spot. You want to talk vibrations? I had to see if anyone else in the room was reacting to the earthquake I felt under my feet. They were not, which indicated it was imaginary. I stood rooted to the spot, wanting to scream that they should trust the lawyer with the law and the spiritual advisor with . . . spiritual advice. Or something. But as usual, Patrick rose up to my rescue. Which was almost always a bad idea.

Literally, he rose. To his feet. 'Sandy is right,' he said to his sister. 'The law is what is coming for you and Sandy knows the law. I've been there and I know. I wouldn't have gotten through it without Sandy. So do whatever it is she tells you to do and be assured she'll do everything possible for you. Because Sandy is the best there is.'

He might have expected applause. He didn't get any.

I decided it was best to show that I was a busy woman working hard to keep Cynthia out of jail, so while the others were sitting and staring at Patrick and me, I turned and headed toward the door. Patrick appeared at my side after a moment.

Behind me I heard Emily say, 'Patrick . . .' with impatience audible in her voice.

'Well, it doesn't appear to have changed anyone's mind, but thanks for the defense,' I said quietly to him as we walked.

'What else would I do?' he asked. 'I'm in love with you.'

'No, you're not.'

TWENTY-SIX

Michael Bryan was a dark-haired man who looked to be auditioning for the role of mannequin, should such a need arise. He had a face that could be described as attractive but had no outstanding characteristics. A police sketch artist could draw a picture of him and have every man in the city arrested on its merits.

He sat at the Seaton, Taylor conference table with his hands folded in front of him, a very good boy who was paying attention to his lessons and was ready if the teacher were to call on him. It was a wonder he wasn't wearing a bow tie.

'I didn't text Cynthia the night my mother died,' he said. Thankfully Michael did not try to choke back tears on the word *died* as so many might. I'm sure he must have used inflection occasionally, but only when prescribed by his doctor. 'I have no idea why she said that I did.'

Judy, standing in the corner, was looking around constantly, probably trying to determine why no one had decided to put a window into the conference room for her to look through and be vigilant. Finally her gaze landed on the door, the only point of entry for a possible attacker, and stayed there.

'What did you do that night?' I asked. My dreams of Michael being the key defense witness were rapidly fading. I figured now the best thing to do was to see where he might actually hurt Cynthia's case and avoid those areas, or skip calling him as a witness at all.

'Are you suggesting I'm a suspect in the murder of my mother?' Michael asked. He might just as well have been asking me which bus would take him to the Staples Center, and he'd have just as lousy a chance of getting an answer from me.

'I'm the defense attorney, Michael,' I told him. 'I don't decide who's a suspect. The police do and they've arrested your wife in that matter. So please tell me what you did that night.'

'I had a business meeting. On Zoom.'

Well, that was not impossible to verify but not easy either. 'With whom?' I asked.

'The police have already been over this, and so has your investigator when he and Patrick McNabb came to see me.' The words were somewhat confrontational. The tone was absolutely bland.

'I'm aware of that. I'm asking so I can have some context.' That sounded reasonable and meant nothing, but I was willing to bet Michael wouldn't call me on it.

He didn't. In fact, he didn't even sigh, which most aggrieved financial analysts would do under the circumstances, particularly the successful ones. 'My partner Daniel Reeves, a client of ours whom I will not name to protect their privacy, and a representative of Highsmith Financial.'

'That's another financial services company like your own?' I said.

The slightest tic around the right corner of his mouth. 'Yes.'

'Why were you collaborating with a competitor?'

This time there was the slightest hint of condescension in his eyes. 'It's not uncommon on a larger transaction.'

'So this was a large transaction.' He'd already said that, but now I wanted to irritate Michael a bit and see what happened. Judy, laser-focused on the door, did not seem to care.

'Most of the ones we are involved in are large.'

Now for the stuff I *really* wanted to ask Michael. 'What can you tell me about Rafael?'

His brow furrowed. Given his demeanor up to now, I feared for his health. 'My mother's gallery? I had no business interest in that.'

'None?' I feigned surprise. 'Not even on an advisory level?'

'My mother preferred it that way,' Michael said.

'How did you feel about that?' I asked.

'Are you my therapist now?' Michael's veneer of impassiveness was beginning to dissolve. He had emotions after all. Chiefly anger.

'It just seems to me that a man with your level of expertise in finance might feel somewhat insulted, even upset, when his own mother turned to someone else for all her business needs.' Before he could ask me again if I considered him a suspect I added, 'I'm told that the gallery was in a good deal of financial trouble. Do you think you could have helped if your mother had asked?'

'Where have you heard that Rafael was having difficulties?' Michael was tamping down the anger again. I was starting to agree with Patrick: What did Cynthia ever see in this guy?

'I'm not at liberty to say. To protect my source's privacy. *Was* the gallery going under?'

Michael looked directly into my eyes. 'How would I know?' he asked.

'If you don't know, who would?'

'That,' Michael Bryan said, 'is an excellent question.'

TWENTY-SEVEN

The opening of Cynthia Sutton's trial was scheduled for ten a.m., so naturally we were waiting in the courtroom, not nearly as packed as it used to be but with plenty of cameras to record the famous actress's trial, at 10.38.

I had my usual pretrial butterflies, exacerbated by the fact that this was only my second case as a defense attorney at a murder trial. And both of those cases involved the same family. I wasn't even a mob lawyer. My life had taken some weird turns since I'd navigated I-80 out of New Jersey.

The fact that my most recent criminal case had ended in a conviction for a woman who had done nothing wrong . . . oh, why go on? It wasn't helping me calm down.

The defense table was peopled by me and Jon Irvin, who had insisted on being my second chair. Jon had jammed his two weeks back on the job with the case and now actually knew more about it than I did, truth be told. Jon is a great researcher and tactician but (sorry if you're reading this, Jon) not the best on his feet in a courtroom situation. He was the perfect second chair and I was happy to have him beside me.

To my right was my client. Cynthia and I had spent a good deal of time together preparing this case and I thought she was ready for what was to come, but she was clearly shaking despite the heat (the air conditioning in the courtroom was turned on, but it was not exactly state-of-the-art) and paler than I was used to seeing her. She had not attended Patrick's trial the year before, which explained why I hadn't ever heard about her before this happened. Cynthia said she had been in Wales filming a movie when Patrick and I were in court, and that she had offered to come but her brother had insisted she stay and finish the job.

He was seated directly behind me, projecting confidence as he always did, but I saw the tension around his eyes and the corners of his mouth. I think Patrick was more nervous at Cynthia's trial than he had been at his own. To his right was Angie, of course, representing the brand and being in front of the cameras so Patrick, who normally would relish such a thing, didn't have to be. Angie understood this part of the business perfectly.

Behind them was, again without explanation, Emily Webster, who never said much but could have been captain of the Olympic glowering team. The woman could glower with the best of them.

Across the aisle from me was Marcus Valencia, the deputy district attorney who had caught the case and was preparing to make a name for himself in the annals of Southern California law. I stifled a smile. Prosecutors in Los Angeles didn't have a fabulous track record in handling celebrity murder cases. Not terrible, but certainly somewhat tarnished.

Valencia was a tall, slim man who probably spent some time in the gym but not enough to bulk up. He wanted to look like . . . well, he wanted to look like Patrick when he was on *Legality*. There were, I would admit, worse things to look like. Valencia was fiddling with the file on his table, trying to exude calm but letting his hands run the perimeter of the file over and over again. I couldn't tell whether it was nervousness or simple anticipation, but I got the feeling the prosecutor was restraining an impulse to leap up and dance just to get the energy out of his muscles.

Right behind him was Michael Bryan. He and Cynthia had actually had a short conversation before we'd all sat down and hadn't been vicious with each other. For a couple divorcing and at the wife's trial for stabbing the husband's mother to death, that was something of a minor miracle.

'What's going to happen first?' Cynthia whispered to me, despite there being no need to whisper while court wasn't in session.

I'd run through the sequence of the trial with her a number of times, but she was nervous and I knew that. 'First will be jury selection and that'll probably take the whole day, if not part of tomorrow. You don't have to worry about anything that's going to happen today.'

Cynthia smiled, but it wasn't terribly convincing, a problem for an actress. 'I'm glad to hear that,' she said. 'I wish we had found the person who really killed Wendy.'

What was it with this family and thinking lawyers went around solving crimes? 'Nate has been doing some good work,' I assured her. 'We don't have to prove who committed the murder, just that you didn't, and within a reasonable doubt. We have a strong case.' I might not have been as convincing on that last part because I was not so sure myself of the evidence we'd compiled. Nate *had* done a good job and had some physical evidence to help going ahead. But we didn't have the slam dunk I'd wanted.

The bailiff rescued me by announcing the judge and we all stood. Judge Hawthorne was a tall and imposing woman. There's a reason they make them wear robes (it doesn't take much convincing; judges love the pomp). You couldn't walk into that courtroom and wonder who was in charge.

I'd done my homework on Hawthorne, before whom I'd never appeared until now. This was not a surprise, since I was primarily a family law practitioner and Hawthorne was assigned to the criminal court. From what I'd been able to find out about her, she would not accept a lot in terms of informality, and she would rule pretty much right down the center lane. If there was precedent, Hawthorne would rule with it. She loved a nice precedent. I had compiled (OK, Jon and some paralegals had compiled) as many as I could anticipate needing and four more than that.

Valencia was easier to read as an example of bro culture than as a lawyer. I'd looked into some of the cases he'd prosecuted and found no discernible pattern, no style that was particularly his. He had a high conviction rate, which wasn't fabulous news for me, but he wasn't infallible. Which was lucky, because neither was I.

Nate Garrigan was not in the courtroom. He was investigating two other cases for my firm but had told me he was continuing to look into Michael Bryan's financial records and the dealings of Wendy Bryan and trying to locate Leopold Kolensky, Wendy's financial wizard, who was such a good magician he'd made himself disappear.

We took our seats again after Judge Hawthorne settled in behind the bench. She looked completely unaffected by the weight of the trial, the level of celebrity and media coverage or the relatively stifling heat in the courtroom. That was probably because I was monopolizing all the worry around those things.

'Any motions?' Hawthorne asked. It's not unusual at all for a judge to suggest that just to get all the piddly stuff out of the way before the real trial begins.

'Move to dismiss,' I said, standing. Why not? It didn't have a prayer of working but you give it a shot. 'The evidence against the defendant is circumstantial at best.'

'Denied,' Hawthorne said. Which part of, 'it didn't have a prayer of working' was unclear?

'Move to dismiss a defense witness,' Valencia said. He was standing too, but the way he did it looked more like strutting while standing still.

Dismiss one of my witnesses? 'Which witness?' Hawthorne asked him.

'Gail Adams,' Valencia said, reading off a document in front of him. 'The representative of the TV academy.'

That made no sense at all. Why would Valencia even care, unless he knew why I was calling Gail to begin with?

'On what grounds?' the judge asked.

'Relevance. The TV and Video Academy distributes TeeVee awards. The victim was murdered with a TeeVee award. I don't see how the connection goes beyond that.'

There was something he didn't want to come out and now I was more determined than ever that Gail Adams would testify for the defense. 'I object,' I told Hawthorne. 'There is a great deal of relevance, as the award found in my client's hands is considered the murder weapon and the design and construction of that award are certainly relevant topics.'

'Your motion is denied,' Hawthorne told Valencia. 'Hearing no others, we can move on to jury selection.'

We all sat down but there was an odd look on Valencia's face. It wasn't defeat, which I was hoping for. It was something like satisfaction and that wasn't good.

'I thought nothing was going to happen,' Cynthia whispered to me.

'Nothing did,' I whispered back.

But I wasn't certain. Of course, I never am.

TWENTY-EIGHT

Jury selection is a very odd process. People think it consists of an attorney reading juror profiles, trying to find unique markers that indicate the person is predisposed to vote one way or another on a verdict for a case they haven't heard a word about yet and then being clever about getting the favorable ones on the jury and removing the people who will vote against them.

About ten percent of that is true. We do look over profiles of jurors and we highlight dangerous ones to question should they be called. The favorable ones are considerably more iffy. Just because someone has a redheaded daughter, for example, doesn't mean she won't vote to convict a fellow ginger accused of selling cocaine. It's risky to ask a potential juror a question to which you don't know the answer, but you do have to get a sense of the person that's not in the documents you get from the court or from consultants.

The fourth juror we were considering was Melvin Benson, a man in his sixties who had retired from a job as a forklift operator only the year before. Mr Benson had never heard of Cynthia Sutton, he said, which was either a lie or good for my side. I needed to find out which was the case.

'Mr Benson, have you ever seen a film called *Traitor-in-Chief*?' I asked. It was one of Cynthia's more high-profile roles, in which she played a secretary of state deciding whether to rat on a president who had collaborated with foreign spies. I'd never seen it, but I've been told by the star's brother that she was very good.

'I can't remember,' Benson answered. 'What's it about?'

I gave him roughly the same plot summary I just gave you and Benson sat there looking bewildered. 'I don't think I saw that one,' he said.

(Later, Angie told me that Cynthia looked annoyed when he said that. I held a brief conversation with my client after that about not appearing to get pissed off at a juror because he hadn't seen one of her movies.)

I went through a list of Cynthia's credits for two reasons: first, I wanted to see how Benson would react to them (he was at best impassive and did not admit to having seen any of them). Second, I wanted to let the three empaneled jurors be impressed with the actress.

'Guess I didn't see any of them,' Benson said when I'd finished.

I gave him a friendly smile and nodded in his direction, then I looked at the judge. 'I'd like to exercise one of my peremptory challenges, Your Honor.'

The courtroom didn't explode into chaos as I walked back to my table, but Valencia, who was already standing up to do his questioning of Benson, looked slightly stunned. He sat back down.

Hawthorne, of course, didn't ask any questions but nodded

and made a note on the tablet computer in front of her. When I sat back down, Cynthia was smiling slightly, probably because she thought I'd dismissed Benson (who was walking away from the witness box shaking his head with incredulity) because he'd never had the good taste to watch any of her performances.

Angie, however, leaned over the rail with her own agenda. 'Why?' she hissed at me.

I couldn't speak without being heard by others so I wrote, 'He was lying', on a piece of scrap paper and passed it discreetly to her. She read it and nodded: Yes, she'd thought so too.

Patrick, ever the overseer, clearly asked Angie to see the note and looked mildly surprised by what it said. Angie whispered to him and he sat back, probably not completely satisfied with the answer but certainly not shaken in his trust for me because I was (in his mind) the best lawyer who ever walked the earth except perhaps Perry Mason. Who never actually walked the earth.

Michael Bryan, I noticed, had been impassive through the whole process. There was a strange air about him that indicated he might still be trying to decide which side he was rooting for in this trial.

I leaned over to Cynthia. 'He's seen you in movies and thinks you need to be taken down a peg or two. Can't have that on the jury.'

She blinked twice. 'How do you know?' she asked in a whisper.

'I slipped two Helen Mirren movies and a superhero film into the list and he never even blinked,' I explained. 'He was ready to say he'd never seen you in anything, no matter what, because he wanted to get the best of you.'

'I was wondering about that,' she said. 'I never played Queen Elizabeth.'

Jury selection went on another four hours with Valencia challenging three potential jurors who were watching Cynthia's HBO miniseries and smiled. I dismissed two on more conventional grounds, given that one of them said she thought movie stars were treated too preferentially by society (which they are), and another was upset with his ex-wife over the terms of his divorce. The judge immediately dismissed one who said she'd seen coverage of the murder, including pictures of the body (which were not supposed to be released and were probably fake) on the internet.

When we had twelve jurors and two alternates everyone could agree upon, Hawthorne declared the day over, banged her gavel and sent us all home. Well, she sent Cynthia home. Patrick went back to whatever shooting schedule had been arranged around his attendance at the trial ('luckily it's all night scenes'), Angie in tow.

Emily stopped me just before she went charging after Patrick. 'Patrick says he's in love with you now,' she said.

'He's not,' I assured her. 'He just thinks he is.'

'Are you the reason he broke our engagement?'

'Go show a house,' I told her. She glowered some more and hurried after Patrick and Angie.

I packed up my stuff so Jon and I could take my car – he wasn't driving yet – back to our office.

On the way there I got a call from Nate. Because during Patrick's trial my car had been . . . incapacitated, and Patrick had made sure Bluetooth was installed in my Hyundai when he was having it essentially rebuilt from scratch, I could talk to the investigator without taking my hands off the wheel. Technology is a wonderful thing, when it works.

'What's going on?' I asked him.

'I have some security video you're going to want to see,' he said. Nate greets people with the facts. He never buries the lead. He should have been a newspaper.

'Security video from where?' I asked.

'The house across the street from Wendy Bryan's,' Nate answered. I could hear the smirk in his voice. He wanted to show me how smart he was, and if it helped my case, I was happy to let him.

'From the night of the murder?' Of course from the night of the murder. What would security footage from a random Tuesday do for Cynthia's case? 'What does footage from across the street show us?'

Nate was ready to drop the bomb and he did it well. 'It shows a municipal car parked right in front, across the street from Wendy's,' he said.

So, somebody from the Department of Public Works lived near Wendy. An unlikely zip code for a civil employee, to be sure, but maybe the person had married well. 'So what?' I said, delivering the straight line as was clearly intended.

'So sitting in the driver's seat of that car on the night Cynthia Bryan was killed, but before the nine-one-one call was made, was Detective Lieutenant K.C. Trench.'

TWENTY-NINE

'I f you wish to interview me regarding the case, I am at your disposal,' Trench said. 'But I am under no obligation to tell you any facts about what I saw outside of the context of your defense.'

We were seated, except Jon who insisted on standing, in Trench's immaculate if impersonal office, all business. I had no idea if Trench was married, if he had children, if he liked to golf, surf, play chess or poker. I couldn't have told you what baseball team he rooted for, or even if he'd ever seen a baseball game. I knew absolutely nothing about Lieutenant Trench. Part of the reason that was true was that his office, where I'd mostly seen him in our short history, was absolutely devoid of any personal mementos, photographs or souvenirs. For all I knew this was a prop office Trench used for visitors. Maybe he had a real one somewhere that showed him in the company of strippers, drug dealers, dominatrixes and/or his loving wife of twenty-three years. Anything was possible. But right now I was livid with him and couldn't properly articulate why.

'You've been walking around with knowledge of my case for months and you've seen me a number of times since this happened,' I said through lightly clenched teeth. 'You didn't mention once that you were present at the scene of the crime while it was happening.'

'It is not within my responsibilities to report everything I see to the defense attorney,' he said with no inflection whatsoever. 'You should have contacted me.'

I closed my eyes and imagined myself on a beach. Oddly, despite living in a city that was famous for its beaches, I was thinking of sitting on a beach chair in Belmar, New Jersey. I took two breaths. It was almost possible to smell the salt air.

Then I started to picture Patrick and I didn't need to imagine him with me on a beach in Belmar, so I opened my eyes again.

'Your name appears on none of my records or the witness list,' I told him. 'Now, why do you suppose that happened?'

'I would imagine it is because I was not questioned by Deputy District Attorney Valencia until this morning, and that would mean he hasn't had time yet to revise his witness list and get the judge's approval,' Trench said. He might just as well have been saying it was going to be cloudy tomorrow with a thirty percent chance of rain.

I sighed. 'Don't make me pull teeth, Lieutenant. We've known each other a while now. What did you see and why didn't you mention it until today?'

'Ms Moss,' Trench said with a pained look on his face, 'I can't say I am an eyewitness to the crime and I will testify to that. I did see Ms Sutton enter the home. She was, for the record, not carrying a TeeVee award with her upon her entrance. I did not hear or see anything that would have alerted me to a brutal murder being committed. Do you think I would have stayed in my car if I'd been aware of that?'

That question had occurred to me. 'No. I don't think you would have. But I don't understand why you didn't mention this until today. And you've been very careful not to answer that question.'

Trench didn't move a facial muscle. 'When I saw the report of the murder, I realized I'd been there just before it happened. I hadn't seen the crime occur, and the person I saw enter the house had already been arrested and charged. Frankly, I didn't see how I could testify in court to anything other than what had already been established. And it is borne out by the security video taken from the street, so you tell me.'

Jon and I exchanged a glance because we were both thinking the same thing.

'Lieutenant,' I said, 'why were you there?'

'At Wendy Bryan's house the night she was murdered?' That was stalling if ever I heard it.

Jersey girls don't take kindly to people being coy. 'No, why were you at the Staples Center the night LeBron hit a triple triple.' Sarcasm doesn't make up for the fact that I don't understand anything about basketball. 'Yes. Why were you at Wendy Bryan's house that night? What were you investigating? You're a homicide detective from Los Angeles and the homicide, which took place in Santa Monica, didn't happen, by your account, until after you left. What were you doing in that part of town?'

'Ms Moss, you are not a member of the Los Angeles Police Department and you certainly do not outrank me. So I will keep my motivations to myself for the time being.'

'I'll ask you about it on the stand,' I warned him.

'And I will give you the same answer. My presence there that night is relevant to your case only to highlight the coincidence that I have outlined, and to prove that Cynthia Sutton was there at the approximate time of the killing, which I do not believe you're going to dispute.' Trench sat straight up in his chair. He rarely leaned back on it and did not appear to have the capability to relax. It was like his entire mind and body had been starched.

'You're sure it was Cynthia?' I said.

'Yes, and I ran the license plate on her car. It was her.' Trench likes to run license plates. For him it's a form of recreation. Everybody has their thing.

'Well, this has been a completely frustrating conversation,' I said as I stood up and grabbed my bag.

'A pleasure as always,' Trench said. I bought a bottle of water from a vending machine in the lobby to get over the dryness in his voice.

Jon and I were back in my car and on the way to our office in five minutes, which in LA is something just short of a miracle. 'There's an awful lot going on in this case that we don't know about and that bothers me,' Jon said while I sweated out a left turn.

'I know.' Los Angeles is a really nice city. Someday it ought to put in a transportation system so people can get around to see it. 'We're done for the day. I'm going to drop you off at the office and go see Nate Garrigan. There must be things we haven't looked into, not the least of which is what Trench was doing at Wendy's house the night she died.'

'Don't drop me off,' Jon said. 'Let's go see Nate.'

I knew he'd say that and I was sure he wouldn't listen to any arguments about how he must be tired, so I had already plugged Nate's address into my GPS. 'Call him,' I said.

Nate Garrigan lived in Sherman Oaks, which took about forty minutes from Trench's office. I'd been to Nate's home office before, but it had been a while so I didn't remember which house was his by sight. Luckily Google Maps knew for certain, so Jon and I approached the mother/daughter home (the daughter part was the office Nate had set up) with a good deal of confidence.

Nate had told Jon on the phone that he was out but would probably beat us back to his place. It wasn't a surprise, then, when he opened the separate door on his office suite and ushered us in out of the heat, which we'd been sweltering in for close to a minute.

'I was going to call you,' he told me. 'I've got a few details to fill in. But there's nothing yet that's going to be a slam dunk in the courtroom tomorrow.'

'We just saw Trench,' I informed him, and his face changed to show interest.

'What was he doing there that night?' he asked.

'That's the question we were hoping you could answer,' I told him. 'Trench is Trench. He's never going to tell us everything he knows because he sees us as the adversary. But he also knows something is up – that's got to be why he was sitting in his car that night – and he wants us to be aware he knows. He's probably got four investigations going on now that we don't know about.'

'Actually, I think I have a decent idea that's just beginning to fit,' Nate said. 'Because I located our old pal Leopold.'

'Leopold Kolensky? Wendy's financial manager?' Jon asked. I was glad Jon was there. I could never remember the name *Kolensky*.

'That's the guy,' Nate told us. 'It took some doing but he is now located in Glendale.'

'Glendale?' I asked. 'Can we go see him?'

'Yeah, but don't expect much information. Leopold's in Forest Lawn. He's dead.'

Well, that was certainly a downer, especially for Leopold. 'Dead?' I said. I was a little stunned. Don't judge.

'Yup. Cardiac arrest. A week *before* Wendy Bryan was killed.' There was less of a grin on Nate's face now because we were heading for questions he couldn't answer.

'Are we sure it was cardiac arrest?' Jon asked. It was an appropriate question. This was a big coincidence, and when I'm trying a case, I hate even small coincidences.

'That's what it says on the death certificate,' Nate said, shrugging. 'He died in his sleep one night. Lived alone since his wife died four years ago.'

I looked at his face. 'There's something you're not telling me,' I said.

Nate nodded. 'The night he died, our pal Leopold had dinner with a client.'

'Don't tell me,' Jon said, 'Wendy Bryan.'

Again Nate nodded. 'At her house.'

THIRTY

Patrick McNabb was never far away while Cynthia's trial was ongoing. On those rare days when it seemed he actually needed to be on set filming *Torn*, he made sure his presence was felt by having Angie sit directly behind me at the defense table. I didn't mind having my best friend watch and offer tips, but it was a little intimidating coming from Patrick's executive assistant.

Emily, it should be noted, showed up only on days Patrick was in attendance, and not all of them.

On this day, though, Patrick was present and going stag, immediately to Angie's right, and watching with an intensity he probably had in reserve from scenes where he had to appear, you know, intense. He didn't look happy and I didn't blame him, but I had no time to pay attention to that. He could remind himself that he believed he was in love with me later.

The reason Patrick wasn't happy was the same reason I was fairly perplexed at the same time. One of the Los Angeles County medical examiners, Dr Leona Ramsey, was answering Valencia's questions and digging me a deeper hole with each answer. I'd have to lift Cynthia out of that hole, and wasn't sure my upper-body strength would be sufficient for the task.

(Don't think for a second that we'd forgotten about Leopold Kolensky. Nate had gotten a copy of the police report from the night of Leopold's death. It was as routine as could be. The 911 call came from Leopold's assistant who had used her key to get into the house when Leopold had not shown up at his office. The ME had determined it was a heart attack and the cops had filed it away and released the body to Leopold's next of kin, who was a nephew. Leopold had no children. Nate was looking into the disposition of Leopold's will, which is something you always do when you're being suspicious. I'll keep you informed.)

'Dr Ramsey,' Valencia was saying. He loved nothing better than to emphasize that the witness was a doctor. I'm not sure what effect that had on the jury, since I doubted any of them would have expected the medical examiner to be an air-compressor mechanic. 'Would it have taken a person of extraordinary strength to penetrate Wendy Bryan's rib cage with the sharp points of a TeeVee award?'

'Objection,' I said without standing up. 'The prosecution is asking the witness to draw a conclusion.'

'I am asking a medical expert to report on the type of wound sustained by the victim.' Valencia countered.

'Objection is overruled.' Judge Hawthorne wasn't going to give me any special consideration. It was what I'd expected, as was her ruling, but it was worth getting the objection on the record just to break up the prosecutor's momentum. 'Mr Valencia?'

'Once again, Dr Ramsey. Did the wounds sustained by Wendy Bryan, in your *medical* opinion, require an unusual amount of strength to inflict?'

'Well, the statuette itself was altered,' Ramsey answered. She pointed to a video screen above her head that showed a photograph of the TeeVee with its globe pushed down and out of the way to better emphasize the sharp wings. 'I'd say it took a pretty strong pair of hands to bend the metal that dramatically. A person who could do that could certainly have plunged the blades of the statue into Wendy Bryan's chest, most certainly.'

Valencia, no doubt anticipating the question I would have asked had he not, said, 'Is Cynthia Sutton capable of that kind of force?'

'Theoretically, anyone with functioning muscles in the hands and upper body could have done so if they were motivated,' Ramsey said, not actually answering the question.

'So Cynthia Sutton, in your estimation, *could* have killed her mother-in-law Wendy,' Valencia said. He wanted to make sure the jury heard Ramsey speak directly to the hypothetical he was asking.

'Yes,' Ramsey answered. She had been on the stand before and knew to answer only that which was asked. Good.

'No further questions,' Valencia said, looking especially pleased with himself. Frankly, if this was as devastating a blow as he expected to deliver to Cynthia Sutton's case, it would be a ridiculously easy trial to win. But I knew he had more firepower yet to come. I'd seen his witness list and his discovery materials. This was just the first inning. Valencia walked back to the prosecution table and sat down.

'Ms Moss?' Judge Hawthorne made it sound like a question. It was a summons.

I gave my client a reassuring smile – not too big, so as not to appear arrogant to the jury – and approached the witness stand. 'Dr Ramsey, what tests have you performed on Cynthia Sutton?'

That clearly was not the first question the medical examiner was anticipating. 'On Cynthia Sutton?' she asked. 'Do you mean Wendy Bryan?'

'No. I mean the defendant, Cynthia Sutton.' For dramatic effect I moved to one side so Ramsey could ostensibly get a more direct view of Cynthia.

'I don't understand. I did not perform any tests on the defendant,' Ramsey said.

'Why not?'

'Because Cynthia Sutton is alive,' Ramsey said. As expected, it drew a light chuckle from the spectators.

'And as a medical examiner, you don't perform physical examinations or tests on living people, just the ones who show up in the morgue. Is that correct?' I asked.

'Yes.' Back to a comfortable answer for the doctor.

'Given that, the fact that you never examined Cynthia Sutton at all, how can you be certain she is strong enough to have killed Wendy Bryan with an award statuette?'

'I did not say I was certain. I said it was my opinion.' Doctors can, when they want to (and often when they don't) take on an air of superiority in their voices. I'm a lawyer, so I know pompous when I hear it.

'And on what did you base that opinion?' I asked.

Valencia stood up, in my opinion because he wanted to give his expert witness a moment to breathe easy. 'Objection. The question has been asked and answered.'

'No it hasn't,' I told Hawthorne. 'The prosecutor asked whether or not the defendant could have killed her mother-in-law. The witness said it was her opinion that was possible. I'm asking on what data that opinion is based. It's a different question.'

'I'll allow it,' Hawthorne said. Valencia sat.

Ramsey was now looking at me with something other than the eyes of a caring physician. Of course she was a pathologist and hadn't had a live patient in years, so maybe it comes with the territory. Or maybe she thought I was trying to impugn her credibility in the case. Because I was.

'Can I hear the question again?' she said.

The court reporter read, 'And on what did you base that opinion?'

Ramsey, who clearly remembered the question but simply wanted to take another second, answered, 'On twenty-seven years of medical experience and study.'

'Can you be more specific?' If she wanted to play hardball, I could play hardball. Cynthia looked petrified. Patrick was sitting forward, leaning his elbows on his thighs and resting his chin on his hands. 'Without assessing the defendant physically, what data do you have to make a judgment on her upper-body strength?'

Angie was chewing something.

Ramsey appeared to be grinding her teeth. Her dentist would no doubt send me a thank-you note after this performance. 'None,' she managed to squeeze out. 'But she appears to be a healthy woman.'

'Is that a *medical* opinion, doctor?' I asked.

'No.'

'Thank you. Now. Concerning a patient you *did* get a chance to examine . . .'

Valencia was once again on his feet, doing the slowest aerobic exercise regimen in recorded history – stand up every three minutes. 'Your Honor,' was all he said.

'Watch your tone, Ms Moss.'

'My apologies, Your Honor,' I said. 'Sometimes I can't help it. I'm from New Jersey.' Again a little laugh from the people watching.

Not from Hawthorne, though. 'Is that right?' she said. 'I'm from Millburn, myself.'

Really! She'd obviously been out here long enough to lose some of her Jersey-ness. 'Edison,' I told the judge.

'Great. Now get on with your questioning and please take note that I managed to not sound sarcastic through this entire exchange.' So we weren't going to get together and reminisce about the Garden State anytime soon.

'Yes, Your Honor.' I turned to face the witness. 'Dr Ramsey, in your examination of Wendy Bryan's body, you found stab wounds in the chest and the back, is that correct?'

Ramsey nodded. 'It is.'

'Could you tell which of those wounds was the fatal one?'

The medical examiner was looking more confident, on familiar ground, but she was still wary because I'd made her look bad – she thought – once before. 'The wound in the chest caused death,' she said. 'It was the deeper one. It collapsed a lung and caused irreparable damage to the heart. Even if she had been found by an EMT and treatment had started immediately, I don't believe she could have been revived.'

Most of this was in her report, which was fine. It gave me a roadmap to where I wanted to end up. 'Can you tell which of the wounds was inflicted first?' I asked.

'It's difficult, but based on the depth of the wounds, the position of the body and the amount of blood that was lost, I would guess that the wound in the back was inflicted first.'

'Thank you, doctor. One last question: is there any doubt that the TeeVee award was the murder weapon?'

'No.' She'd memorized the shortest answer in the human language.

'How do you know?'

'There were traces of the metal from the statuette and from the gold veneer it was sprayed with found in the body,' Ramsey answered.

'Is there any other way they could have found their way into Wendy Bryan's body?' I asked.

'I suppose it's possible but that would be extremely unlikely,' she said.

I had to admit I agreed with that assessment. But I had a witness coming up who could elaborate.

THIRTY-ONE

'There's a question I should have asked you and I never have,' I said to Cynthia.

We were taking our lunch break at the courthouse. The spectacle of a famous actress on trial for murder, coupled with the speculation in the media about why the famously single (widower) TV star Patrick McNabb was taking such an active interest in the case, was driving press coverage to a very high level. So we were eating on the roof, at a table very kindly left for us by the courthouse support staff.

It was a typically furnace-like August day in Southern California and heat rises, so taking our break up here had turned out to be one of the less-great ideas I'd had lately. But I was thinking hard now about the proceedings and was rapidly coming to the conclusion that I'd made no progress in the trial so far.

True enough, I didn't seem to be losing ground in my effort to prove that Cynthia hadn't killed her mother-in-law with a Best Dramatic Actress (in a miniseries, movie or limited series) award. But the trial was treading water. We were still in the early days and the less interesting (to the jurors) witnesses. I wasn't getting anywhere and I was starting to think I knew why.

'What's that?' Cynthia wiped her mouth with a paper napkin. She had another in her lap and a third tucked into her neckline. It was one thing to be on trial for murder. It was another to be an actress in Hollywood photographed with marinara sauce on her blouse. That is exacerbated when you're on trial for murder because marinara in photographs looks like blood. And Cynthia was not to be denied her eggplant parm sandwich.

'Who do you think killed Wendy?'

Jon leaned forward. It was windy up here, which made the heat about two percent more tolerable but also made it harder to hear from across the table. He wanted to hear the answer because I was sure he had his own theories, but hadn't voiced them because he didn't want to step on my toes. I believed my toes could handle it and would have to articulate that to Jon. Because I didn't have a clue who might have stuck a TeeVee in Wendy.

Cynthia gave it some visible thought, and not the kind that actresses usually make a show of having. I have met actresses who were very intelligent in my time here, and I have met some (as well as actors, I should note) who had one thought in their heads, and it was usually about how to get further ahead in 'the business'.

'I honestly don't have a real strong feeling about it,' Cynthia said. 'Let me check with Chrys.' She reached for her mobile phone to text her spiritual advisor and find out who the universe thought should be the subject of the LAPD's investigation, which was not ongoing because they thought they'd found their woman two minutes after entering Wendy Bryan's house the night of the killing.

'No,' I said. I didn't reach for Cynthia's phone because in LA that might prompt yet another murder and it would be my own. 'I don't want to know what Chrys thinks. I want the opinion of someone who was close to the victim. You knew Wendy and what was going on with her. What do you think was going on with Rafael? Were Pete and Penelope and Leopold all taking Wendy Bryan for a ride?'

Emily, who had appeared at the lunch break as if summoned by Patrick (or Angie, at Patrick's behest), rolled her eyes. All this talk about murder when we could be discussing real estate. She had not spoken a word to me since arriving. Good.

Cynthia shook her head. 'I was never on the inside with that,' she said. 'I don't even think Michael was allowed to look over the books at the gallery, which bugged him. But I know Michael didn't like Leopold.'

'Do you think Pete or Penelope might have killed Wendy?' Jon asked at a shout.

Cynthia shrugged. 'Anything's possible.'

I texted Nate for more information on Leopold's death, which I had not yet disclosed to Cynthia because I wasn't sure it was relevant, although I thought it was. A lot of things look like heart attacks. Electrocutions look like heart attacks.

No answer came immediately so I turned back toward Cynthia. 'You've told me that a lot of people hated Wendy. Pete and Penelope could have been among them, right?'

She shrugged. 'Everybody hated her,' she said.

I didn't respond. Instead I looked at Patrick while Jon typed notes frantically into his iPad.

I made serious eye contact with Patrick because I knew the way his mind worked, and he was already thinking of how he could progress using the information I'd gathered at this lunch. 'Remember that it is *not* the defense attorney's job to find the real culprit,' I said deliberately. 'I deal with the information I have and my job is to prove that Cynthia *didn't* kill Wendy, not that somebody else did. We're clear?'

'Crystal, my love,' Patrick said.

'Stop that.' That was me, not Emily, for the record. She was still sitting there looking infuriated.

'Of course.' Patrick spoke with an air of tolerance; at some point I'd understand that I was in love with him. Angie, to my chagrin, grinned. 'So we have quite the array of suspects.'

'Did you not hear what I just said?' What was the point, exactly? I'd had this conversation with him thirty times before, either on his trial or on this one. What was it with the Dunwoody family and murders, anyway? 'We are not looking for suspects. We're looking for evidence that proves Cynthia didn't kill her mother-in-law.'

'I didn't,' Cynthia said.

'I know, but you saying that isn't quite enough.' My turkey club just wasn't as appealing anymore. The crinkle-cut potato chips that had come with it were, though. I'd think about that when I went running tomorrow morning at six. Court days suck.

'I have one idea,' Jon offered. I immediately turned my attention to him. Patrick, who considered him a distraction from me, didn't mind Jon exactly but thought he was unnecessary. So he engrossed himself in his phone.

'Talk to me,' I said to Jon.

'What we have in evidence right now is all what the prosecution doesn't have. They don't have a clear motive. Yeah, the two women didn't like each other but that rarely leads to murder. They don't have proof that Cynthia is strong enough to bend the metal in a TeeVee. They don't have a witness. All that's true, but it's proving a negative. They don't have the evidence they need, but they have a *lot* of innuendo and theory, and that might be enough to convince a jury.'

I felt myself squint a little and the sun was behind me. 'So what's your idea?' I asked Jon.

'We need to prove a positive. The ME's report is vague on the time of death, giving us a two-hour window. Lieutenant Trench, who was outside in his car, saw Cynthia go inside but didn't have any idea there was a murder occurring, which means he didn't hear a cry of pain or terror. It's entirely possible that Wendy had been dead up to an hour before Cynthia arrived.' Jon turned to face our client and raised his voice so she could hear him. 'What were you doing right before you went to Wendy's house?' he asked.

'I was getting my nails done, as a matter of fact.' Cynthia seemed to take the question as a challenge.

'You have someone come to your house for that?'

'Yeah.' You didn't hear the British accent as much with Cynthia as her brother. She had been born in America and, from what they'd told me, only visited England occasionally when she was young despite her father being British. There was still a tinge of it here and there, but mostly she could have been born anywhere. 'So what?'

'I'm not implying anything,' Jon said. 'Please just answer my questions. How much time was there between the manicure and when you left for Wendy's house?'

Cynthia's defensive posture softened. 'Just a couple of minutes. I was running late.'

Jon looked at Cynthia and me. He probably looked at Angie too, because all men do, but she was too far away to be in one glance with the two of us. 'How long does it take nail polish to *really* dry?' he asked.

'Just a few minutes,' I said. 'Cynthia, I'm sure, had no trouble driving.'

'Yeah, but that's not *really* dry.' Cynthia was now on Jon's wavelength. 'With the kind of stuff Sevda uses, it could actually take an hour or so.'

'How long did it take to drive to Wendy's?' Jon said. He was very much in cross-examination mode right now.

'About twenty minutes.'

'So let's say it was half an hour between the application of the nail polish and when you found Wendy's body,' Jon said. 'Would that be about right?'

'On the outside.' Cynthia nodded.

Jon manipulated his phone until the photograph of Cynthia, doused in blood on the floor of Wendy's den and clutching what she thought was her TeeVee award, showed on the screen. He handed it to me. 'Look at her hands.'

I did, and they had a lot of blood on them, but her nails looked great. 'I'm still not there with you,' I told Jon.

'Was there any mention of nail polish found in the police report or the ME's report?' he asked me.

'No, but it wasn't on Wendy; it was on Cynthia.'

'Yeah, but think,' Cynthia said. She was catching on faster than me. 'If my nails were still even a little wet and I picked up the TeeVee to kill Wendy, wouldn't there have been some polish in the blood they found?'

I looked at Jon with new admiration. 'You're a genius,' I said.

He grinned. 'I try.'

THIRTY-TWO

'A manicurist, Ms Moss?' Judge Hawthorne looked, let's say, skeptical.

'I'm merely asking for her to be added to the witness list as an expert on nail polish,' I explained. 'I don't expect to call her to the stand for some time.'

We were in sidebar, which meant that the judge had stopped recording the proceedings so Valencia and I could approach the bench. This was a question of procedure and the jury didn't need to hear it. I'd asked to add Sevda Lakonya, Cynthia's manicurist, to the witness list, which in theory had been set in stone weeks before. But this kind of thing happens all the time and Valencia had no reason to object to it. So he'd objected to it.

'What relevance can the defendant's fingernails have to do with this murder?' he asked the judge. Because, you know, girls.

'It goes to the physical evidence and the photographs submitted by the LAPD,' I told Hawthorne. 'I believe there is a good deal of relevance, but of course Your Honor can rule on that when the witness is on the stand.'

Hawthorne nodded and Valencia knew he had no more chance on the subject. Why he cared, aside from being a frat boy jerk, was difficult to know. 'I'll allow it,' the judge said. 'Everybody back to your tables.' She actually shooed us off like so many bumblebees. 'Proceed, Mr Valencia.'

'The people call Detective Lieutenant K. C. Trench.' Valencia had been rehearsing that bit into a mirror; you could tell.

Trench, willing himself not to sweat in the overheated courtroom, strode to the stand, took his oath and sat down without creating so much as an unwanted crease in his trousers. The man was impeccable from head to toe. It was unnerving.

After the preliminaries, during which Trench's curriculum vitae was made to sound as if he was a cross between Sherlock Holmes and Iron Man, Valencia asked if he'd been in the vicinity of Wendy Bryan's house the night she died.

'Yes,' Trench said. I had seen him testify before and knew he would offer nothing but what was asked in the fewest possible words.

Valencia had clearly questioned Trench before too because he didn't seem the least bit thrown by his witness's brevity. 'And did you see anyone enter the house?' he asked.

'Yes.' A couple of the jurors rolled their eyes. Just as well. Trench was a prosecution witness.

'Approximately how long after you saw someone enter did the police call come in and officers dispatched to the house in Santa Monica?' Valencia said.

'I was not present by then, but according to the records from the Santa Monica dispatcher, it was three minutes later,' Trench answered.

'Did you know . . . Is the person who walked into Wendy Bryan's house the night she was murdered here in the courtroom today?' Valencia was trying to build to a TV moment worthy of . . . well, Patrick McNabb.

'Yes,' Trench said. He was trying to build a TV moment worthy of the test pattern.

'Can you tell us who that was?' Valencia had anticipated Trench's taciturn response and used it to fit his rhythm. Clever.

'It was the defendant, Cynthia Sutton,' Trench answered. He did not point as witnesses do if they've seen too many movies. I doubted Trench had ever seen a movie. He probably went home every night and read through his unsolved cases. If he had any unsolved cases.

There was no gasp among the spectators. They weren't surprised. Who *else* would Trench have been called to identify?

'Thank you, Lieutenant.' Valencia appeared to be terribly pleased with himself. He walked back to his table and sat down.

Judge Hawthorne, apparently waiting for more from the DA, got nothing and waited a moment to turn to me. 'Ms Moss?'

'Thank you, Your Honor.' I stood up and approached the witness box. 'Lieutenant Trench, how long did Cynthia Sutton stay inside the house after you saw her go inside?' I asked.

'I don't know.'

'Why don't you know?'

'Because I left almost as soon as she went inside. I had no idea a crime was being committed or had been committed inside the home.' Trench was being careful, which was not in the least uncharacteristic of him. But I did see Valencia flinch a tiny bit at 'or had been committed'.

'Was the defendant carrying a TeeVee award when she went inside?' I asked.

'No.'

Valencia gave a thought to standing up and objecting that the TeeVee was kept inside the house but decided against it. If he had redirect he could clarify that; if not he could simply mention it in his closing statement.

'Lieutenant, were you staking out Wendy Bryan's home?' I really wanted to know why Trench was there the night of the murder and he wouldn't tell me in conversation.

'No.' The man must have been a riot at dinner parties.

'But you were parked in front of it at a very crucial time.'

'Yes.'

'Your Honor, the defense is not asking a question.' Valencia didn't bother to stand.

'Please ask a question, Ms Moss.' Neither did the judge. To be fair, if she stood everybody would probably leave the courtroom so that was better.

'Certainly,' I said, as if I had an alternative. 'Lieutenant Trench, how far from the other car were you parked when the person you saw enter the house got out?'

'Roughly seventeen yards,' Trench answered. Roughly.

'Are you certain the person you saw was Cynthia Sutton?'

'Yes. I checked her license plates when she drove up.' For Trench that was an emotional outburst. 'They matched the vehicle registered to Cynthia Sutton. In addition, I had seen the defendant in a film and recognized her.' So he *did* go to the movies!

Trench identifying Cynthia was not exactly a devastating blow to my defense. The police had found her inside the house holding the murder weapon so we were conceding the point that she was there. 'Lieutenant Trench,' I said, 'did you see the defendant stab Wendy Bryan with the TeeVee award?'

'No,' Trench said.

'Did you hear her say she wanted to kill her mother-in-law?'

'No.'

'Do you have any facts at all that would indicate the defendant is the one who killed Wendy Bryan?'

'I have no access to data that the arresting officers and Detective Brisbane, who led the investigation, already have,' Trench answered. 'I did not investigate the crime on my own.'

'Why not?' I asked. 'You were already very near the crime scene.'

'I am not a member of the Santa Monica Police Department,' Trench answered. 'The case was assigned to Detective Brisbane. I had no relevant information to give him so I did not attempt to do so.'

'So you can't personally tie the defendant to this crime, is that correct?' Make sure to frame it in the form of a question, *Jeopardy!* fans.

'No, I cannot,' Trench answered.

I thanked him and sat down. When asked, Valencia said he would like to ask the lieutenant one question on redirect and Judge Hawthorne allowed it. Valencia stood up, buttoning his suit jacket, and approached Trench the way a dog approaches a cat that has scratched its nose more than once.

'Lieutenant, you said, when the defense counsel asked you so cleverly, that you have no information that ties the defendant to the murder.' He did not wait for the judge to tell him to ask a question. 'Do you have any information that proves the defendant did *not* murder Wendy Bryan?'

Trench didn't exactly sneer but his left eyelid twitched a little. 'No.'

Valencia smiled and nodded. 'Thank you, Lieutenant.' He sat down, indicating his questioning of Trench was completed.

'What was that?' Cynthia asked me in a whisper.

'He thinks that helped him,' I answered. 'I don't know why he thinks that, but he thinks it.'

THIRTY-THREE

'Trench wasn't assigned to investigate Leopold Kolensky's death, but I'm betting that's what he was doing,' Nate Garrigan said. 'Kolensky died in his home, not in Santa Monica.'

Nate rarely came to my apartment. In fact, he had never come to my apartment before. But he'd called and said he wanted to talk about some case-related stuff and was in my area. Angie and I were taking it easy after the day in court. Angie was taking it easier than I was, so she had to go get dressed when I told her Nate was on his way.

I was in a pair of running shorts and a T-shirt with the Ben & Jerry's logo on it because I'm incredibly classy, but Nate had insisted and I was too tired and too hot to change back into professional clothing. To Nate's credit, he did not comment. I know men who would.

Nate burped. 'Sorry,' he said. It was a lie. 'I'm here because there's definitely something going on with the finances at Rafael.'

'The art gallery Wendy Bryan ran,' Angie said.

'Yeah. It's under water.'

I looked hard at him. 'I assume you don't mean the building has been flooded,' I said. 'You're saying Wendy wasn't paying the rent?'

'Worse than that,' Nate told me. 'She owned the building. She wasn't paying the mortgage and she wasn't paying an equity loan she took out on the place two years ago. Wendy, as we say in the business, was broke.'

'How much water?' Angie asked.

Nate looked at her. 'What?'

'How much water was Wendy under? How much did she owe?'

There is nothing an ex-cop likes better than to pretend to still be a cop. So Nate was downright smug in his ability to shock people while remaining world-weary at the same time. 'About eleven million dollars,' Nate said, barely hiding his satisfaction.

I refused to be amazed even as my brain was saying, *Eleven million dollars!* I like Nate but I needed him to remember who his employer was right at the moment. 'How did we not know this until now?' I said. 'This has got to be a matter of public record.'

'Not where she got the money.' Nate's smugness had a secret and it was dying to tell me.

'You're kidding,' I said, just to let him know I knew what he meant. And for a change, I actually did.

Angie didn't. 'What?' she asked.

I kept my gaze on the investigator. 'You're saying Wendy Bryan, mother of a major stockbroker and mother-in-law of an actual movie star, was borrowing money from the mob? Do you guys even have a mob out here?' In New Jersey they practically had storefronts that said 'MOB' on them, but Los Angeles seemed so . . . sunny. It was hard to picture Tony Soprano doing well in Bel Air.

'Of *course* there's organized crime in Los Angeles.' Nate

seemed almost insulted. 'But these guys, well, *organized* might be overstating it. They're a group of overgrown petty criminals who ended up building their business into something that could afford to loan Wendy Bryan millions. But they wouldn't be happy with her once she stopped paying. No matter how high the interest rate is, it doesn't matter if the customer doesn't pay.'

Angie was already shaking her head. 'I don't get it. Wendy had this great big house and this prestigious art gallery. She could go to a real bank if she needed money that badly.'

'She did.' Nate was becoming less insufferable as we discussed the facts of the case. He was a good investigator and was serious about his work. 'Part of what she was doing with the money she'd borrowed was to pay off loans she'd gotten from Bank of America, legit. When her credit rating got low enough that she couldn't pay those off on time, she went to our pals and that's when the real fun began.'

This was getting to be too much. Everything I'd heard about Wendy Bryan over these months was that she was practically a reincarnation of Pearl Mesta, the original society grande dame. She'd worn expensive clothes and jewelry. She had an enormous mansion decorated to the nth degree. She threw dinner parties that would be the talk of the town for months. This did not in any way seem like a woman who was at all concerned about her finances.

'Was it her spending that did her in?' I asked. 'All the jewels and the clothes and all that? Was she taking from the business to pay for all that?'

'The opposite.' Nate shook his head and took another swig of beer. He didn't seem that interested in the drink, frankly, except to use it as a prop. 'She had pawned most of her really good jewelry and was wearing fakes. The house was a rental. She'd sold it to a dentist who needed a deficit to show on his taxes three years ago. Everything she did was a pretense. None of it was real except the gallery. She cared about that and would do pretty much anything to keep it from going under.'

'I've got to go into court tomorrow,' I told him. 'The prosecution is still putting on its case but I don't think it'll last past lunch. He'll rest and then it'll be my turn. I can't put an anonymous group of Southern California mobsters on trial. I need to raise the possibility that maybe Wendy Bryan *didn't* die because her daughter-in-law couldn't stand her. So what can I say that I can prove?'

'Nothing yet.' Nate wasn't happy about bringing the bad news but he'd do it if he had to. 'I know what I know but I don't have hard evidence yet. That'll take a couple of days at least.'

Angie walked over to him and looked deeply into his eyes. Nate seemed bewildered by her sudden attention but, like most men who met Angie, didn't mind it at all. 'Are you in danger?' she asked him.

Nate busted out laughing. 'Me? From these guys? Oh, you had me worried there for a minute. No. I can handle them, especially since I don't need to name them to prove that Bryan was in debt up to her neck and then some.'

'Leopold,' I said.

'Yes. About Leopold. Like I told you, he had dinner with Wendy the night he died. The ME was called because he died alone, and ruled it natural causes. Myocardial infarction. But the timing is at least a signal that more needed to be asked, so I started asking.'

'And?' Angie doesn't have a lot of patience for the outcome. That has proven to be quite a boon for some men she's known.

'And we have some local wise guys on the finances and then her "executive director" decides to have a heart attack and die. What I've found out from doctors is that there are a lot of poisons that can cause heart problems or look like heart problems to the degree that even a trained pathologist won't notice the flags. It's a tough case but there are signs all over the place that it's hinky.'

'Geez, Nate,' I said. 'Do you think you can get Edward G. Robinson to play you in the movie?'

Nate stood up, leaving half the bottle of beer full on the table beside him. 'I'll go see the ME,' he said, giving my remark all the attention it deserved. 'And about that up-and-coming star in the art world, Pete Conway and his manager. From what I've found out so far, Pete has an inflated opinion of his own talent and his manager Ms Hannigan helped inflate it. So maybe they were mad at Wendy for running her gallery into the ground. Because the odds were that she'd have been closing the doors two months ago if not sooner.'

He turned toward the door, thinking he'd been macho enough to exit on that pronouncement. But I stopped him and made him look me in the eye. 'Nate. Do we have any idea who killed Wendy Bryan?'

Nate took a long moment and his face changed from one of complete conviction (perhaps that's not the word I wanted to use in this case) to slight embarrassment, like the young student who has been caught having not read the book for the book report.

'No,' he said, and left.

THIRTY-FOUR

'Did you ever witness an argument between the defendant and Wendy Bryan?'

Valencia was questioning Isobel Sanchez, who held advanced degrees in economics and finance from Universidad Nacional Autónoma de México in Mexico City and had been Wendy Bryan's housekeeper since arriving in Los Angeles seven years earlier. Sanchez, who wore a look of mild irritation, did not betray any emotion in her voice and spoke English almost without an accent. I took four years of Spanish in high school and can order paella with confidence, but that's about it.

'I saw a number of arguments between them,' she answered. She was trying not to look at Valencia, although she was a witness he had called. She didn't appear to like him much.

'Can you tell us what those arguments were about?'

'They varied.' Sanchez said. I think even the prosecutor who had clearly instructed the witness to offer no more than a direct answer was probably just a little bit disappointed in the tenor of her answers. Could I expect she'd be more welcoming when I cross-examined her?

'Was there one topic they disagreed on more than anything else?' Valencia asked.

'Yes.'

Valencia, no doubt lamenting his lack of a dental license given all the teeth he was pulling, did his best to get to the point. 'What was that topic?'

'Her son.'

'Michael Bryan, Wendy Bryan's son and the defendant's husband,' Valencia clarified.

I stood. 'Estranged husband,' I said. I could do some clarifying of my own. I glanced at Michael, sitting in the front row as usual, and he cringed just a little bit when I said that, which was the effect I'd been hoping to create.

'Sit down, Ms Moss, unless you have some legal objection,' Judge Hawthorne, well, ordered. So I sat.

'What about Mr Bryan did the defendant and her victim disagree upon?' Valencia asked.

I stood up. 'Now I have an objection,' I said to the judge.

Hawthorne nodded. 'Mr Valencia, you'll restrain yourself from referring to Mrs Bryan as the defendant's victim. The defendant is considered innocent until proven guilty and you are well aware of that, I assume, having graduated from law school.'

'Sorry, Your Honor. Her *alleged* victim.' Valencia started toward the witness box again.

'Mr Valencia.' Hawthorne was having none of the prosecutor's hilarious wit.

'Sorry, Your Honor. It won't happen again.' Before the judge could tell him that it sure as hell wouldn't, he got back to questioning his witness, who looked as though she wanted to stab him with a well-polished salad fork. 'Mrs Sanchez, you said that you witnessed a number of arguments between the defendant Ms Sutton and the victim. What specifically did they argue about concerning Mrs Bryan's son?'

'Ms Sutton believed that Mrs Bryan dominated her son and kept him from doing things he wanted to do,' Sanchez said. 'Mrs Bryan believed her son should have more respect for his mother and that Ms Sutton was a negative influence on him.'

Valencia, having finally gotten more than three words out of his witness, nodded appreciatively. 'What kind of things did Ms Sutton suggest her husband' – he looked at me – 'sorry, *estranged* husband, might have wanted to do that his mother was in some way making him forgo?'

'The last time I heard them yelling at each other it was about

Mr Bryan's work. Mr Bryan wanted to become a movie producer and his mother thought that was because his wife was an actress,' Sanchez said, looking at Michael. 'She believed that Ms Sutton was trying to drive a wedge between her husband and his mother and that making him a producer on her films would have been the final blow. She told Mr Bryan if he gave up his successful career to take a chance on that because of a pretty girl, he would never see any of her estate.'

'How did Ms Sutton respond?'

'She called Mrs Bryan a bitch.'

Valencia looked around, perhaps expecting a gasp from the spectators. He got none, so he moved on. He was a professional.

'Did Ms Sutton ever threaten violence on Mrs Bryan?' he asked.

What? If you never ask a question that you don't know the answer to, and Valencia clearly wanted an affirmative answer . . .

'Yes,' Sanchez said.

Oh boy.

'In what terms?' the prosecutor asked.

'She said that if Mrs Bryan tried to turn her husband against her, she'd cut out Mrs Bryan's heart.' Sanchez was looking at her shoes now, upset with the information she had to impart.

I didn't look at my client because I didn't want the jury to know this was news to me. But Cynthia passed me a note that read, *'I said that.'*

'And that was how long before Mrs Bryan was murdered?' Valencia asked.

'About two weeks,' the witness answered.

'No further questions.' Valencia, this time having actually scored some points, did his best not to sport the obnoxious grin as he sat down. He mostly succeeded.

I felt it was important in my cross-examination not to look like I was berating Isobel Sanchez. This was partially because I wanted the jury on my side and partially because I wanted Sanchez on my side. It also had vaguely to do with the fact that I really didn't *want* to berate Isobel Sanchez.

'Ms Sanchez,' I began.

'It's Mrs,' the witness corrected me. Not a great start.

I nodded and smiled at her. She didn't smile back. 'Mrs Sanchez, you said that Mrs Bryan was upset that her son was intending to go into film production with his wife, Ms Sutton. Did that impact her finances at all?'

Sanchez gave me a withering look. 'How would I know?' she asked.

'Fair enough.' The whole be-nice-to-the-witness thing wasn't going quite as I'd hoped. 'Did Mrs Bryan pay you on time?'

'On time?' Surely Sanchez didn't need an explanation of the term.

I gave her one anyway. 'Yes. Was Mrs Bryan ever late in her payment?'

Sanchez looked away, which was interesting. She looked at the judge. 'Do I have to answer that?' she asked.

'I agree,' said Valencia, on his feet. 'Mrs Bryan is not being accused of her own murder. What does the frequency with which she paid her maid have to do with this case?'

Sanchez's eyes flashed at the word *maid* but she didn't say anything.

'Ms Moss?' Judge Hawthorne was asking me for some clarification on Valencia's question.

'The defense is curious as to the state of Mrs Bryan's finances, as we will discuss when presenting our case,' I explained. 'I believe it goes to motive. Ms Sutton had no reason to kill her mother-in-law for her money, but Mrs Bryan might very well have been in some financial difficulty with people who might have been very angry with her.'

'It's shaky but I'll allow it,' Hawthorne said. Valencia looked disappointed. Sanchez looked back up to the judge, who told her, 'Please answer the question.'

'Mrs Bryan didn't owe me any money when she died,' Sanchez said.

'I appreciate that, but it doesn't answer the question,' I countered. So much for being friendly with the witness. 'Were there times when Mrs Bryan couldn't afford to pay you on time?'

Sanchez looked like she wanted to swallow her lips. 'There were times she didn't pay me right away. I don't know if it's because she couldn't afford it.'

'Did she tell you why she wasn't paying you at those times?' I asked.

'That was just answered, Your Honor,' Valencia piped up.

'No, it wasn't. Please answer the question, Mrs Sanchez.'

Now Sanchez looked like she wanted to swallow *my* lips, and more in a Hannibal Lecter sort of way. 'Mrs Bryan said that she was having some problems with the bank,' she answered.

'Thank you. Mrs Sanchez, you said that Ms Sutton said she would cut out her mother-in-law's heart if Mrs Bryan, and I'm quoting, "tried to turn her husband against her." What was the context of that remark?'

This time Sanchez seemed genuinely confused. 'The context? She was angry at Mrs Bryan.'

'Yes,' I said. 'And as you said, they were angry at each other over Mr Bryan's intention to change careers.' I was looking at Michael Bryan when I said that and he looked exactly as I would have hoped – surprised. 'Had Mr Bryan told his mother that was what he was going to do?'

'Yes.' Sanchez was more comfortable with that answer. It only had three letters.

'Do you think Ms Sutton actually meant she would cut out her mother-in-law's heart?' I asked.

Predictably, and somewhat to my relief, Valencia was on his feet. 'Objection. The witness is being asked to judge the intentions of the defendant.'

'Sustained.'

I nodded again, as if acknowledging that I'd asked an improper question and regretted it. The question might have been unorthodox but I didn't regret it one iota. 'One last area to ask about, Ms Sanchez. Were you ever present during a conversation between Mrs Bryan and her son when she asked him to loan her money?'

Sanchez suddenly found her shoes fascinating; she looked down at them with intense interest. She said something very faintly.

'Please speak up, Mrs Sanchez,' Judge Hawthorne said as I mentally thanked her. I didn't want to have to do that myself.

Sanchez looked up. 'I said, "Yes. One time."'

'What were the circumstances of that conversation?' I asked.

'Mrs Bryan asked Mr Bryan if he could loan her some money to help pay for a special event she wanted to host at Rafael. It was going to launch a new series of works by Pierre Chirac.'

'How much money was she asking for?'

'I don't know.' Sanchez's eyes were burning holes in my forehead. No doubt they would serve as ventilation for my brain.

'Did Mr Bryan loan his mother the money?' I asked.

'Yes.'

'Did he add any conditions to the loan?' I said. Cynthia had already told me about this and I needed to head it off as efficiently as possible.

'Mr Bryan said he'd loan his mother the money as long as she never told his wife about it.'

People in the gallery looked at each other knowingly. No doubt they were wondering why the defense would elicit such a damning piece of evidence against its own client.

It was a calculated risk. 'To your knowledge, *did* Mrs Bryan tell Ms Sutton about the loan?'

'Yes. She told Ms Sutton the next day when they were having lunch together.'

'And how did Ms Sutton react?' It was crucial that Sanchez answer this question honestly.

'She said it was OK with her.' Sanchez looked over at Cynthia and came as close to smiling as she had the whole time she was on the witness stand, which wasn't especially close. 'She said she wanted the art show to succeed.'

Cynthia had told me a little about this. 'And how did Mrs Bryan react to that?' I asked.

Sanchez put great effort into putting no inflection into her answer. 'She said that Ms Sutton could shove her support.'

I dismissed the witness. Valencia saw no reason to redirect. We broke for lunch.

Patrick and Angie were right in front of Cynthia and me as we headed out of the courtroom. Michael Bryan stepped out into the aisle and stopped just as Cynthia reached his row.

'Cindy,' he said. The man looked positively stricken.

'It's too late for that, Michael,' my client told him and walked by.

But we didn't make it all the way out of the courtroom. Patrick must have spotted the two uniformed police officers first because he stopped and backed up and turned so he was facing into the aisle, his back to the seats on the right side of the room. It wasn't a wide aisle and with me, Angie, Cynthia and Jon all going to the door, there wasn't much room to breathe, which was a real problem in this heat. You don't get to go to court in a T-shirt and shorts, much to my chagrin.

The cops walked in like cops do, backs straight and shoulders back, certain they're in charge of everything and nobody will question that. Cops can be hilarious and understanding. These weren't.

The taller, broader one, whose name tag read *Mancini*, fixed his gaze on Angie and me, which was not easy since we weren't standing next to each other. 'Which one of you is Sandra Moss?' he asked.

I didn't care for his tone, but I took a step forward just as Angie said, 'I am. Is there a problem, officer?' Angie will protect me even when she doesn't know what she's protecting me from. Everyone should have an Angie.

'No, *I'm* Sandra Moss,' I said clearly. But I didn't ask if he had a problem, which would have been the next sequential thing in New Jersey. This was California. People were, at least in theory, polite.

'Which one of you?' the shorter, slighter cop asked. He looked supremely confused.

Before Angie could claim to be Spartacus again, I said, 'I am.' Again, I asked no question. I figured it was their responsibility to explain themselves and not mine.

'Then who are you?' the bigger cop asked Angie.

'I'm her attorney.' Maybe only some people should have an Angie.

The big cop shook his head as if declaring the whole matter unimportant. He looked at me. 'Sandra Moss, I have a warrant for your arrest. You have the right to remain silent. Anything you say—'

'*What?*' Patrick demanded. The smaller cop looked at him, seemed to recognize him, took one step toward him as if about to ask for an autograph, corrected himself and turned back in my direction.

I think the world of Patrick. I do. But he tends to think everything is about him. I ignored that and kept my eyes on the cop while something in my digestive system tightened just a little. I'm not afraid of police officers generally, but this one had something in his eyes that lowered my body temperature about

three degrees. Normally in heat like this I'd have considered that
a positive. Not this time.

'On what charge am I being arrested?' I said in a voice
that I hoped wasn't quavering.

The smaller cop actually pulled out his phone and called up
a note to read it to me. 'Obstruction of justice, bribery and
extortion.'

Before I knew it, I was in a holding cell in the building's
basement.

THIRTY-FIVE

'This is an outrage,' Patrick said.

'The fact is, it's three outrages,' I corrected him. 'But
that's not my main problem right now.'

You'll ask me how Patrick managed to get himself inside a
secure section of the criminal courts building of Los Angeles to
talk to me in my cell while my attorney, Jon, was still trying
to get an explanation of the charges against me and hadn't
actually shown up to discuss it with me yet.

(For the record, Holiday Wentworth had offered on the phone
to represent me, but she had no criminal law experience at all
and Jon did. The fact that I knew Jon was an excellent attorney
everywhere but in front of a judge wasn't making me feel especially better at the moment.)

'I don't understand what they're charging you with, Sandy.'
Patrick reached through the bars for my hand. I felt like I
shouldn't give it to him, that the prisoner in the other cell (an
actual prostitute who was not Madelyn Forsythe) would see
it as a sign of weakness and the guard, who must have let
Patrick in on the basis of him being a famous actor, would
think I was Patrick's girlfriend. 'What is the LAPD trying to
do to you?'

On the other hand (so to speak), Patrick was trying to comfort
me and he was a dear person. I put my hand on his in a gesture
of my own strength. I doubt anyone else was watching and

therefore the move and all the thought I'd put into it were meaningless. So be it.

'It's a good question,' I told him. 'Are they trying to keep me out of court for Cynthia's trial? If so, it's a bad strategy. No judge is going to hold me in jail on what even the cops are calling non-violent crimes and certainly Jon is out there getting me into an arraignment as we speak, hopefully in front of a judge who knows me.'

'If it's not Cynthia's trial, then what?' Patrick asked, trying to turn his hand so that he was holding mine and not the other way around. But I was insisting for reasons I couldn't even explain to myself. 'How do they benefit if you go to jail?'

If I'd had an answer for him I would have given it. But if what Trench had told me was true, that people at the upper levels of the LAPD were actually targeting me personally, there had to be a reason for it. I wasn't a big enough deal, especially in California, to have annoyed officials that high up. It was somehow flattering that they even knew my name.

As well-known as Wendy Bryan had been, could she have had friends in positions that elevated, and if so, would they (assuming they were involved somehow in law enforcement) have been angry enough to try to stop me from defending Cynthia? That seemed like an awfully long stretch.

And Trench had warned about what could happen if a person who had annoyed the higher-ups ended up in prison, even for one night.

'I can't begin to say,' I told Patrick. 'What I know for sure is that we've got to get me out of here as quickly as possible. Where's Jon?'

'I don't know, but when I leave here and they give me back my phone I'll text him,' Patrick said, smiling at me. 'Can't let the woman I love languish in a cell.'

That again. 'Not now, Patrick.'

But there was no need to wait for Jon; the door opened and he walked in with an expression of . . . something on his face. Fear? I hoped not.

'What's the deal?' I said when he got close enough.

Before he answered he looked at Patrick. 'You're going to have to leave. This is attorney-client stuff.'

Patrick believes he knows all about being a lawyer because he played one on television. It's sort of like if the cast of *Gray's Anatomy* started doing surgery. He nodded and took his hand back through the bars. Through what I could only assume were Method tears welling up in his eyes, he said, 'I'll see you soon,' and managed not to choke on the words as he said them. Then he turned and walked out of the door. I'm sure he imagined the camera was aimed at him leaving bravely and not me sitting in the cell. Actors.

'So what's the deal?' I repeated.

'Somebody out there wants you in here,' he answered. 'They want to schedule the arraignment for the day after tomorrow.'

The day after *tomorrow*? These things never take that long, especially when the accused (whatever I was accused of) has private counsel. 'How is the court justifying that?' I asked. 'What the hell is it they say I did, anyway?'

'Apparently the idea, which is total crap, is that you are paying off court officials to get Judge Klemperer off another case you're working.'

Judge Klemperer! 'The Madelyn Forsythe case? This is about *that*?' I'd been so deeply engrossed in the murder trial I hadn't considered the prostitution case. 'At most that case would result in a ninety-day sentence! Who the . . . who cares enough about that?' Then I thought for a second, in particular about the video surveillance that was no doubt trained at this cell. 'And by the way, no, I'm not paying off anybody to do anything. How stupid am I supposed to be in this soap opera?'

'Pretty stupid,' Jon admitted. 'They say you're paying the court clerk under the table to transfer Klemperer off the case and get yourself a panel of three judges to hear it.'

My dream scenario. 'I won't lie, Jon. I'd love to see that happen. Klemperer hates women and isn't giving me or my client a chance. But there's no way I would try to go about doing it like that. I'm a lawyer, not a second-rate bail bondsman.' My immediate apologies to all bail bondsmen. I'm sure none of you bribe anybody and you're all first rate. I was under stress, in a holding cell. I'm sure you can sympathize, if not empathize.

'Well, they have some bank records that have clearly been doctored showing this employee of the court clerk's office with deposits of three thousand dollars, a thousand dollars each for three months, in cash. They're going to try and tie those to you. You'd better check your accounts and make sure nobody's hacked in and withdrawn that exact amount of money.' Jon's mouth twitched and for a moment I thought he believed I'd committed this ridiculous crime. Then I realized that was his way of showing anger when he was trying to conceal it.

'Three thousand bucks,' I said. 'Not only am I guilty of bribery, I'm cheap on top of it. What's the clerk saying?'

'So far nothing. Apparently he took the three grand and booked a trip to Chichen Itza for the weekend. But there is good news. You're not going to be spending the next two days in jail. I got you an arraignment for six o'clock tonight.'

Suddenly life seemed better. Funny how quickly that changes. Yesterday, if you'd told me the good news was that I'd be arraigned for bribing a public official today, I would not have thought that a terrific deal. 'Jon! How'd you do that?'

'Thank Judge Hawthorne. Nobody's going to delay her trial and remove the lead defense attorney, charges or no charges. You'll be back in her courtroom tomorrow morning by her order.'

I wanted to hug him more than I had wanted to hug Patrick when he was taking my hand, which pretty much summed up our relationship at this moment. 'Thank you,' I said. 'I appreciate you taking this on. You didn't have to do it.'

'Yes, I did.'

That was sweet. 'You're taking this personally,' I said, thinking I should have been the one who was doing that.

'I got shot over this and lost a kidney,' Jon said. Fair point.

'Well, I appreciate it.' That certainly seemed an inadequate thing to say.

Jon stood and put a determined look on his face. 'Get yourself presentable as much as you can,' he told me. 'We're gonna get you arraigned.'

THIRTY-SIX

The arraignment took four minutes, according to my iPhone. Jon entered my plea of (completely) not guilty, the judge (Harmon Evans, whom I had never seen before) noted the state of my ongoing murder case and the letter from Judge Hawthorne and released me on my own recognizance while doing an admirable job of not rolling his eyes at the sheer absurdity of the whole situation.

I was home in an hour, soaking my feet in front of Patrick (which should have disabused him from any notion that he was in love with me but didn't), Cynthia, who was probably wondering why I didn't have someone on staff to take care of my feet properly, and Angie as soon as I could arrange it. (Emily was probably fuming that she hadn't been invited to the foot-soaking.) My feet seemed to be taking the brunt of the punishment I'd endured today. Jon went home to relax for the night. He didn't say anything, but I knew the many surgeries he'd undergone had depleted him and he needed more rest than he had before.

'Emmie called me today,' Patrick said out of nowhere. Naturally. 'She still wants to know why I called off the engagement.' This was a periodic occurrence, he had noted over the past few months. Was he trying to make the point that he cared more for me than for the woman he had been planning to marry? Did that matter?

'Did you tell her it was because she was a controlling bitch who wanted to micromanage your life?' Angie, when she was 'off the clock' as Patrick's assistant, tended to speak a little more bluntly than when she was working on his behalf.

Patrick smiled that beguiling smile with the hint of sadness in it, the one that probably had gotten Emily to fall in love with him to begin with. 'I think I put it a tiny bit more diplomatically.'

I wanted to deflect any further talk of Patrick's love life for . . . the rest of my life. 'I don't think I got arrested today because of your case, Cynthia,' I said. If Patrick could change conversational gears without so much as a segue, so could I.

Cynthia, who had been sort of staring into the middle distance as if acting in a scene in which her character didn't want to betray the pain in her heart at the revelation of her husband's infidelity (or perhaps I was taking the analogy too far), turned sharply at the mention of her name. 'Why not?' she asked with an edge to her voice. Was she offended that I'd get arrested for something other than defending her?

'Because there's no upside in it for the upper echelons of the LAPD to get me off your case. I'm not the world's most renowned criminal defense attorney. And as accomplished as you are, Cynthia, I don't really think it matters enough to those men' (they were pretty much all men) 'to bother with arresting me. Besides, I think the attempts to shoot Patrick and me and the attack on Jon were all related, and they started before Wendy Bryan died.'

My feet were feeling better. Was it weird that I didn't want to dry them in front of Patrick? I sat with them in the mini-tub I had bought at the CVS and pondered my neuroses.

Angie's eyes narrowed. 'If it's not the murder case, what is it?' she asked. 'They wouldn't try to kill you over a couple of parking tickets, would they?' I had gotten two parking tickets in one week six months ago and refused to pay them because I felt the citing officer had been acting out of an inflated sense of power. It's a long story and Angie won't let me forget it. The tickets were still pending.

'I've been racking my brain trying to answer that one,' I told Angie. 'And the only thing I can come up with is the Forsythe case.'

'The suburban prostitute?' Patrick said. Never let it be said he wasn't attentive to discussions of my work.

'The *alleged* prostitute and for the record, non-prostitute,' I corrected him. The heck with it; if that was going to be his attitude, I'd towel off my feet right in front of him. I took to doing just that. It didn't seem to bother anybody but me. 'But it seems to me that this started right around the time I took her case.'

'How does that fit?' Cynthia said. 'Could there be people in

the police department who were using her services and don't
want their wives to know?'

What was it with that family? 'She's *not* a prostitute,' I said.
It's best not to yell at your clients and, truthfully, I didn't. It just
felt like I had. 'Sorry, Cynthia. I get worked up about my clients.'

'I noticed,' she said with a little smile.

'But that's the problem,' I went on. 'Maddie isn't a call girl.
She wasn't trying to sell sexual acts in exchange for money. But
the charges continue to be pressed and someone keeps trying to
kill or incarcerate me. So what does that tell us?'

'The chief of police has her mistaken for someone else?'
Patrick offered.

Feet now operational, I stood and drained the tub into the
sink in the galley kitchen to wash it out. 'That's a highly
unlikely possibility,' I told Patrick. 'If you don't want the client
to talk, no matter how mistaken you might be, eliminating her
lawyer is hardly the way to do it. There *was* that one attempt
on her by the guy with the knife, but it was the only time that
happened.' (He had been released and was no doubt out in the
world knifing people just as a hobby now.) 'I've been shot
at three times and jailed once.' I got out the cleanser and
washed the sink.

I put the tub away under the sink and sat down, picking up
the pair of socks I'd taken out before I started my foot therapy.
I put the socks on. 'Maybe it's not Maddie's case. Maybe somebody just hates me because I'm obnoxious and disliked.'

'Don't be absurd.' Patrick didn't approach me. I thought it
was the feet. 'Everyone loves you.'

'The men with the guns would disagree,' I said. I picked up
my phone and dialed (if that's the word, because 'pushed for'
seems odd) Nate Garrigan.

'What can I do for you *now*?' Nate is a man of deep feelings,
most of them aggravation. And it's not like I hadn't asked him
to look into quite a number of things in relation to Cynthia's
trial. But hey, I was paying him (OK, so the firm was paying
him, but whose idea was *that*?), so you'd think he might at least
try to take a more civil tone. That's what you'd think.

'I'm trying to figure out why people are shooting at me and
having me arrested,' I said. 'Consider it more of a personal favor.'

Nate sighed for effect. 'Fine. Who do you want me to follow this time?'

'The deputy chief of police.'

THIRTY-SEVEN

'Detective Brisbane, what did you find when you entered Wendy Bryan's house on the night in question?' Valencia, now that he didn't have to question Trench anymore, was practically throwing Brisbane a testimonial dinner, that's how excited he was to have the detective who had investigated the case now testifying.

'I discovered a body on the floor of the center hall, having bled profusely from a chest wound,' Brisbane said. He was a man of about fifty, his hair what I'm sure he thought was a distinguished salt-and-pepper but was just gray. He was neither thin nor overweight, not especially tall or short, and his eyes were the color that boredom would be if it could take on pigment. He was speaking in a tone that indicated this wasn't his first homicide and he certainly hoped it wouldn't be his last. 'But the officers on the scene informed me she had no pulse and the EMTs said she was dead. That was confirmed by the medical examiner when she arrived.'

'Was the murder weapon found with the body?' Valencia asked, despite the jury having been told the story twice before during testimony from the two uniformed officers.

'No. The officers found the award in the adjoining room with the defendant clutching it in her arms,' Brisbane said. I considered objecting to the word *clutching* but let it go. You don't want to be seen as a nag or a nitpicker. Juries don't like that, and they especially don't like it if you're a woman. Juries were brought up in this society too.

'Was there any doubt that the TeeVee award was the murder weapon?'

He gave exactly the response I was hoping for: 'No. It had the victim's blood all over it and the defendant's fingerprints everywhere. The ME's report made it clear that the wings on the statue, which were very sharp, had been what made the wounds in the victim's chest and back.'

'Thank you, Detective Brisbane,' Valencia said. His case had been made. He thought.

I stood up and started talking as I approached the witness box. 'Detective, you arrived in the house after the uniformed offices and the emergency medical technicians, is that right?'

'Yes. It's not unusual. I don't get called until the officers on the scene suspect they have a homicide on their hands.' Great. Not only was Brisbane a witness who would answer more than the question, he was also keen on making sure he came out looking great. He was the anti-Trench.

'Of course,' I said. 'Did you notice any markings on the floor between the body and the entrance to the den, where Cynthia Sutton was discovered?'

'Markings?'

'Yes. A trail of blood, let's say. If the defendant had stabbed her mother-in-law with the statue and then carried it into the den, wouldn't the blood on the award have dripped on the floor?'

'I would assume so.' Brisbane was also not like Trench in one particularly relevant area: he wasn't a good detective.

I nodded to Jon, who produced a very big enlargement of one of the crime-scene photographs, which he brought up to the bench. I approached and looked at Judge Hawthorne. 'Your Honor, this is an enlargement of a crime-scene photograph that has already been entered into evidence by the prosecution. May I show it to the jury?'

Hawthorne beckoned to Valencia, who walked up to the bench. 'Mr Valencia, the defense wants to show this photograph to the jury. Ms Moss says it is one that you have already introduced. Do you recognize it?'

Valencia looked at the picture, grimaced, and then nodded to the judge. 'I recognize it.'

'In that case I will allow the photograph,' the judge said. Valencia didn't look happy walking back to the prosecution table, but his happiness was not my responsibility. Thank goodness.

Jon put up an easel we had brought for this exact purpose and put the picture, mounted on card stock, up for the jury to see. 'This photograph, taken at the scene of the murder, clearly shows part of the victim's body on the floor,' I told them. I had made sure to crop out some of the more gory areas. They'd seen these pictures already and I wanted it to be the prosecution's fault they'd had to look at all that blood. There was a little in this picture because I needed to make a point, but every juror knew it could have been much worse. 'This is the side of the room that leads to the door into the den, where the defendant was found. Yet there is no blood trail leading from the body to the door.'

'Is the defense questioning the witness?' Valencia said, hand in the air.

'Please ask the witness a question,' Hawthorne agreed.

'Detective, why no blood?'

'I really couldn't say,' Brisbane answered. All that fuss for *I don't know*.

'Why can't you say?' I asked.

'There are any number of possible reasons. She might have wrapped the statue in her clothing so it didn't drip.' Brisbane looked pleased with himself for thinking that one up.

I made a point of looking at him for a moment, but not too long a moment. 'The defendant was found in the next room wearing a T-shirt and linen trousers and clutching the statue,' I said. 'How could she have possibly wrapped it in her clothing?'

'Objection.' Valencia. Who else? 'The defense is asking the witness to speculate.'

'I'll withdraw the question, Your Honor. Detective Brisbane, is it possible that someone else killed Wendy Bryan, did indeed wrap the TeeVee in something else or take it elsewhere, and then the defendant found it, discovered the body and was so shocked that she is unable to remember those few seconds before she ended up curled on the floor of the den and crying her eyes out?'

'Again, Your Honor.' Guess who. 'The defense counsel is once again calling upon Detective Brisbane to speculate on something he was not there to witness.'

That gave me an opening. 'Your Honor, the prosecution has been doing nothing but that since Detective Brisbane sat down. He was not there when the crime was being committed and yet

Mr Valencia has asked him a number of questions about his opinions regarding how it was done. How it this different?'

'Objection overruled,' the judge said. 'The witness will answer.'

'Is it possible,' I reiterated, 'that someone other than Cynthia Sutton killed Wendy Bryan and then left the TeeVee there for her to find, thus causing the fingerprints and the bloodstains?'

'A lot of things are possible,' Brisbane said, unwittingly giving me a 'reasonable doubt' argument for my closing statement.

'Is that one of them?' I asked.

'I guess so.'

'No more questions.' I sat back down at the defense table.

Once prompted, Valencia stood up for redirect. 'In your opinion as an experienced homicide detective, is it likely someone else killed Wendy Bryan and then made the murder weapon disappear until they could miraculously hand it to Cynthia Sutton in another room?'

'No,' Brisbane said.

'No further questions.' Valencia made a point of looking self-righteous as he walked back and sat down.

'*I'm* beginning to wonder if I did it,' Cynthia whispered to me.

'Trust me,' I said. 'You didn't.'

I got the chance to prove it once Valencia, having exhausted the number of law enforcement officials he could trot out (plus Wendy's housekeeper and a few lesser 'experts') rested his case, I began calling witnesses for the defense. Because I'd promised to give Valencia some time before I trotted out the star witness on nail polish, I began with Gail Adams, the representative of the Academy of TV and Video. Gail, with whom I'd spoken three times before, couldn't have been a better rep for a body that liked to project dignity. She was polite, soft-spoken, but authoritative and as proper as a fourth-grade teacher.

After some back-and-forth from Valencia, which ended up in pretty much the same exchange we'd had before about Gail, she was sworn in and seated in the witness box. I began by asking about the academy and her position there, to get the jury acquainted and establish that Gail would know about such things. But I kept that part of the questioning brief, because not just the jury but the judge certainly was wondering what strange point I might be trying to make.

And make no mistake: it was indeed a strange point.

'Ms Adams, what is the composition of a TeeVee award?'

Gail nodded once, having known in advance I'd ask the question. But she had known the answer off the top of her head the first time I'd called and asked her. Gail knew everything there was to know about TeeVee awards and television. I had been holding back on introducing her to Angie, who probably would have monopolized the rest of Gail's natural life asking her questions about actors and shows.

'The TeeVee is made of copper, nickel and silver and has a veneer of gold on its outside, except for the base,' she said.

'Aside from the gold, those are not soft metals,' I noted.

'No. It's quite a sturdy statue.' Gail seemed proud of the construction of the award that had been identified as the weapon responsible for the death of Wendy Bryan.

'How much does it weigh?' I asked.

'A little under seven pounds.'

'Your Honor,' Valencia said, standing and looking pouty. 'I'm sure this is very interesting testimony, but what does it have to do with this case?'

I looked at Judge Hawthorne. 'If Mr Valencia waits another minute, the relevancy will become very clear,' I said.

Hawthorne nodded. 'Proceed.'

I turned back to face Gail and caught a glimpse of the jury, who mostly seemed to be accepting her well. You do see facial expressions and these were – at the worst – respectful. 'As you said, the TeeVee is a very sturdy award. Now, I'm going to show you a photograph and I'd appreciate it if you'd tell me what you can discern from it.'

The picture, of the statuette that had been taken from Cynthia at the scene, was one I'd shown to Gail before when we were prepping her for testimony. I'd already entered into evidence and Valencia had seen it and, for once, not offered an objection, so he and the jurors knew it had been identified as the murder weapon. Hawthorne had it projected onto the flat screen mounted overhead so the jury could see it. But I handed the original print to Gail for her examination.

It took her only a few seconds. 'That's not a real TeeVee award,' she said.

For the first time in this trial there was a murmur among the spectators, and a few members of the jury looked at each other in something like disbelief.

Cynthia looked positively stricken.

I didn't feign surprise because the jurors surely knew that I had been expecting Gail to say that, but I did ask her, 'How can you be sure after such a quick look at that picture?'

'The physics of the statue are wrong,' she answered. 'It's the same general shape but it's proportionally incorrect, and the fact that the figure has been bent forward like that proves it's not authentic.' Gail spoke with authority but not in a way that made her seem like a know-it-all. I knew from our conversations that she'd never testified in court before, but the experience certainly wasn't overwhelming her.

'A real TeeVee wouldn't bend like that?' I asked, just to drive the point home.

'Absolutely not. It's too dense and the metal is too hard. You'd need some very strong tools and probably superhuman dexterity to bend a TeeVee like that.' I wanted to get Gail to testify at all my trials, even the divorces.

'But Cynthia Sutton was awarded a genuine TeeVee award, wasn't she?' That was to make my client feel better and to establish that such an object did exist in her possession.

'Oh, goodness yes,' Gail said. 'She won it fair and square and it was given to her at the Prime Time TeeVee Awards show three years ago. If the real one was lost or stolen, it would be replaced by the Academy.'

At the defense table Cynthia's shoulders relaxed a little. She looked at Angie, seated behind her. Angie smiled reassuringly and nodded. Actors are so insecure.

'So if this was what killed Wendy Bryan . . .' I said.

'It was not Cynthia Sutton's TeeVee,' Gail assured me.

'Agreed. One last question, Ms Adams. Can a TeeVee winner sell her award for money?'

'The Academy tends to frown on that and will take legal action if someone, even the original recipient, attempts to sell a TeeVee award,' Gail said.

That was all I could possibly have wanted so I turned her over to Valencia, who looked just a little flustered as he approached the witness stand. 'Ms Adams, are you an expert in metallurgy?' he began. Oh, good. He was going to try to make my witness, who was anything but, look silly.

'No,' Gail told him. 'I am an expert in the TeeVee awards.' She was gracious enough not to add, *And that isn't one*, which I thought was awfully telling about her character.

'So you can't say for certain that the metal couldn't have been bent in order to create a weapon,' Valencia went on, seemingly having missed Gail's answer to his previous question.

'Yes, I can. I'm very familiar with the composition of these awards, and they can't be bent that severely by hand, or even with most household tools.'

Valencia thought he had an opening there. 'Then what sort of tool *could* do that kind of alteration on the statuette?'

'Probably an industrial vice or a blacksmith,' Gail told him.

I could see the heave of his chest as he sighed, but he rallied. 'But even if this pictured object is not an official TeeVee award, it might still be strong enough to stab a woman to death, is that correct?'

'I would have no way of knowing,' Gail said. 'I'm not an expert on *fake* TeeVee awards.'

'No further questions.' Valencia, having made the point he needed to make but none of the others, sat down and looked exhausted.

I stood up. 'If Mr Valencia prefers, I could ask Ms Adams to bring in a real TeeVee award and Mr Valencia could bring in a professional wrestler to see if he can bend it as we see in the photograph.'

'Sit down, Ms Moss,' the judge said. I always listen to judges.

THIRTY-EIGHT

'Leopold Kolensky was poisoned,' Nate said.

We were standing on the steps of the courthouse. I'd planned on going home with Angie, getting some Thai food and absolutely not thinking about Cynthia's case, except all the time because who was I kidding? But Nate had shown up just as we left the building and dropped this particular bomb on me.

'OK,' I said. 'I know you, and you don't just make stuff like that up. So who have you been talking to and what do you have to prove that Leopold didn't die of a heart attack?'

Nate was in such an urgent frame of mind that he didn't ogle Angie at all and he forgot to show us how smug he was about how well he did his job. 'Talked to a friend of mine who works in the ME's office and had him look at some samples taken at the time. Nobody bothered to check for poisons because the guy had a heart attack, but sure enough when he ran the tests it came back positive for lily of the valley.'

Angie, who was probably quite pleased not to be ogled for once (although she likes Nate fine) looked at him with confusion. 'Lily of the valley?'

'Yah. Apparently it's a cardiac glycoside, and if you get enough of one of those, it can look a lot like you had a heart attack.'

I was starting to see a theory develop. 'And how do you get too much of it?' I asked Nate.

'It has a slightly sweet taste.'

'So it can be hidden in food,' I said. I wasn't really talking to Nate so much as thinking out loud. 'Probably dessert.'

'And . . . this guy Leopold ate too much of it because it reminded him of candy?' Angie is very smart. Don't let her fool you, because she'll try.

'I think the important thing right now is to find out what was on the menu at Wendy Bryan's house,' I said.

When I called Lieutenant Trench with my theory, which he

described as 'wild-eyed', despite not being able to see my eyes at all, he used his best Vulcan ability to suppress emotion and did not let out an exasperated sigh. I know he wanted to. But instead he suggested that Nate and I (and Angie, but Trench didn't suggest that) drop by his office to work things out.

'I don't see how this helps you with your case,' he said after Nate explained what he had discovered. 'Your client is not charged with killing Leopold Kolensky.'

'Come on, Lieutenant, you're a homicide detective,' I said, although I was pretty sure he had not in any way forgotten that. 'Doesn't the possibility of a second, or in this case, a first murder taking place and involving the same woman tingle your spidey-sense just a tad?'

'My . . . spidey-sense.' Trench seemed to roll the term around in his mouth for a moment and, for lack of a spittoon, did nothing about it. 'Trust me, Ms Moss, I will be perfectly happy to investigate something when I'm assigned to do it by the chief of detectives. And if there is a police report filed that indicates the need for a homicide detective, I'm sure that I or one of my fellow peace officers will look into it to the best of his or her ability.'

I wanted to make a wry comment on the idea of 'peace officers', but I liked Trench in a way and didn't want to insult him specifically. 'I'm surprised at you, Lieutenant,' I said. 'I didn't think procedure would get in your way when a possible murder victim hasn't received justice.'

That's when things got weird. Trench wrinkled his nose. No, really. Just like a real person with a problem on his mind. Trench! I know!

He took in a breath and looked at me. 'I would greatly appreciate it if you did no more about this for the time being,' he said. 'As I said, I see no benefit to your efforts to acquit Ms Sutton of her mother-in-law's murder.'

'I think it has a *lot* to do with Wendy Bryan's murder and I think it will direct suspicion away from my client,' I told Trench, trying to goad him into revealing something he knew. Because he knew something. He *always* knows something. 'And I intend to bring it up in court tomorrow. Can you give me a reason that I shouldn't?'

Trent remained silent for a moment, which was his way of

groaning. 'Ms Moss, I have no authority to tell you what you can or cannot do in a court of law. But I can inform you that it would seriously jeopardize an investigation I have been conducting for months if you were to make public what you think you know about the death of Leopold Kolensky.'

'Leopold Kolensky was poisoned with lily of the valley, a cardiac glycoside that can simulate a heart attack,' Angie told him, while Nate looked surprised. He might have wanted to drop this bomb himself but he seemed more shocked that Angie would remember all the words in the right order. People – OK, men – tend to underestimate Angie, usually at their own expense. 'He probably ate it in a chocolate mousse he had at dinner at Wendy Bryan's house the night he died, on an evening we know for a fact that Cynthia Sutton was not present.'

'She was filming for her series that night, and we have a sign-in file from the studio that confirms it,' Nate said. No matter what he needed to get some of his own back. Which was fair, since he was the one who'd unearthed all this information, including the studio records.

Trench sat back in his chair and laced his fingers behind his head, a typical position he used when thinking. Of course, he was thinking all the time, but when he was really concentrating, the finger-lacing thing was his go-to posture.

He looked at me. 'You bring an unusually loyal team with you,' he said. 'The level of commitment is impressive.'

'You're trying not to say anything, Lieutenant, and I respect you well enough to understand that you have good reasons. But my job is to keep an innocent woman out of prison for the rest of her life and you are playing it cagey with me.' I leaned forward and put my chin on my hands, elbows on the edge of Trench's desk, which I knew he wouldn't like. It was for effect. 'If you know something that can help me, I'd like you to consider that when we knew something that could help *you*, we came straight here to tell you about it. And I *can* decide not to mention this information in court tomorrow, but I need a reason.'

Trench stood up, probably because of the proximity of my face, and walked around a bit behind his desk. He wasn't exactly pacing, but it would be hard to say he definitely wasn't. 'This is what I can tell you, Ms Moss,' he said. 'Mrs Bryan's business, which was being managed by the late Mr Kolensky, was leveraged beyond normal limits. In other words, she was going broke. She had Mr Kolensky to her house weekly for dinner as a gesture of support and confidence in him. But that practice ended about seven months ago, and she did not invite him again for two months. Then he visited her for dinner once more and died that evening. You say it was a result of poisoning, the pathologist who did the autopsy said it was a coronary issue. You may take from that what you will. Now if you don't mind, I have other pressing business.'

And that's when it dawned on me. 'You've been investigating Kolensky's death the whole time,' I said to Trench. 'That's why you were outside Wendy Bryan's house the night she was murdered. Did you suspect her housekeeper, Isobel Sanchez?'

'You are speculating,' Trench said, his voice a bit sterner. 'And you are speculating without sufficient facts. That's a dangerous game, Ms Moss. I'd advise you to reconsider what I've told you before and pay special attention to the people who have made several attempts on your life, and why they might be doing so.' Just because Judy had stayed outside, he thought I'd relaxed my security efforts. I made no move to change his mind.

I stood up, which probably was a relief to Trench. 'I have just one question for you, Lieutenant.'

'Ask it quickly so you can leave,' he suggested.

'Do you know which nights Isobel Sanchez used to have off?'

THIRTY-NINE

'**M**r Conway, did Wendy Bryan ever delay a payment to you?'

Against my better judgment I'd listed Pete Conway as a defense witness, on the hope that he could speak to the financial problems at Rafael that I believed were among the reasons she had been murdered, which would help put my client, who was *not* having financial problems, in the clear. Pete wasn't exactly a friendly witness, but Valencia hadn't seen a reason to call him as a prosecution witness, which made sense. I wasn't sure Pete and Cynthia had actually ever met, so he'd have a serious problem implicating her.

'It's Chirac,' Pete said.

The stenographer, because yes, we still use them, looked up. 'Excuse me?' she said. Judge Hawthorne, who was visibly displeased by the stenographer performing an end run around her, decided not to say anything about it. But she nodded to Pete that he should answer.

'My name. It's Pierre Chirac.'

'That isn't your legal name, is it?' I asked.

'I am in the process of making it my legal name,' Pete sniffed.

It's a one-hour process (including waiting in line) to change your name at a clerk's office, but I let it go. I had to remember Pete was supposedly on my side. 'Of course. Mr Chirac, would you please answer the question? Did Wendy Bryan ever delay paying you after she sold your artwork at her gallery?'

I knew the answer to that question but I needed to have Pete say it. 'I had not sold a piece at Rafael at the time Wendy died,' he said, barely containing a sniffle. 'My debut show was still being planned.'

From there on, his testimony virtually matched Penelope Hannigan's but for choice of words. Wendy, it seemed, was a secular saint who had propelled the careers of young artists (although neither could name one) and was about to send Pete – sorry, Pierre – hurtling into the stratosphere.

Pierre: She found me literally painting in an attic and saw something no one else had seen.

Penelope: Wendy had the best eye for talent I've ever known.

Pierre: I practically lived at her house for three months when I couldn't pay the rent in my boarding house.

*Penelope: She advanced Pierre fifty thousand dollars before the opening but didn't live long enough to pay it.**

'Wendy Bryan promised Pierre fifty thousand dollars in advance of his gallery show?' I asked. 'Is that commonplace in the art industry?'

---

* Testimony taken from the transcript of State of California v. Cynthia D. Sutton

Penelope winced a bit at the use of the word *industry*. 'The art world,' she said. 'No, galleries virtually never pay in anticipation of sales. Most take art on consignment, meaning the artist makes the piece available and then he and the gallery split the profit when the piece sells. Some galleries even charge artists to showcase their work. Wendy paid Pierre an advance. That was one way in which she was extraordinary.'

'How did you find out about Wendy's death?' I asked Pierre. It was a polite way of saying, *Where were you when someone stabbed her?*

'Penelope called me with the news.'

'So you were not living in Wendy's house when she died?' I said.

'Oh, no. I hadn't been living in the guest bungalow for months.' *The guest bungalow. F. Scott Fitzgerald was right about the rich. Except that he was wrong.*

Still, I had to go on asking Pete questions. 'How did you react?'

'I was devastated.'

'I have no doubt you were' (especially since the fifty grand was now gone) 'but what did you do?' I asked.

'I went right over there because, I don't know, I guess I wasn't going to believe it until I saw it.' Pete blinked a few times in an attempt to conjure tears. It had the effect of making him look as if he was choking them back, which I guess was pretty much the same thing.

'What did you do when you got to Wendy's house?'

'Oh, nothing.' Pete seemed baffled by the question. 'The police were all over the place and wouldn't let anyone in.'

'How did you hear about Wendy Bryan's death?' I asked Penelope.

'Isobel Sanchez called me,' she answered. 'I guess she was off that night because she was calling from her apartment in the Hollywood hills. She tried to break it to me gently, but there's no easy way to tell someone a dear friend has been murdered with a TV award.' There was something about the way Penelope said *TV award* that made me wonder if I was a snob about television and should give Patrick a break.

'Was there any discussion, that night or after, of the fifty thousand dollars . . . *Pierre* had been promised by Wendy?' I said. If she could be a snob about TV, I could be a snot about Pete's desire to become French for no particular reason.

'We asked about it, of course, but Wendy's finances were in such a chaotic state. Her executive manager had just died of a heart attack and I don't think there was anyone in charge of her money at all.'

'Was that matter ever resolved?'

'No,' Penelope said. She looked away as if the lack of eye contact might mean I wasn't paying attention to what she said. 'The estate has been . . . well, there has not been clarity about the financial situation so far.'

'Aren't you and Mr Conway' (because he had not legally changed his name) 'suing Wendy Bryan's estate for the fifty thousand?' It was a matter of public record and I'm a lawyer. You thought I wouldn't find out?

Penelope mumbled a bit and Judge Hawthorne leaned down toward her. 'Speak up please, Ms Hannigan.'

'I said it's really two hundred thousand,' Penelope said too loudly. 'We are also seeking relief for emotional suffering.'

I walked directly in front of Penelope so she couldn't avoid my gaze and, for a witness I'd called on my own, I leaned over a little aggressively. 'Think carefully, Ms Hannigan, and remember there are penalties for perjury.'

Valencia stood up. 'Your Honor, does the defense attorney realize she called Ms Hannigan as a friendly witness?' He was posturing to make me look mean to the jury, and in this case I really didn't mind very much. It would be a passing moment and my closing statement was a couple of days away. I could win them back.

'Is there an objection there, Mr Valencia?' Hawthorne was playing it by the book. Good for her and not bad for me.

'No, Your Honor.' Valencia sat down. The jury probably didn't even understand what had just happened.

'Proceed, Ms Moss.'

I didn't lean in as far this time; my point had been made. 'Ms Hannigan, were you aware *before* she died that Wendy Bryan was in financial trouble and that she couldn't pay Mr Conway the fifty thousand dollars?'

Penelope's eyes flashed anger and a few of the jurors at least probably saw it. 'No,' she said.

'And yet you had contacted a Mr M.H. Brady, a lawyer special-
izing in breach of promise suits, a week before Wendy Bryan
died,' I said. 'Didn't you? Weren't you asking him about suing
her for the fifty grand?'

Again Valencia leapt to his feet. 'This time I have an objection, Your Honor. Counsel is badgering her own witness.'

'I have the records from Mr Brady's office and can produce
Mr Brady's executive secretary if necessary, Your Honor,' I said.
Everybody in Hollywood is an executive something.

'Then she doesn't need an answer from Ms Hannigan,' Valencia
argued.

'Maybe not, but I'd like to hear it,' Hawthorne told him.
'Overruled. Ms Hannigan?'

Penelope stared forward. 'What?'

'Please answer the question.' Hawthorne didn't have the court
stenographer read it back because she knew perfectly well that
Penelope had heard my question the first time.

Still, she took a moment to compose herself, as if she'd been
horribly insulted and needed a break to contain her horrified
emotions. 'We were in touch with Mr Brady to discuss the possibility of a lawsuit, but it was not filed until after Wendy had
passed away.'

'How long before she died did you know about the tenuous
state of Mrs Bryan's finances?' I asked.

'As I said before, I *didn't* know,' Penelope fairly snarled.

'Then why were you consulting about a possible lawsuit, which
became a real lawsuit?'

'Because she hadn't paid Pierre,' Penelope answered. 'I didn't
know that she hadn't paid anyone else, either.'

I had asked one last question of Pete. 'Did you and Wendy
Bryan have a romantic relationship?'

Valencia: 'Objection!'

'I withdraw the question.'

FORTY

'How do you think we're doing?' Patrick asked me.

The court was in recess for half an hour because Judge Hawthorne had business she needed to oversee and we (Patrick, Cynthia, Jon, Angie, the inescapable Emily and I) had taken over a conference room with the help of a custodian named Will, who was clearly hoping Angie would smile upon him. Which she did. Smile. That was it.

'We're holding our own,' I said honestly, sipping from a water bottle I'd gotten from a hallway vending machine. Talking makes my voice raspy, which sounds threatening to a jury. I was trying to avoid that. Hot tea would have been better, except that I hate tea. 'But we haven't scored the knockout blow we need just yet.'

Cynthia who, as in most of our conferences, was trying to distract herself because, she'd told me, 'I get scared when I think about it,' looked up from the paperback novel she was reading. 'Do you have that ready, Sandy?' she asked. 'Is there a knockout on its way?'

'We haven't found the real killer yet,' Patrick said, then saw the look I gave him and held up his hands in a defensive position. 'Sorry, love.'

'Don't call me that.'

'I can't help it. I'm British.'

Jon, who had been obsessing over his phone from the time Hawthorne had banged her gavel for recess, didn't look up now. 'I think we have enough for reasonable doubt.'

I nodded in his direction even though he didn't see me. What was going on with his phone was too fascinating and probably incredibly nerdish. Jon follows sites about comic books, horror movies and superhero TV shows. Jon is complex.

'I agree,' I told him, 'but juries are funny. I'd feel better if we could cover over *unreasonable* doubt as well. I want each and every one of those people to be absolutely certain Cynthia didn't kill Wendy Bryan.'

'I didn't,' Cynthia said for, by my count, the zillionth time. We left a pause in the conversation out of habit.

'Will you have Cynthia testify?' Patrick asked. He knew that I'd been waffling on the subject because of Cynthia's fame. Anything she said, no matter how affecting, could be described by the prosecution as a 'terrific acting performance', much in the way that Patrick's testimony had been during his trial. I wasn't sure if that had affected the jury because we'd never actually made it to a verdict.

I decided that for once I'd find out what my client wanted instead of telling her what she should want. 'What do you think, Cynthia?'

'I'd be terrified,' she said without hesitation.

'I understand that,' her brother told her, 'but it might help convince the jury of your innocence. You are the best actress I've ever seen at evoking sympathy.'

'The last thing we need is Cynthia acting on the—' was as far as I got.

'Aha!' Jon said from his corner, hunched over his phone. He looked up at me, grinning. 'Sandy, the charges against you have been dropped.'

I blinked a couple of times, partially because I'd been so engrossed in Cynthia's case that I'd forgotten I was an alleged criminal myself, but also because the news came so completely out of left field. 'They have?' That was the best I could do.

'Yes.' Jon stood up and brought his phone to where I was sitting. On the screen, which he indicated, was a message from Judge Evans, who had presided over my arraignment. It read: *DA has withdrawn charges v. S. Moss. Documents forwarded to your email.*

'Well, that was heartfelt,' I said. 'What made this happen? What did you do, Jon?'

'Surely the district attorney realized the charges were absurd,' Patrick said. Like that ever happens.

'I didn't do anything,' Jon answered. Neither of us said anything to Patrick, who was speaking quietly to Angie at the moment. Emily, as was her habit, was looking displeased, mostly in my direction. 'I mean, I had filed a brief calling for the charges to be dismissed due to lack of evidence, but it wasn't with Judge

Evans. This started happening while we were in session but I
didn't see it until just now.'

That didn't make much sense. The Los Angeles DA wasn't
going to reverse a decision based on a brief that probably
hadn't had time to be seen by anyone yet. I wasn't that high a
priority within the city's criminal justice system.

Was I?

'I sense Lieutenant Trench's presence in all this, but there's
no use in saying anything to him because he'll deflect or deny
it outright,' I told Jon. 'Either way, thank you!'

Just then Jon's phone pinged again and his face got more
serious when he scanned it. 'There appears to be one provision,'
he reported. This time he didn't show me the screen. 'They want
a look at your client Madelyn Forsythe's book.'

Her book? Was Maddie an author? 'What book?'

'According to this, her book of clients. From her prostitution
ring.' Jon looked at me. 'I thought you said she was innocent.'

'She is! They're being crazy and using me for leverage against
Maddie for something she doesn't have!' I took a deep breath
because crying seemed unprofessional and that's when Will
opened the door.

'They're ready for you,' he said.

I couldn't try Maddie Forsythe's case now, nor could I agree
to the asinine provisions that Longabaugh (because it had to be
the prosecutor) had attached in offering a possible end to my
own criminal charges. If this was an attempt on some high-flyers
to distract me from Cynthia Sutton's murder trial . . . well, it
was actually working pretty well.

'I'd like to recall Isobel Sanchez,' I told Judge Hawthorne
when we resumed. This move had been included in my witness
list to make it impossible for Valencia to leap up and object to
my calling one of his witnesses when I'd already had a chance
to cross-examine her after he'd finished his questioning. To his
credit he didn't even flinch. Hawthorne nodded and the bailiff,
a guy named Bart, called Sanchez, who obviously knew that
was going to happen. She walked to the stand and was reminded
of her oath to tell the truth, which I have always thought was
kind of funny. We're told that we're on our honor to be honest
in the witness box and the penalties for perjury are rarely

mentioned. This is mandated under the You Promised Act of 1958.

Sanchez got herself comfortable in the witness chair, no doubt reminding herself that she had sort of resented me the last time she was here, so she should start by scowling. She was good but she couldn't hold a candle to Emily, who was seated to the side of Patrick that wasn't occupied by Angie. I wasn't intimidated by either one, but it was a little odd to see from a witness before I'd asked my first question.

'Mrs Sanchez,' I began, remembering that *Ms* appeared to be a disliked term by the witness, 'what were your hours when you were working as Wendy Bryan's housekeeper?'

'I lived in the house five days a week, and the schedule would vary,' she answered. I saw Sanchez relax a bit, just a bit, after I'd asked such a mundane question. She didn't know what was coming.

'If Mrs Bryan had a dinner guest, would you always be on call? Did you have to work every evening she invited someone over for dinner?'

It'd be interesting to see how she answered, I thought. Sanchez might have been getting an inkling of what I was going for and she didn't want to lie, either for moral or practical reasons. The skin around her mouth got a little taut.

'I would almost always be expected to work on those nights. We had a small staff and I would be called upon to help with the dinner parties.' It was the *almost* that gave her away. She did know where I was going and she wasn't happy about it.

'Were you working a night not long before Mrs Bryan died when she had invited her executive manager Leopold Kolensky to dinner?' I asked.

Sanchez looked at the judge, perhaps to ask for permission not to answer, but thought better of it. 'She had Mr Kolensky in for dinner many times,' she said. 'I was there almost every time.' Again, that word *almost*.

'But not this time. It was the first occasion that Mrs Bryan had invited Mr Kolensky in for a very long stretch, wasn't it? They hadn't really been social for quite some time, had they?'

'I was not involved in Mrs Bryan's social affairs,' Sanchez said.

'Do you recall seeing Mr Kolensky there many times in the year before Mrs Bryan died?' I asked.

'No.'

'So on the night he came back for a dinner, just the two of them, were you working?' I said.

'No.'

I didn't do the showy thing of looking surprised, because it wouldn't have helped me and no one would have believed it anyway. I'm a lousy actress and would never have showcased my amateur skills in front of Cynthia Sutton and Patrick McNabb. Instead, I simply asked, 'Why not?'

'Mrs Bryan said she wanted it to be friendly and so she wanted them to be alone.'

'Did you cook the dinner?'

Her eyes flashed as she looked at me. She knew I knew. '*No*,' she said.

'Was there a full-time chef on the premises?' I asked.

'No.'

'So who cooked that evening?'

Sanchez, cornered, had no choice but to implicate herself in a crime she didn't commit, or to give up her employer, and she wisely went for the latter. 'Mrs Bryan did.'

'Are you aware of what happened later that night?' I asked.

Very calmly and evenly, she answered, 'Mr Kolensky passed away of a heart attack.'

'Is that what happened?'

Now Valencia, probably not knowing why he felt like he should, objected. 'What relevance does this have to the case of Wendy Bryan's murder?' he asked Hawthorne.

'It has a great deal of relevance, Your Honor,' I said. 'Because we have evidence that Leopold Kolensky did not die of a heart attack. He was poisoned at the dinner he ate in Wendy Bryan's house that night.' I'd cleared it with Trench before bringing this up.

There was an actual gasp, an audible one, in the room. Even a couple of the jurors looked shocked, but no doubt they were also wondering exactly what Valencia professed to be next: 'There is no evidence on the record that Mr Kolensky was poisoned but, even if he was, Your Honor, what does that have to do with Wendy Bryan being stabbed with a TeeVee award?'

'Ms Moss?' the judge said.

'I believe it goes to motive, Your Honor, and if you'll give us a little time to show that it is what happened, the court will see the relevance.'

Hawthorne considered and Valencia got a little sweatier in this hot courtroom. 'I'll give you a *little* leeway, Ms Moss, but I don't intend to turn this trial into an investigation of Mr Kolensky's death, is that clear?'

'Perfectly, Your Honor, and I'll see to it that doesn't happen. Now, Mrs Sanchez, were you aware of the implication that Mrs Bryan might have poisoned Mr Kolensky?'

Sanchez, who had no doubt been hoping the judge would rule that she didn't have to talk about Kolensky anymore, exhaled. 'Not at the time, no,' she said.

'Not at the time. So you became aware of the possibility later?'

Sanchez clearly didn't want to answer that one. She looked up at the bench. 'I don't know anything, Your Honor,' she said. 'Do I have to say things I'm not sure of?'

'You should just answer the question as honestly and clearly as you can,' Hawthorne said. 'If you feel that you would be implicated in a criminal act, you have the option of citing the Fifth Amendment to the Constitution, which says you can't be compelled to do that.'

The witness nodded and took a moment to collect her thoughts. 'Mrs Bryan told me not to ask about the dinner with Mr Kolensky and to say that he left the house that night feeling fine if anyone asked me,' she said. She did not look at me, Hawthorne, Valencia or any of the jurors. She seemed ashamed.

'You also brought some vegetation to Mrs Bryan from your home, didn't you?' I asked.

'Yes. I knew that Mrs Bryan had asked me to pick some flowers for her because I live in the hills and she said the things that grew near her weren't pretty. And she asked me for lily of the valley, but I didn't think that was such a pretty flower. It wasn't until she asked me again that I brought some.'

I gestured to Jon, who brought a folder with him to the bailiff. 'Your Honor, my associate has a revised autopsy report on

Leopold Kolensky. It indicates that he was poisoned with lily of the valley, which can cause symptoms very similar to a heart attack in people who have already had some coronary conditions. I'd like to enter it into evidence.'

'Your Honor, the prosecution hasn't had a chance to review this report and wasn't aware of its existence until this minute.' Valencia didn't want the autopsy report to be part of the trial and I didn't blame him. It pointed at a great many things going on in Wendy Bryan's household that Cynthia Sutton had absolutely no authority over or knowledge of.

So I wasn't surprised when Hawthorne said, 'I think the prosecution should have time to study the report. But I'm still waiting to hear how it is relevant to the murder of Wendy Bryan, Ms Moss.'

'Yes, Your Honor. Mrs Sanchez, let's discuss another matter. What kind of car do you drive?'

Valencia, who had been huddling over the autopsy report with his second chair, flung his hands into the air. (Some will ask how he caught them. We passed that joke in Jersey decades ago.) 'What kind of car? Your Honor? Relevance?'

Hawthorne gestured him down. 'Go on, Ms Moss.'

'I have a Prius,' Sanchez said.

'Yes, you do. In fact, you have a brand-new Prius you bought just a month after Wendy Bryan died. Now, given that you have already testified that Mrs Bryan was having some difficulty paying you in a timely fashion for months before she died, can you tell us how, according to the dealer where you bought that new Prius, you paid cash for it, and the car cost over thirty thousand dollars. Are you just that good at saving money?'

Sanchez looked me straight in the eye. 'I had some money saved, yes. Because I knew that the job wouldn't last forever.'

'Mrs Sanchez,' I said. 'Are you familiar with an eBay account with the name *mujer poderosa*? Roughly translated, "mighty woman"?'

Sanchez got visibly flustered. Her cheeks reddened a little. She bit in on her lips. I saw some tremble in her head, as if she were holding back rage. 'I don't know about that account.'

'No?' I said. 'Because eBay records suggest it's registered to a Rosa Rodriguez. Isn't Rodriguez your maiden name?'

'Yes, but my first name is Isobel.'

'And your sister's name is Rosa. Mrs Sanchez, the eBay account I mentioned sold, over the past year and a half, a large number of items whose original bills of sale could be traced to Wendy Bryan. And, according to a clerk at Mighty Mike's Pawn Shop on Sepulveda Avenue, someone came in six months ago trying to get cash for a TeeVee award whose nameplate suggested it was Cynthia Sutton's. Are you aware of these sales?'

Sanchez didn't miss a beat. 'Judge, I think I need to use the Fifth Amendment.'

FORTY-ONE

'She had a scheme with her sister,' Nate Garrigan said. 'It's clear from the eBay records that Isobel was taking things from Wendy's house, either with or without her permission, and selling them for cash. She must have taken a lot of jewelry and silver because those were the most prominent things on the eBay account over the last year and a half.'

'If we could get bank records, we'd see the deposits, wouldn't we?' Angie asked.

'Probably, but we'd need a subpoena for that,' I told her. 'If it comes to it, I'll request one.'

We were at a bar around the corner from the courthouse. Cynthia, exhausted from the day's testimony, had gone home, as had Jon, but Patrick was there in his 'civilian' disguise, a baseball cap down over his eyebrows and sunglasses below that. I was having a margarita because I was an adult and I could; Nate had a beer (Rolling Rock, which he considers exotic because it's 'imported from Pennsylvania'), Patrick was drinking club soda and Angie had a glass of white wine which she was downing in swigs.

Emily, life of the party that she always was, was drinking still water from the tap because why should bartenders and wait staff make a living?

'How'd you find the eBay account in the first place?' I asked Nate.

'They actually tried to list the TeeVee there and then pulled it,' he said. 'The TV Academy doesn't care much for something like that.' He hadn't been in court when Gail Adams had told us exactly the same thing, almost in those words, and I didn't see the point in stomping on his good mood.

'But eBay records are public?' Angie said. 'That doesn't seem right.'

'You don't have to ask for records,' Nate pointed out. 'Once you get the name, and I got that from the attempt to sell the TeeVee, you can trace someone's posts as far back as you want to go. I just didn't know where to look until just now. And finding out that Sanchez had a sister named Rosa Rodriguez was very helpful.'

'Does this really help Cynthia's case?' Patrick asked. His focus is always on the person he cares about, which is admirable even when it's harshing your mellow.

'The idea that they were trying to sell the TeeVee makes a big difference,' I suggested. 'Cynthia clearly wasn't doing that. And if she'd found the fake TeeVee, the one that *could* be bent into a weapon . . .' Suddenly it dawned on me.

'She could get mad and kill the person she thought sold her TeeVee,' Angie said.

'But she didn't,' Patrick insisted. Cynthia wasn't there to say it, so he had to take up the slack.

We all sat there looking at each other for a long moment. I was already devising arguments against Valencia making exactly that insinuation. Nate took another gulp of Rolling Rock. Angie, to whom it would never occur to feel guilty, looked as though she felt guilty. Patrick, for the first time since I'd met him, appeared frightened. Emily looked over at me and mouthed, *'Bitch.'*

You know. Thursday.

Judy, sitting at another table to have a better vantage point of the door, said nothing, but that was Judy.

'Where'd they get the fake TeeVee?' I asked no one in particular. No sense engaging with Emily.

Nate answered because of course he would. He had the best chance of actually knowing. 'Probably online, but those are records I can't get without a subpoena. Or they could walk into any one of a hundred novelty shops in Hollywood and find something.'

'That one was especially realistic,' Patrick said. 'It fooled Cynthia.'

'There are probably only a couple of companies making fakes that good,' Nate said, rubbing his chin. That was a 'thinking' gesture that was either meant for theatrical purposes or had morphed into a real thing over the years. He looked at me specifically. 'Does it really matter where they got it? I can do some looking around.'

But I was already on to the next thing in my mind and couldn't believe it had taken me this long to consider it. 'Patrick, how well did the people who worked for Wendy and Cynthia know each other?'

Patrick didn't look like he understood. 'You mean were they sleeping together? Not that I know about.'

'No, that's not what I mean. Were there any people who were working for both of them, maybe on a part-time basis?'

I don't know why but suddenly Emily looked excited, like a third-grader who *finally* knew one of the answers for a favorite teacher.

'The spiritual advisor,' she said. 'Crystalis.'

'Chrysanthemum,' Patrick corrected her. 'What about her?'

I was a few feet ahead. 'Did she advise Wendy as well?' I asked Patrick.

'I don't think so,' he said. 'I'll text Cynthia and ask.' He pulled out his phone. 'But I am almost certain she didn't.'

But that hadn't been my original idea anyway. 'What about the manicurist?'

Angie grinned.

FORTY-TWO

'My name is Sevda Lakonya.' The woman being sworn in as a defense witness was in her early thirties and dressed considerably more expensively than I was.

And, I noticed, her fingernails were polished and shaped so artistically they almost looked like no one had worked for hours on them.

Bart the bailiff finished swearing Sevda in and she sat down gracefully. She'd looked like she was traveling inside a cloud since the moment she had arrived in the courtroom. It wasn't a flashy thing, not like a major Hollywood star entering the room (as I'd seen with Patrick and Cynthia). Sevda clearly was a confident woman and accustomed to being treated as someone with influence. She was, after all, in charge of most of the cuticles in the entertainment industry, I'd discovered when researching her.

'Ms Lakonya,' I began, 'are you the manicurist who does the nails of the defendant, Cynthia Sutton?'

'I'm not sure I know what you mean by *does*,' Sevda answered. 'I treat the fingernails and toenails for many very important clients, and Cynthia is one of them.'

So, yes. 'Were you at Ms Sutton's house the night Wendy Bryan died?'

'Yes. We did a mani/pedi and I did some work on her eyebrows.' Cynthia didn't look pleased at that last mention; ironically, her eyebrows knotted in the middle.

'What kind of nail polish did you use on her fingernails?' Might as well start with the stuff Valencia was expecting.

'It's my own blend,' Sevda said. 'I don't like to give out the formula.'

'Well, I might ask you to do that because it's important to know how long it would take the polish to be fully and completely dry.'

'I can tell you that,' Sevda said, waving a hand like we were dishing it after a number of mojitos. 'That color and sheen would be dry to the touch in ten minutes.'

'Yes, but how long before it would be completely dry all the way to the nail, so that it would not be subject to, say, deterioration if immersed in liquid?' *Why say blood if you don't have to?*

'I mean, if you're talking about *absolutely* dry, that would take forty-five minutes to an hour based on the humidity level in the air.' Sevda, still pleased with herself, smiled at me. I was such a nice peasant.

'What time did you finish the appointment and leave Ms Sutton's house?' I asked.

'According to my log it was six fifty-five.' Clearly Sevda was very thorough. She did not have to think for a moment or consult notes.

I paced a little and nodded, acknowledging her answer. 'Now, Officer Crawford has testified that the nine-one-one call came in and he was dispatched at seven thirty-eight. That's forty-three minutes after you left Ms Sutton's. If her nails had been drenched in blood' – there are times you can't help it – 'after that amount of time, would the polish have deteriorated, even a little?'

'You wouldn't have seen anything.' Sevda was being protective of her work and her reputation.

'No, certainly,' I agreed, 'but would it have broken down at all chemically?'

'I imagine so,' Sevda said. 'It dries to the touch, but not that completely in that amount of time.'

'So at least traces of it, elements, would have shown up in the medical examiner's report, wouldn't you say?'

Valencia objected out of reflex. 'The witness is not the medical examiner,' he noted. As if we didn't know that.

'Sustained.' Hawthorne wasn't going to let Sevda testify to what should have been in the autopsy report. That was fine. The idea had been planted in the jurors' minds, and it wasn't the point I most wanted to make anyway.

'Did you also work with the victim, Wendy Bryan?' I asked Sevda.

She sat up proudly. 'Yes, I did Wendy's nails for the past ten years. In fact, that is how I met Cynthia.'

Perfect. 'So you had been to Mrs Bryan's house many times before.'

The smile got broader. 'I couldn't begin to count,' Sevda said.

'So, did you get to know the people who worked for Mrs Bryan?'

'Some of them,' Sevda said. She looked puzzled that I would bring other people into the equation when we could have been talking exclusively about her.

'Do you know Isobel Sanchez?' I asked.

'Yes.' She clearly didn't want to talk about Isobel Sanchez.

'Did you have occasion to talk to Mrs Sanchez often about the goings-on at Mrs Bryan's house?' I said.

'Oh, I don't know that I'd say it was often,' Sevda answered. 'Maybe once or twice.'

'Don't be modest,' I said. 'I could note that you and Mrs Sanchez were seen by other employees on numerous occasions having detailed conversations. A chauffeur named Otto specifically mentioned that to me when I was talking to him about testifying.' Otto had not had anything else of any interest to say and had not been working the week Wendy was killed because he was on vacation in Aix-en-Provence, France, leading me to wonder why I'd gone to law school when a driver's license had clearly been more than enough.

Sevda's face colored a little. 'Isobel and I would talk occasionally,' she said.

'Did you see Pierre Chirac at the house very often?'

Apparently considering Pete Conway less of a sensitive subject than Isobel Sanchez, Sevda relaxed a little in the box. 'I did for a while. He was living there. I came in on him once when Wendy wasn't even home; he had his own key. Luckily he was fully dressed. But then there was a falling-out of some sort, I was told, and Pierre moved out.'

'When was the last time you saw Wendy Bryan?' I asked Sevda.

'I did her nails the day she died.' The tear she sniffed away appeared to be authentic. 'Maybe three or four hours before I went to see Cynthia.'

'When you were at Wendy's house that day, was Pierre Chirac on the premises?' I wasn't sure and was taking a chance but there was some security video from the camera across the street that wasn't all about Lieutenant Trench, and I'd seen a figure drive up, too far away for a clear view.

'No,' Sevda said. 'Not that I saw.'

Oh. That was not a good surprise. I looked at Cynthia, who shrugged.

As I turned back toward the witness, Sevda added, 'But I did see Penelope Hannigan drive up when I was leaving, and that's just about the same thing.'

Bingo!

I thanked Sevda and let Valencia ask her about the particulars of the nail polish for a half-hour, something the jury would surely punish him for later. Then Hawthorne dismissed Sevda and said, 'Ms Moss?'

'Your Honor, I would like to recall Penelope Hannigan.'

FORTY-THREE

'**M**s Hannigan, you remember that you are under oath?' Judge Hawthorne asked.

'Yes,' Penelope said. She was not at all crazy about being back on the stand and she hadn't even heard Sevda's testimony. It had taken us the entire lunch break to locate her and bring her back to the courtroom. Luckily Penelope had been nearby, checking on the status of her lawsuit against Wendy Bryan's estate.

Hawthorne nodded in my direction and I approached the witness stand. 'Ms Hannigan, why didn't you tell us you had been at Wendy Bryan's house the day she died?' No sense beating around the bush this time. There was blood in the water. Does that constitute a mixed metaphor?

'I was not asked,' Penelope answered. That was true enough, but it was also evasive.

'I'm asking now. Were you at Wendy Bryan's house that day?'

Penelope's lips pursed as if she were sucking the juice out of a lemon. 'Yes.'

You don't often get a murmur from the spectators, but there it was. Just like in the movies.

'Why did you go there that day?' I asked. I knew what she'd say and I knew what was true. It's good to know both things, especially when they're not the same.

'I was going to check on the details of Pierre's show, which was scheduled to open two weeks later,' Penelope said. 'There were questions about the placement of certain works and the prices to be ascribed to others.'

'So you weren't there to threaten Wendy with a two-hundred-thousand-dollar lawsuit and complain that Pete Conway hadn't been paid yet?' I asked.

Valencia twitched but said nothing. Patrick looked like he was watching the most engrossing movie he'd ever seen. Angie, recognizing the look on my face, was grinning widely. Emily looked bored.

'No. Of course not.'

'Interesting,' I said. 'Your lawyer Mr Brady's schedule notes a phone call from you – that he billed you for, by the way – that took place less than two hours before Wendy Bryan died, but you weren't going there to talk about the lawsuit?'

Penelope's eyes flashed daggers – or perhaps bent fake TeeVee awards – at me. 'No. As I said, I was there to discuss the details of Pierre's show.'

I didn't press the point. 'In which room of the house did your meeting with Wendy take place?' I asked.

'I believe it was in the den,' Penelope said.

'You believe?'

The scowl. 'It was in the den.'

Pete Conway walked through the door into the courtroom just at that moment and Penelope definitely saw him enter. Her eyes widened a bit and she swallowed heavily. She picked up the bottle of water that was left there for her and took a sip. And that was when I knew what to do.

'Did you notice any special decorations in the den, on that day or on any other you might have happened to visit?' I asked.

'I'm not sure I know what you mean.' Penelope was looking past me directly at Pete.

'Say on the shelf over the bar,' I said. 'Did you notice any particular object?'

'No. I don't recall anything special.'

'That is where the statuette that Wendy thought was Cynthia Sutton's TeeVee award was kept,' I noted. 'Wendy's housekeeper Isobel Sanchez testified it was prominently displayed and couldn't be missed by anyone who came in.'

'Well, I had been there many times before, and I guess it became one of those things that you see but you don't notice, you know?' Penelope's eyes never left Pete and seemed to be sad, like she was hoping he'd leave, or that she thought she'd never see him again. Or that she was sitting on something sharp. It was hard to tell, except she could have gotten up if she was sitting on something sharp.

'I guess so. Ms Hannigan, was anyone else in the house when you visited Mrs Bryan that day? Or was it early evening?'

'I don't remember what time it was, but no, there was no one else in the house. Even Isobel the *maid* wasn't there.'

'Be careful, Ms Hannigan. What if I could produce security footage, taken from across the street, that showed Mr Conway – that is Mr Chirac – letting you into the house when you arrived?' I saw Cynthia lean over and ask Jon a question and he shook his head negatively.

'I'd say that footage is not accurate. Pierre was not in the house when I got there.' Now Pete was looking like something was dawning on him and he looked back at the door as if deciding whether to leave.

'So he arrived later?' I said.

'Yes. No. He wasn't there.'

'Make up your mind, Ms Hannigan.'

Valencia, riding a white horse, rose to defend my witness. 'Badgering, Your Honor.'

'Ask a question, Ms Moss. Don't editorialize.'

'Yes, Your Honor. Ms Hannigan, one last time. Was Mr Conway at Wendy Bryan's house at any time during your visit the day she died?'

Penelope's panic-stricken face did not move or change. Later Angie told me she thought that Pete might have nodded at her just a tiny bit, but she said he looked terribly distressed too.

'I think he might have come later,' she said. 'I don't recall exactly.'

I took a deep breath because this was the big plunge and I wanted to do it right. If I made Penelope worry about Pete, things might go Cynthia's way. If you know what I mean. 'Ms Hannigan. The security footage shows no one but you entering Wendy Bryan's house after four p.m. until Cynthia Sutton arrived at seven thirty-five. But it shows you arriving in a taxi and it never shows you leaving.'

Having seen the video footage, Detective Brisbane had declared it irrelevant because he said the camera occasionally turned away

from a view in which Wendy's door was visible for ten seconds.
I didn't think a car could drive up, Penelope could leave the
house and get in, and it could drive away out of camera range
in ten seconds. If I'd told Trench what Brisbane had said,
he probably would have pulled out hanks of his own cop-short
hair. 'Now, can you tell me if you were in the house when Wendy
Bryan died?'

'No!' Penelope practically barked the word out. It seemed to
escape from her rather than her sending it. 'I wasn't.'

'Then what time did you leave? If you arrived after four and
the defendant got there just after seven thirty, what time did you
leave Mrs Bryan's house that day?'

'I don't know. I can't remember. You're confusing me.'
Penelope had not expected to testify today, then thought it would
be about particulars and now was finding herself placed at the
scene of a murder. In all, she was having a rough day. She took
another sip of water. She'd have to ask for a bathroom break
soon.

'I didn't intend to confuse you, Ms Hannigan,' I said.
'But I'm trying to figure out how, if you were in the house when
Wendy Bryan was murdered with a TeeVee award, you didn't
see or hear anything and you don't remember the award being
in the same room as you when you met with the victim. Did Mr
Chirac come in at some point to take you out of the room?' Turn
up the heat.

'Pierre . . . Pierre wasn't *there*,' she insisted. 'You said there
was no footage of him coming into the house.'

'That's true, but Mr Chirac had a key from the time he'd been
living in Mrs Bryan's house. Where was he living on the day
she died, do you know?'

Penelope sat up straight. 'He was living with me,' she said.

'Then why didn't you go to the house together? Had you and
Mr Conway had a falling-out of some sort? Because a neighbor
of yours called the police the night before saying she heard raised
voices at two in the morning, followed by a slamming door.'

'That might have come from another apartment,' Penelope
said.

'It might have, but it didn't. The neighbor specified which
apartment was generating the noise, and it was yours. So I'll ask

again, Ms Hannigan: why didn't you and Pete Conway go to Wendy Bryan's house together?'

Penelope was red in the face and her neck showed tension. I won't say the veins were popping but clearly not enough blood was making it to her brain because she forgot to lie. 'He took his own car! I don't see what the big deal is about that.'

In the spectators' area, Pete Conway put his hand over his eyes.

'So Mr Conway *was*—'

'*Stop calling him that!*' Penelope's lips were pursed and for a moment I flinched, thinking she might spit at me. 'His name is *Pierre Chirac!*'

'Very well. So Mr Chirac *was* in the house when you arrived?'

Penelope looked out into the courtroom but Pete wasn't looking at her. He wasn't shaking his head. She wasn't getting any instructions. 'Yes,' she said in a very small voice. Hawthorne asked her to repeat herself, and she did.

'And neither of you saw or heard the murder take place? Why were you out of the room when Cynthia Sutton arrived?'

'I don't know.' We were back to that.

'Your Honor.' Valencia was on his feet again. He might need a recess to iron the wrinkles out of his pants. 'I'm not aware of Ms Hannigan being on trial here.' Again an objection without an objection.

'Let's try to stick to the case at hand,' Hawthorne said. Which sort of sustained the non-objection, but not really.

'Certainly,' I said, like I had a choice. 'Ms Hannigan, you testified that you didn't see the TeeVee award in the room when you met with Wendy Bryan. Did you see it at any other time that day?'

'I don't think . . . wait. Yes. I saw it in the center hall which was unusual because that's not where Wendy had been keeping it. She said she was going to give it back to Cynthia that night.'

Valencia smiled. Cynthia shook her head.

'Where in the center hall?' I asked.

'What?'

'Where in the center hall was Wendy keeping the TeeVee when you saw it that day?'

Penelope's eyes really wanted to pop out of her head and spin around the room a couple of times, but the laws of physics prohibit such things. 'On a shelf.'

'That is a very distinctively designed room and the jury has seen pictures of it,' I told Penelope. 'There are no shelves there large enough to hold an object the size of a TeeVee award. Ms Hannigan, is Mr Chirac a strong man, physically?'

Stunned by the change in direction, it took Penelope a moment to answer, but she did so quite proudly. 'Yes, he is,' she said. 'It infuses his art, particularly his sculptures.'

'So he could probably bend a metal statue down in the way that the counterfeit TeeVee was bent, would you say?'

Penelope was shaken but had composed herself again. 'I wouldn't know.'

'Did you know the TeeVee was not real?' I asked.

'No. How would I have known?'

'Well, you were fairly friendly with Isobel Sanchez, and she knew because she had replaced the real TeeVee, which she sold for three thousand dollars on a dark web site, with the fake one. She has given that statement to the police. She also says she told you about it because she knew you were upset with Mrs Bryan and wanted to let you know she wasn't paying you because she didn't have the money, and not because she had lost faith in Mr Chirac's artwork.'

'I don't remember her saying anything about the TeeVee,' Penelope's mouth said. Her eyes said something along the lines of *If I had that TeeVee now I would stab* you *with it.*

'I'd like to get back to the time of the murder,' I said. Valencia, behind me, made a gesture that was supposed to communicate he was glad we were heading in that direction. I mentally added him to my Christmas card list so I could take him off of it later. 'According to the medical examiner's report, the stabbing took place somewhere between six twenty and eight p.m. Since we've established that you and Mr Chirac were in the house at that time, can you account for your whereabouts at that time?'

Penelope's eyes narrowed to slits. She wasn't mad; she was thinking. 'Between six twenty and eight o'clock? That's a long time. We were in various rooms, I guess.'

Time to increase the pressure. On Pete. 'Well, you said you

started out in the den talking to Mrs Bryan, and then you were in the center hall, where you saw the TeeVee on a shelf that doesn't exist. So where did you go after that?'

'I don't know. You'd have to ask Pierre.'

'I intend to. But I think the question that finally needs to be answered is whether it was you or Mr Chirac who stabbed Wendy Bryan, because it sure wasn't Cynthia Sutton.'

Valencia didn't even have time to object. Penelope was literally vibrating in the witness chair and she just couldn't contain herself. 'It was Pierre!' she said. 'He got mad about the money and stabbed her after he bent the statue down!'

That was what I'd needed. 'So you're saying Cynthia Sutton did not—'

Valencia was on his feet before I could finish the sentence. The courtroom went from murmur to tumult quickly, but it got worse when Pete Conway stood up and shouted, 'It was her! Penelope stabbed her! I was an innocent bystander!'

The only thing I remember right after he said it was that Patrick McNabb was grinning from ear to ear and I didn't blame him. It was the most TV moment I'd ever been part of in my life.

FORTY-FOUR

'We find for the defendant,' said Judge Madison. Madelyn Forsythe's appeal had been completed in record time. I'd managed to get a panel of three reasonable judges, they heard the 'merits' of the case the prosecution had brought and found in Maddie's favor in approximately six minutes. Once and for all I'd proven that the DA's office had been incredibly overzealous and had targeted the wrong woman.

Even Longabaugh walked over and offered to shake my hand, which I declined, citing sanitary standards. I did nod graciously in his direction.

'Sandy, I can't thank you enough.' Maddie was all warm smiles as we packed up to leave the courthouse. Patrick, who couldn't be persuaded to leave me alone for a minute since Cynthia's trial, stood grinning near the door and gave me a thumbs-up. Philip, ever discreet, was 'chatting' with Judy. I wondered if now that Maddie's trial was over, I wouldn't need to have Judy around anymore. 'I don't think any other lawyer could have gotten me off,' Maddie said.

Flattering though that was, I couldn't take credit. 'They had no case,' I said. 'The idea that you were convicted in the first place should have gotten me fired. I appreciate your sticking with me.'

'Oh, that wasn't your fault,' Maddie said, waving a hand. 'The chief of police wanted me convicted, and he generally gets what he wants. I'm sorry that ended up getting you arrested for nothing.'

I stopped and looked at her closely for a moment. I hadn't told Maddie about my arrest because I didn't want her to feel it was her responsibility. I thought she'd had enough to worry about. 'You knew about that?' I asked.

Her face indicated I was being amusingly naïve. 'Of course I did,' she said. 'They wanted my book and they were using you as a bargaining chip. But you were so smart getting these three judges. They couldn't be bought. And the DA so didn't have a case. You really are brilliant.'

Right now I felt about as brilliant as a ten-watt lightbulb. 'Your book?' She knew about that crazy ploy too?

'Yeah. I keep client records exactly for situations like this. They want to put the screws to me? I can make it very uncomfortable for some very highly placed men.' She winked. 'A few women, too.'

'But the man with the knife came after you,' I protested, trying to convince Maddie that she really wasn't in the sex-for-money business.

'I know. You inspired me! After you were attacked, I thought that would work great so I called a guy, and he was worth every dime I paid in sympathy and deflection. Nice touch, right?'

She started up the aisle toward Patrick. 'So you really are a prostitute.' The words just slipped out of my mouth.

Maddie turned and gave me a haughty look. 'I am *not* a prostitute,' she said. 'I'm a *madam*. Besides, they're called sex workers these days. Thanks a lot, Sandy. The check will be in the mail.'

I stood there, unable to do anything but shake my head in

wonder for two full minutes, before Patrick came over, looking concerned. 'Are you all right, love?' he said.

'She really is . . . you know, she really is . . .'

'I tried to tell you,' he said. 'I know a few producers and at least one studio executive who have availed themselves of her services.'

The only thing I could think to say was, 'Let's get out of here.'

'Are you all out of courtrooms to be in?' Patrick asked.

'For the time being.'

We walked toward the door but Patrick stopped me. 'I still don't understand what happened in Cynthia's trial,' he said. 'Of course I'm grateful she's free, but everyone was accusing everyone else. I never really got the whole story.'

I didn't blame him. By contrast to Maddie's turbo-speed appeal, it had taken another two days after Pete Conway had accused Penelope of Wendy Bryan's murder for the trial to be ended by Judge Hawthorne and the charges to be dropped by whoever Valencia's boss was.

At first the prosecution had refused to accept the confession as authentic, I told Patrick. 'Valencia was so determined to believe that Cynthia had killed her mother-in-law that he dismissed Pete's outburst as emotional and coerced. It wasn't until Penelope said *Pete* had committed the same murder that he asked Trench to step in and "assist" Brisbane, who looked for all the world like there were tiny airplanes circling his head.'

'It's always good to summon the lieutenant,' said Patrick, suddenly Trench's biggest fan.

'Wendy Bryan almost certainly poisoned Leopold Kolensky over dinner at her house,' I went on. 'But she wasn't alive, so Trench didn't have anyone to charge in that murder. He could have been petty and brought charges against Isobel Sanchez, but he's not a petty man. Anyway, Sanchez was facing charges of theft because she'd taken items from Wendy's house when Wendy was alive and pawned or sold them in lieu of the salary she was supposed to have been paid. It's even unclear whether Sanchez had told Wendy what she was doing and was cutting her in on the profits. Wendy Bryan's business is indeed buried under piles of debt.'

Nate Garrigan's assertion that Wendy had been borrowing from organized crime figures (Why are they always 'figures'? Why aren't they 'organized criminals'? It's like how everyone who makes a dirty movie is a 'porn star'. I guess there are no porn character actors.) had panned out and four arrests had been made, but the accused weren't exactly Don Corleone. These were low-level guys who thought they'd get their hooks into a big art dealer and instead got Wendy Bryan, who wasn't going to pay off for anybody. Even an attempt to try to cash in with Wendy's son Michael was caught on a recording. Michael told his contact that his mother would claim any money he got in a divorce settlement and that his attorney was working it out with Cynthia's as they spoke. It turned out Cynthia's lawyer, who was subsequently disbarred, had worked with her mother-in-law when Wendy had suggested that she get any money recovered in the divorce and Michael, doormat that he was, had agreed. Cynthia wisely fired her attorney even without knowing that and hired me, and that was a problem for Wendy, Michael and the lawyer. Any idea of coming after Cynthia's money was sort of put on hold when she'd been accused of killing the debtor. For the LA mob, this had not been a successful operation. They could have used a few lessons from the guys back in Jersey.

'You're adorable when you speak legalese,' Patrick said, thinking that was an endearment. 'Go on.'

To avoid any more words like 'adorable', I did. 'Once Valencia had finally given up on his fantastical quest, I asked the judge to dismiss the charges and she did with the DA's blessing, seeing as they'd gotten dual confessions from Penelope and Pete and had to sort out what had actually happened. You know that part.'

'How did they sort it all out? That's the part where I got lost. Everyone accusing everyone else.' Patrick sat down in the last row, figuring this part might take a while.

'I wasn't present at the questioning of course, but Nate and Judy checked in with their sources at the LAPD, who confirmed that the two were accusing each other, each presumably attempting to shield him-/herself from the long arm of the law. Unfortunately, it was fairly obvious after a few hours of this that both of them had played a role in Wendy's murder.

'Pete got there first, the night before the killing. We knew that. Their neighbor reported Penelope and Pete had gotten into a major argument that night and Pete had stormed out. Penelope claimed the fight was about Pete's loyalty to Wendy and that he had killed Wendy when he realized she wasn't so loyal to him, which in Pete's case meant she wouldn't give him any money.'

'She didn't have any money,' Patrick pointed out.

'True, but Pete didn't entirely know that. Pete doesn't entirely know anything. He admitted he'd used the key from having lived there previously to get into the house and set up camp in an upstairs guest room. He had not told Wendy or anyone else in the house he had returned because Wendy had been, let's say, less than enthusiastic about him ever coming back to live there again.'

'Once again, I can't blame her,' Patrick said.

I nodded, but there was some element of charm in Pete that other people clearly got and I didn't. 'Do you want to hear this?' I asked Patrick.

'Of course.'

'Well, settle in. It's not a short story. Pete admitted he'd slept in that day until two in the afternoon because of course he did. Then Pete had to decide what to do, and being Pete, decided wrong.

'Naturally his first choice was to go downstairs, announce himself to Wendy and cook himself some breakfast. To be honest, Pete's first choice was to have someone else cook him breakfast in Wendy's kitchen, but no such servant – including Wendy, who refused – was available, and that's when the arguing began.

'Wendy, who strikingly was opposed to having someone break into her house demanding an omelet, expressed this thought to Pete and suggested in no uncertain terms that he vacate the premises immediately after turning over the spare key she'd forgotten she'd given him. Pete, who had an angry Penelope waiting for him in her apartment and wasn't sure if he actually had a home at this point, refused, saying room and board was in lieu of (although I doubt he would use those words) the fifty thousand-dollar payment he felt he was owed via a prior arrangement he'd made with Wendy.'

'Cheeky bastard, isn't he?'

'That's not how we'd say it in Jersey,' I informed him. 'Wendy adamantly demanded Pete leave, saying she would call the police if he didn't. Pete, who didn't know that Wendy had been borrowing from the Gang That Couldn't Loan Straight, said he would complain to her bank. Apparently he also didn't understand that banks don't work like that.'

Patrick settled back in his chair, so it was obvious to me that we weren't going anywhere for a while. I put down the briefcase he'd offered to carry for me, gave Judy a glance through the window in the courtroom door, and leaned on the seat across the aisle from Patrick. I wasn't going to sit down. That was my way of establishing authority, I decided. Why I needed to establish authority was something I'd no doubt talk to a therapist about sometime in the future.

'OK. So Wendy was on edge because she *did* know from whom she'd borrowed a great deal of money with the express purpose of showcasing Pete's works. I can only guess she felt he was being ungrateful about the lengths to which she'd gone for him and said she'd call the cops to have him arrested for breaking and entering. Pete – and keep in mind this was from his own admission – said he hadn't broken anything because he had a key.

'Instead he decided to call in the cavalry and phoned Penelope, who was still mad but wanted the money. She said she'd get to Wendy's as soon as she could. Apparently that meant the minute she'd had a bath, dressed, gone out to get her hair done and stopped along the way for a quick bite at a local coffee shop, where she said the chicken salad was "too mayonnaise-y".'

'This part I know from what Cynthia told me,' Patrick said, sounding like the pupil who finally had a correct answer after a long lecture he only partially understood. 'Penelope finally got to Wendy's house and found her and Pete yelling at each other because he wouldn't leave and had ruined a frying pan because he didn't know how to make an omelet, right?'

'Yes, but that wasn't what really got everyone into a heated state. Penelope told Wendy she and Pete would sue her for two hundred thousand dollars. *That* led to Wendy telling the artist and his manager that she was going to cancel his show, sell the gallery and recoup her losses by selling the rights to his work, which she owned via their contract. She said she would give them to Isobel Sanchez to sell, as her housekeeper had made quite a nice profit selling some of Wendy's belongings and splitting the money with her.'

'Well yeah, but she was selling everything on eBay and in pawn shops,' Patrick said.

'Have you *seen* Pete's artwork?' I asked.

'Good point.'

(Wendy didn't know the half of it: Isobel and her sister Rosa had wildly inflated the prices on Wendy's jewelry, electronics, a few small pieces of furniture, decorative knickknacks and – completely unbeknownst to Wendy – Cynthia's TeeVee award, which had been tracked down to its new owner and retrieved since the trial. The TV Academy, in case you hadn't heard, doesn't look kindly on people buying TeeVees. They'd found buyers with deep pockets and bad shopping skills and had netted some six hundred thousand dollars from their efforts, then told Wendy they'd gotten half that, so her cut was one hundred fifty thousand. Perhaps Trench might recommend fraud charges after all.)

'All that was beside the point,' I told Patrick. 'Wendy threatening to cancel his big breakthrough *and* "steal" his work enraged Pete, but here's where the stories diverged depending on who might be doing the telling. Pete said he had idly picked up the statuette pretending to be Cynthia's TeeVee while they were arguing and, once he started getting angry, had bent the head of the figure down without even noticing he'd done so. Nobody disputed that, but when Wendy made her pronouncement, Penelope said Pete said he got so enraged that he touched the wings on the "TeeVee", decided they would hurt someone if they were struck with it hard enough, and in a fit of rage plunged them into Wendy's back and then, when she fell to the floor, her chest.'

'But Pete said no,' Patrick guessed.

'Absolutely. His version differed in the details, mostly in the casting. Pete said he had indeed bent the statue into a weapon shape, but it was totally idle, he was just mad, and that Penelope was the one who'd used it on Wendy. That apparently led to some brouhaha in the examination rooms even though they were questioned separately.'

Penelope's statement that I'd seen typed up suggested that Pete had taken the statue and thrown it out of the den in a fit of rage and into the center hall. She said then that Wendy, upset that the symbol of her power over her daughter-in-law (the award for Cynthia that Cynthia couldn't have) had been damaged that

she hurried into the center hall to get it. Pete said he followed
Wendy and got to the 'TeeVee', but not before Penelope, that
angry accusations and the occasional ethnic slur about the Irish
had followed, and that Penelope Hannigan herself had become
enraged and stabbed their hostess to death.

'Who did it?' Patrick asked. 'Pete or Penelope?'

'Hang on,' I said. 'Once the initial rush of adrenaline had
subsided, no matter who had done the stabbing, our heroes realized exactly what they were in and how deep they were in it.
They were heading for the garage to find something in
which they could transport and dispose of the body.'

'And that was when Cynthia showed up and provided the
perfect fall guy,' Patrick said.

'Exactly. Cynthia came in while the two actual murderers (or
one and an accomplice, if you want to go that way) were out of
the room, found the body of a woman she had detested bleeding
out on the floor and completely crumbled. She ran into the den
and sat there until someone – Penelope – came in and handed
her the bloody trophy, which she still doesn't remember happening.

'Once they heard Cynthia, Penelope (everyone was in agreement it was Penelope) suggested a plan of action: They picked
up the bent, sad little false statuette and wrapped it in a towel
because Pete said it would be a shame to stain the rug any further.
They dropped the TeeVee in Cynthia's lap from behind, and she
never even turned to see who had done that. Then they took
the towel back to their apartment and burned it.

'The cops were alerted when Penelope picked up Wendy's cell
phone, called nine-one-one and reported a murder in the house,
smashing Wendy's phone to bits immediately after disconnecting
the call.'

Patrick shook his head. 'It all seemed so complicated and now
it all seems so stupid. Wendy was killed by two people who
really had no idea what they were doing.'

I shook my head. 'They knew enough to cover their asses.
They took Penelope's car back to their apartment and started
planning for the questions from the police that wouldn't start
coming for days because the Santa Monica police were positive
they had apprehended the killer.'

'I'll ask one more time,' Patrick said. '*Who did it?*'

'Trench did his usual thorough job, pored over every possible piece of physical evidence that Brisbane had glanced at before and recommended to the DA that Leopold Kolensky's death be reclassified as a homicide, that Wendy Bryan be recorded as the killer, that Wendy had indeed borrowed money from mobsters and that she had done so on the recommendation of Penelope Hannigan, who – he suggested – had been in some debt to the sharks of her own accord.

'Then he told the DA that, based on what he could tell from the physical evidence, Isobel Sanchez had sold the real TeeVee, Pete had twisted the fake one into a weapon, and Penelope had done the stabbing, probably before Pete had made it into the room. Part of this conclusion was reached based on the study Trench had made about Wendy's character. He deemed it plausible that she'd be upset about not have something to lord over Cynthia and that she would undoubtedly have used slurs and insults when dealing with Penelope.'

'So Penelope killed Wendy.' Patrick sat back. 'I thought it was Pete because he was that stupid.'

'Pete *is* stupid, but he isn't mean enough to kill someone in cold blood,' I said. 'Polygraph tests, which are not admissible in court for good reasons, indicated that Penelope's story was more plausible than Pete's. And while there were no fingerprints from either suspect on the TeeVee, because the "important parts" had been wiped before giving it to Cynthia, there were some of Penelope's in the room and not Pete's. There was a very partial footprint from Pete's designer shoes on a piece of Wendy's smashed cell phone. Brisbane did a truly awful job and is right now being pressured to retire.'

The rest Patrick knew: Penelope was charged with murder, although only second degree because it was determined that the crime was not premeditated. Pete rolled over hard on his manager/girlfriend/partner-in-crime, and Penelope finally confessed. Patrick knew that, but hadn't been convinced Penelope was the murderer because . . . well, because it was a tangle and Patrick likes things neat.

Cynthia's divorce from Michael became final six weeks later after her husband abruptly dropped his demands for ownership of their house or any money from her. The fact that he'd lied to

Patrick, Nate and the police (!) about texting Cynthia and summoning her to his mother's house the night she died – because Wendy really *did* want to extort some money from her daughter-in-law and hoped to use the TeeVee as a hostage – might have had something to do with it.

So here we were, Cynthia back at her home a free woman, Jon back at the office working on a case of his own, Angie with a rare day off (out buying new clothes to better conform to the Patrick McNabb 'brand'), Maddic Forsythe off to . . . it was better not to think about it . . . and me, standing in the courtroom with my jaw no longer dropped, being ushered out to the hallway by Patrick, who seemed to find the whole thing amusing. Maybe he'd insisted on the recap to get me back to reality, but I was still stunned.

He led me out through the hallway, where there were no reporters waiting for word on a minor prostitution case. A few heads turned as the TV actor appeared, but people were generally respectful of our privacy once they saw my stunned expression and figured I was currently smelling toast and on the way to the nearest Emergency Room.

'It's all right, darling,' Patrick said quietly. 'You just need a minute.' Of course I knew that, but he wanted to be supportive and I let him do it. I didn't even flinch at 'darling', because he called every woman he knew 'darling' or 'love'. He'd seen too many Cary Grant movies on TV when he was growing up.

We made it to the elevator and were about to get on for a quick trip to the parking levels.

And that was when I noticed the man in the denim jacket, reaching into his pocket.

FORTY-FIVE

Immediately my complete torpor in reaction to Maddie's revelation shook loose and I was clear-eyed and activated. No, really.

My first impulse was to push Patrick out of the way. I knew the guy with the gun wasn't there for him and I wasn't about to let another man get shot because he was standing too close to me. Patrick looked astonished, took a step back after I pushed him and said, 'Sandy!'

'Run!' I shouted, and endeavored to do exactly that, away from the elevator (I *knew* I couldn't go in there) and in the direction opposite Patrick. Four people standing at the elevator doors turned in confusion and stared at me.

The man in the denim jacket looked at Patrick, then at me, and started walking in my direction. He wasn't running like I was, he was walking with an accelerated pace. He had the advantage of not wearing heels but I thought this was a bad time to stop and change my shoes.

The Glendale County Building, where the courthouse is located, is not a huge structure like the courthouse in downtown LA. There weren't tons of options to consider when looking for an escape route. I chose the least-crowded option I could see, a corridor off the lobby, with the idea that at least other people in the building wouldn't get shot because of me. Not again.

I ran (drawing curious looks from other people in business clothing) to the turn and went into the corridor, which seemed to lead to offices for county officials. I'd never been down this way before and really didn't want to stop to read each nameplate on the doors. I was heading for the EXIT sign at the end, which led to a stairway and – with any luck at all – an alarm. My current dilemma (among a number of others that I had all of a sudden) concerned whether I would climb the stairs after I hit the door, or descend. Which one would be more likely to confuse my pursuer?

After all those years of trying to get past the tree or the parked car, I finally knew what I'd been running away from my whole life. And I didn't want it to catch up with me.

Right now, I could hear Denim Man's heavier, faster footsteps behind me, and as I ran I anticipated hearing the report of his pistol and then . . . what?

If I could just make it to that EXIT sign . . .

'Hold it!' I heard from behind me. I wondered if that ever worked for him. Would people just stop so they could be shot more efficiently? I ran faster but I was already noticing my breath coming in gulps. 'Stop now or he dies!'

There could only be one 'he'. And of course the next voice I heard was Patrick's. 'Keep running, Sandy! Don't worry about me!'

Whose idea was it to make these corridors so freakin' long?

But my stomach was clenched and not because I was running hard and wasn't in Angie-type shape. My stomach was clenched and it wasn't because I was terrified of being shot, although I was. My stomach was clenched and it wasn't even because I was enraged that this guy had waited *months* to come after me again. Where the hell was Judy?

No, my stomach was clenched because I absolutely couldn't cope with the idea that Patrick McNabb might die and it would be my fault. Even him telling me I shouldn't stop was a reason I chose to stop. I was only about fifteen feet from the EXIT sign. The very definition of 'so near and yet so far.'

I turned and faced the man in the denim jacket, who was indeed standing just about twenty yards away, a very reasonable distance from which to shoot someone. And he was holding a gun to Patrick's head, his other arm holding Patrick close to him to use as a shield, as if I might have a weapon on me.

Now that I thought of it, how did he get a gun into this building? There were metal detectors at the doors and security personnel everywhere except right here where a professional killer (I assumed he was not in it for sport) wanted to shoot me down and then probably kill Patrick out of spite.

And what scared me was that the thought of Patrick dying was even worse than the realization that I might get killed myself. That was something I'd have to mull over a few nights, if I ever saw the sun go down again.

'How'd you get a gun into the county courthouse?' I said. I figured if I engaged him in shoptalk, he might forget to do his job and talk with me like a colleague.

'Sandy,' Patrick said, a catch in his voice. 'Why didn't you run?'

'I don't have to tell you anything,' the gunman said. I was impressed. Back home he would have said, *I don't have to tell you nothing.* It was a higher class of assassin here in the big city. 'I just have to kill you.' That seemed awfully talky for a guy with a gun. Why hadn't he shot me already? It would be a bad idea to ask him, right?

'Who hired you?' I demanded. 'If I'm going to die, I at least deserve to know who asked for it. Was it the chief of police?'

Denim Man looked bemused. 'The chief of *police*?' he said. 'You think the chief of police needs to hire somebody if he wants you to disappear? He's got nine thousand cops under his command. If he wants you to go away, you'd be gone already.' He maneuvered Patrick closer, only ten yards from me.

'Then who?' Trench had filled me up with the idea that the upper echelons of the police department wanted me dead, and now the guy who'd been trying to kill me for months was saying it wasn't them? 'Why do you need to shoot me?'

Patrick struggled, but he neglected to take into account that all the fights he'd been in on television had been carefully choreographed and planned so that he would win. He tried the classic elbow-in-the-ribs move and Denim Man just pivoted and held onto him. 'Slow down, buddy,' he said. 'You're not going anywhere.'

There was considerable commotion in the lobby behind the gunman and he twitched his head to check. He knew he didn't have much time and was eyeing the very same EXIT sign I'd been trying to reach. He was already planning his escape for after my lifeless body was lying on the floor. 'Who hired you?' I demanded again.

'I don't get names. It was some woman. She's mad at you for stealing her fiancé. You shouldn't mess with other people's fiancés, lady.'

I stared at Patrick and he stared at me. '*Emmie* hired you to kill Sandy?' Patrick said. My face must have had the same mixture of horror and exasperation that his did. All this because I'd told him to slow down his wedding plans?

'I told you, I don't know names. Now go over there.' Denim Man spun Patrick around and pushed him toward me. 'All I know is first I was supposed to kill *him* and then I was supposed to kill *you* and now I'm supposed to get both of you. So I get paid double. It's been nice knowing you.'

He raised his gun and pointed it at Patrick and I just couldn't bear the thought or the stupidity of this situation. I fell to my knees.

That seemed to distract Denim Man as he turned to aim at me (or the perceived motion of me) and found me not where he expected. He fired one shot that clearly went over my head. Then he turned again, and instead of adjusting his aim at me on the floor – the much easier shot since I was practically immobile – he took quick aim at Patrick.

Behind me there was a sudden ruckus as the stairwell door burst open and there were Philip and Judy, who (as I saw once I lay down and rolled over to look) were both holding automatic weapons on the gunman. *'Freeze!'* That was Judy. She took her job seriously. She took *everything* seriously. Judy probably would have taken Woody Woodpecker seriously.

Stairs work in both directions, I reminded myself. The element of surprise had gotten Judy and Philip to the right place at exactly the right time.

Denim Man, professional that he was, knew when he was outgunned. He very carefully lowered the gun to the floor, left it there and stood up, hands behind his head. 'I'm unarmed,' he said carefully.

Philip held him and then there was building security there and before I knew it county officers joined them. There was quite the swarm around us. I was amazed Trench didn't show up, but in my mind he was watching through security cameras suspended from the ceiling that broadcast directly to his cell phone. No doubt Emily Webster, Patrick's ex-fiancée, was already in custody.

My main thoughts, however, were on Patrick. I rushed over to him and threw my arms around him. 'I'm so glad you're OK,' I said.

He sounded amused in my left ear. 'I have always been. But I was worried about you.'

'That's because you're in love with me,' I said.

'Don't mock me, darling,' he said.

I moved back and looked him straight in the eye. 'I'm not.' And I kissed him very seriously for as long as I wanted to, which was long. 'I love you too,' I said when I came up for air.

FORTY-SIX

'**M**s Moss,' Lieutenant Trench said, 'we must stop meeting like this.'

To say the scene after our latest narrow escape had

been frantic would be something of an understatement. Philip held Denim Man's hands behind him and applied zip strips while being offered no resistance. I was willing to bet Denim Man had been through this ritual more than once before.

Angie appeared minutes later. I didn't see when Patrick had texted her (because I knew I hadn't), but she might have just been hovering over the Glendale County Building waiting for something to happen that required her attention. With Angie anything's possible. She used to run some Dairy Queens. Now she ran Patrick.

She was beside herself with unnecessary guilt. 'The fourth time you get shot at and I wasn't there for any of them!' she wailed. To me, I'm pretty sure. Patrick had only been shot at three times.

'I'm glad you weren't there. *You* could have gotten shot.'

Then, as if teleported by Captain Kirk himself, Trench had shown up, without Sergeant Roberts this time. I asked the lieutenant why his shadow was not shadowing him and he said that, as I'd expected, there was the matter of arresting Emily Webster and Roberts was seeing to that.

'You should send a SWAT team,' I told him seriously. 'She hired a guy to kill me because I had a conversation with her boyfriend.'

Denim Man, who was being led away by two uniformed officers, stopped for a moment. 'At first it was just to kill him,' he said, nodding his head in Patrick's direction. 'Something about forgetting an anniversary.' He looked straight at Patrick. 'You're better off with this one, buddy.'

'I agree,' Patrick said and Angie, her eyebrows now orbiting her head, opened her mouth. I shook my head and she closed it again but her eyes were full of mischief. It was going to be a long haul.

'Take him,' Trench said to the officers. 'And write down anything he says.'

Patrick shook his head. 'Emmie. How could I have been so wrong?'

'You don't have the best history,' I told him. Then I turned toward Trench. 'Speaking of being wrong, Lieutenant. You warned me that the upper echelons of your very own department were angry with me and it turned out to be Patrick's ex-fiancée.'

'I am sure it will come as a surprise to you, Ms Moss, but I am actually not infallible. However, I did *not* say that anyone in the LAPD would try to kill you because that would be absurd. And they *were* angry with you about the prostitution case. You persisted far beyond what had been expected.'

My head was still reeling from that one. 'Yeah. Maybe beyond what I should have done,' I said.

Trench raised an eyebrow. 'Once the issue of the client book was settled, I'm told the deputy chief was considerably less concerned,' he said.

'But Maddie kept the book.'

He nodded. 'And will continue to keep it. Confidential. As it has been for years.' He saw to it our statements were taken and then he left, no doubt to go foil the Joker in a plot to contaminate the Los Angeles water supply.

After a minute it felt weird to be standing around in a corridor of the Glendale County Building so we picked up my briefcase (which an accommodating bystander had brought from where I'd dropped it) and started back toward the elevator that would take us to my venerable Hyundai.

'Sooooooo?' Angie said. 'What's going on?'

'We got shot at,' I said. 'Did you miss that part?'

Angie regarded me with a stern look. 'You know what I mean.'

I did know what she meant but for some reason it was embarrassing to discuss. So I said, 'Later,' and for some reason thought that would be that.

Of course it wasn't. Patrick, who had been grinning broadly ever since I'd embraced him out of relief, stopped walking and looked into my eyes.

'What?' I said, noting that people were already starting to look.

He did just what I'd have most wished he would not do. He took my hand and knelt on the incredibly municipal floor.

'Sandra Moss,' he said. 'Would you do the honor of becoming my wife?'

Angie gasped and put her hands to her face.

I pulled him to his feet and hugged him close to me. 'Oh Patrick,' I said. 'Of course not.'

CAST OF CHARACTERS

Sandy Moss: a lawyer in Los Angeles transplanted from New Jersey

Angie: Sandy's best friend from Jersey, who came out to LA to visit and stayed

Patrick McNabb: Famous TV actor whom Sandy defended successfully in a murder trial

Detective Lieutenant K.C. Trench: LAPD homicide detective

Nate Garrigan: An investigator sometimes employed by Sandy's law firm

Holiday Wentworth: Sandy's immediate superior at the firm

Madelyn Forsythe: Sandy's client accused of prostitution

Cynthia Sutton: Sandy's client accused of killing her mother-in-law

Wendy Bryan: Cynthia's late mother-in-law

Michael Bryan: Cynthia's soon-to-be-ex-husband and Wendy's son

Marcus Valencia: Deputy DA prosecuting Cynthia's case

Brian Longabaugh: Deputy DA prosecuting Madelyn's case

Judge Coffey: Madelyn's case

Judge Hawthorne: Cynthia's case

Judge Reinhold: Popular actor in the 1980s and 1990s, not appearing in this book

Leopold Kolensky: Wendy's financial consultant

Pete Conway (Pierre Chirac): Artist associated with Wendy's gallery

Penelope Hannigan: Pete's (Pierre's) representative

Jon Irvin: Sandy's associate and second chair at Cynthia's trial

Detective William Brisbane: Detective assigned to Cynthia's case

Isobel Sanchez: Wendy Bryan's housekeeper

Gail Adams: Expert witness on TeeVee awards

AUTHOR'S NOTES

The last thing a writer wants to do (literally) is run out of words. But with each new book comes the joy of acknowledging those who helped make it possible, and I find myself looking for new ways to express my gratitude that won't sound trite or less than heartfelt.

Sandy Moss and her gang of co-conspirators would never have reached you in any form without the absolutely dogged determination of Josh Getzler, my agent and my friend, who championed the series since we first met in a year that I'd rather not identify. Everyone at HG Literary had a hand in it and all are to be exalted. Special thanks to Jon Cobb, who keeps Josh off the phone with me so he can be on the phone with editors.

Of course the wonderful people at Severn House, whom I hope to meet someday in the post-pandemic world where Sandy lives, have been brilliant (to coin a term) and lovely to work with. Thank you Kate Lyall Grant, Rachel Slatter, Natasha Bell and Penny Isaac, without whom this book would: a) not exist, b) be much worse, c) probably have been sent to the wrong place and d) be riddled with timeline errors, typos, and stupid mistakes. You're all invaluable.

Anytime the subject is a poison of any type, thanks must immediately be sent out to the amazing Luci Hansson Zahray, 'the poison lady,' who makes sure that if I do make a mistake, it's intentional. If there is a misstatement involving lily of the valley, you can rest assured it is not Luci's fault.

Booksellers have been ravaged by the past year and a half and we need booksellers desperately, so even if you don't buy this one, buy other books and get them from a local, independent bookstore if you can. Let the other guys sell you a blender or something.

I get by with a little help from my friends, and my author friends, whether they know it or not, provide backup and support even when I don't tell them I need it. So you should read their books, too: Julia Spencer-Fleming, Ellen Byron, Catriona McPherson, Hank Phillippi Ryan, Naomi Hirahara, Chris Grabenstein, Kellye Garrett and Jack Getze have all been there when I needed them. Thank you for that.

Erin Mitchell is an astonishing person who tries, often against my own efforts, to introduce me to a waiting public. Thanks for never expressing frustration with me for insisting on staying obscure, Erin. I promise you it's not my real goal.

If you've read any E.J. Copperman or Jeff Cohen book, you are a member of my tribe and I am forever beholden to you. Drop me a line sometime and let me know what you're thinking.

E.J. Copperman
Deepest New Jersey
April, 2021

9/2021